THE SOMMIÈRES SUN

By CE Hunt

Copyright © 2021 CE Hunt

All rights reserved

The characters and events portrayed in this book are fictitious. Any similarity to real persons, living or dead, is coincidental and not intended by the author.

No part of this book may be reproduced, or stored in a retrieval system, or transmitted in any form or by any means, electronic, mechanical, photocopying, recording, or otherwise, without express written permission of the publisher.

ISBN-13: 9798736198412
ISBN-10: 1477123456

Cover design by: Art Painter
Library of Congress Control Number: 2018675309
Printed in the United States of America

À Miel et Guillaume

1

"Damn it all to hell, Steve! I was just tryin' t'help!"

"Help, huh? Well, you damn near broke us up. When Pauline left for France the other day, she wasn't mad at me, but she was definitely disturbed about my family…that being you, of course…again. What the hell did you tell her anyway?" I peered over to my ne'er-do-well cousin, Clark. He had managed to really upset my new fiancé.

"You know…the usual shit, man."

"Uh huh, like what?"

Clark grinned and appeared proud of what he told Pauline, "You should have seen her face, man! She was a wildcat full of jealous," he boasted.

"Full of what?"

"Shoulda seen her eyes, man!"

"That 'jealous,' as you call it, was righteous rage I suspect."

"Huh?" Clark pushed his glasses up and looked me in the eye as he stopped arranging food on my table for my "bachelor party" he'd dreamt up.

"Seriously, Clark. What kind of bullshit did you tell her?"

"I told her you were quite the cocksman."

"What?"

"You know, ladies' man…you had 'em coming and going out of your place…never a disappointed customer!"

"What? You made me out to be a male prostitute or something?!"

"Nah, man...they wasn't paying you, Stevie. They was givin' it to you, you being a cocksman and all! Don't you get it?" Again, pushing his new glasses up to give me his best earnest look. I noted his eyes quivering a bit less than in the past. And he was mostly looking me in the eye. The new glasses were actually a nice touch...made him look a little less wild and maybe even a trace smarter. And they slightly distracted from his bad complexion.

"That was way over the top, Clark. You almost screwed everything up. Just watch what you say around Pauline in the future. PLEASE! Besides, what's a cocksman?"

"Don't know really, just heard some guy in the pen use it. I think it's a fancy word for like stud or somethin.' He was a dude, had lots of schooling, like you. He knew stuff, stuff like what those gals from Europe want."

"Huh?"

"He said those Eye-talian women want their men to be studs, you know, to strut around, to be cocksmen. You know that macheese-ism shit."

"Well, Pauline's French, not Italian. I'm no expert, but I think French women are way over the whole machismo business and probably have been for a couple of centuries. Your friend in the pen is a dumbass, Clark. Please don't try to apply what you learned in prison to the real world. And definitely not to my world." Clark appeared to be thinking as he stared at the beige rug in my living room. I took that as a gleam of hope.

Just then Bruce knocked at my front door and I could see Pablo parking his truck on the street in front of my house. My "bachelor party," as Clark insisted on calling it, was just about to launch.

Fifteen minutes later, Pablo and I were out on the patio in the back quaffing an ice cold Tecate, Pablo's favorite. I'd given him a bunch of my Chihuahua Cerveza, the brand I imported into the US, but he preferred his Tecate. I didn't really blame him.

"Amigo, I am very happy for you. I can't wait to meet your Pauline. She sounds like such a good...and interesting woman. The kind of woman you need."

"I can't wait to meet Maria. I'm happy for you two." Pablo had gotten married while I was in France. I expressed my regrets at not being in Marfa for the wedding.

Just then I heard the sound of a woman laughing very loudly from within my house, not a sound one expects at an intimate bachelor's party perhaps. Pablo and I wandered into the house to find Pilar and Amy unloading beer onto the dining room table.

"Where should we put this stuff *muchacho*?" Pilar smiled at me. I must have looked surprised.

"What? Did you expect me and Amy to miss your bachelor's party?"

"Well, I don't know exactly, but I'm damn glad you two are here."

"Steve, I brought Hank, hope you don't mind." Hank was Amy's fiancé and a ranch foreman on a ranch near mine.

"The more the merrier, Amy. Good to see you, Hank!"

"Steve, don't know if you remember me. We met years ago on the ranch. I knew your Uncle Clive real well."

"I think I do, way back, Hank."

"Yep, years ago."

Just then Bruce interjected, "My friend Timothy is coming too Steve, that okay?" Bruce smiled at me. Bruce was the owner of a bookstore/art gallery in town and the guy that my old girlfriend, Stacy, had tried to set me up with on the disastrous evening months ago when she thought I was gay.

"That's great Bruce. I think I know him. 4 dimensions gallery?"

"That's him."

A crowd was gradually appearing in my living room and dining.

Within half an hour, music was blaring, and the attendees of my bachelor party were starting to get drunk, except Pablo and me. Pablo had to drive back out to the XYX ranch and wasn't much of a drinker anyway. He had stayed on and been the foreman at the ranch my Uncle Clive had willed to me but moved on after about six months. I still wasn't sure why he'd left, but he'd assured me it had nothing to do with me. He just thought it best. Maybe it had something to do with my cousins, Clark and Amy, being left out of the will. Uncle Clive left it all to me, "me" being his nephew. He totally left his kids, my cousins, out of the will. I'd tried to make it up to Amy and Clark in a variety of ways.

After figuring out she had a real knack for business, I hired Amy to be my business manager for Clive Miles Enterprises. I named my business after Uncle Clive. My businesses were basically my inherited ranch, art gallery, a few leased buildings and my beer distributorship. None of them set the world on fire, but Amy always managed to keep things in the black, or at least gray, and together they made enough money to pay the employees and put a little extra aside. Thank God for her. I mainly just wanted to write novels. Glad she was a great manager. Even though my first book was selling okay, I was making almost nothing on it after promotions, tours and other trips related to the book. I did sell the movie rights for a little cash and a tiny chunk of the profits of any future success of the movie. I had the good fortune of investing the sizable cash portion of the inheritance wisely across numerous investments and was doing pretty well. Jim, our attorney and kind of investment guy, had advised me well.

"Steve, have a damn drink. Don't look so pouty. This is your bachelor party, *vato*!" Pablo smiled at me. He and I had wound up on the back patio again while the party raged on in the house. The West Texas sun was setting, and cicadas were making their evening music, which I could occasionally hear over the music coming from inside.

I was still slowly nursing a Tecate.

"I'm gonna have to leave soon to get back to the ranch before dark," he continued. "I got a pump I gotta check on, make sure it's working."

"Pablo, I'm glad you came amigo. You're the best. It means a lot you showed up. You're a real friend. Always have been."

"Why you so serious?" Pablo asked. "Lighten up Steve. These people want to celebrate."

"I was just reflecting on how my lifestyle has left me with so few real friends. I had a few buddies, mainly golf and drinking pals, in college that I've pretty much lost touch with. I have a few friends from the Army. The only two I've really kept in touch with are still in and deployed overseas. They couldn't come. My Hill 'friends' dropped my ass as soon as I left their world of DC."

I looked at Pablo and damn near felt like bawling.

"How'd I wind up with so few real friends, Pablo? Shit, they had to invite women to my bachelor party to just have enough, not that I mind at all. How'd I let this happen?" I was reflecting on all the good people who had slipped out of my life.

"Well, Steve, let me leave you on this thought. You always got me as a friend. You took good care of me and my church when *el jefe*, you know, Mr. Miles, died. I'll never forget that. I know Amy has a few rough edges, but she is completely devoted to you, and she is one smart woman. You got a hell of a business partner in her. And it sounds like you have a very special woman in Pauline. Sounds like that's enough good friends in my books. I'd take three or four damn good friends over a mess of half-ass friends."

"Damn straight! Thanks Pablo." I mustered a smile for him. I love the wisdom of folks that have jobs that offer some quiet time that gives them the time to think about what they really feel about life versus some celebrity or some political commentator telling them what to think. Many writers I'd met displayed such wisdom as well.

"Knock the pity party off and get your ass in there with those folks. They want to be your friend, too!"

2

"So have y'all set a date, Steve?" asked Maureen. Maureen owned the Rincon Inn down the street. She had thirty years on me but was flirtatious as ever. I had finally wandered back into my party from my patio after reflecting a bit on Pablo's words. Plus, my beer was empty.

"Not exactly. Soon. I'm heading back to France within a couple of weeks. We need to get some stuff nailed down there and make a few decisions about our future. Where we plan to live, work, all that kind of thing."

"Good. There's still time for you and me to have a romp or two!"

"What about your husband, Maureen?" We'd always enjoyed flirting with each other even though we weren't remotely serious.

"Oh, he won't mind. He's okay me letting off some steam from time t'time." She paused to admire herself thoughtfully in my mirror. "This here's way too much woman for one man. He figur'd that out years ago."

"Uh huh, Maureen. I always thought you were kind of conservative."

Maureen, discreetly hiding a beer-induced burp, replied, "Bible says be fruitful and multiply."

"I think there's a bit more instruction on the topic of sex in the bible, Maureen."

"Oh shit, you damn libs always want to over complicate shit. You almost gettin' me outta the mood, Steve. You know that?"

I started to facetiously apologize before Reverend Burkheisse from the Marfa Episcopalian Church walked over and congratulated me. She had helped me get through a tough break up, and I found her sensitivity and understanding comforting.

"Congratulations, Steve! So happy for you."

"Thanks Judy. So great to see you again."

I love the Reverend, but it seems Clark invited damn near everybody. I half expected our local art "critic," Paco to come around the corner any second and shoot both barrels at me. After a little dust up we had with her at the art gallery, she loved to give me the finger every time she saw me around town.

I mingled as any good host should. I made small talk with pretty much everyone there. The music was getting a bit louder and the drinks were flowing freely. So far only one drink had hit the floor. Somehow Clark had managed to avoid my carpets with the ruby red concoction he was drinking way too much of. He promised me that would be his last drink for the evening.

As I scanned the house to ensure compliance with his commitment, out of the corner of my eye I saw Pilar motioning to me to join her outside on the patio. I wandered over to the door.

"You really going to get married, Steve?" Pilar gave me a strange, crinkled nose look. She too had been drinking a bit. In the past, she and I had a trace of unconsummated romantic history.

"That's the plan." I always seemed to equivocate around Pilar for some reason. I decided to finally change that. "No, seriously, Pauline and I are getting married, Pilar. You just know when it's right."

She just looked at me.

"Well, I want you to know that I'm am very happy for you."

"Thank you, Pilar. How you been doing?"

"Good." She walked off into the dark yard. She nodded with her head for me to follow her.

Once outside in the dark, she took my hand and pulled me to her.

"Here's your bachelor party gift." She proceeded to plant a hard kiss on my lips reminiscent of the one we shared last summer right before she went back to Ithaca for grad school.

After I regained my senses, I finally blurted out, "Wow! What's that all about?"

"Well, every guy is supposed to be tempted at his bachelor party."

"You definitely did that, Pilar."

Pilar laughed and said, "So, lover boy, are you tempted?"

"You know the answer already. We've been through all that. We have chemistry. But remember it's complicated and we both have significant others. Hell, I'm engaged!"

She stared at me a long while with her big brown eyes, slowly smiled, subtly lifted one eyebrow, lightly kissed my cheek and whispered, "I don't have a significant other." With that she slowly drifted back into the house, not looking back. Her short dress allowed the light from the house to silhouette her exquisite legs. Not something I needed to be thinking about.

I stood outside and listened to the crickets and stared into the bazillion stars above. I took a deep breath and let it out into the Marfa night very slowly. I sure missed Pauline.

The rest of the party was inconsequential but mostly fun. Clark kept his word as far as I could tell…no more drinks. Bruce and his friend helped Clark and me clean up the house. I half expected someone to comment on Pilar's kiss. Fortunately, it never came up. Maybe the darkness obscured the little indiscretion.

One thing I knew for sure, though: life was never boring in Marfa.

3

"Steve, you gotta tell'em yes, but only if my cousin gets a role! That'd be me, of course!"

"Clark? What are you talking about?" Clark stood outside on my porch after banging on the door to wake me up me early Sunday morning.

"You know, the damn movie deal!"

"Huh?"

"I want a role, and a good'un! I wanna kiss a star or somthin'!" He had sunglasses on, horn-rimmed, with partial wire frames. Looked good on him.

"What movie?"

"You know, the movie Aim's been working on with that Hollywood feller. Tito's the name I think."

"Okay, Clark. I'm still asleep. I'll find out more later from Amy."

"Thanks Steve, …you know…you still kind of owe me. They took that scholarship thing away from me."

"Clark, you brought that on yourself. I don't see how you figure I owe you anything."

"I was innocent! I never tried to sell nothin'. I was try just trying to give her some pot, you know? She seemed so uptight. Besides, that ain't why I was busted. I was wrongfully charged. I was cleared!"

"Didn't help she was the daughter of the university president, Clark. Whatever, you weren't supposed to have any drugs anyway."

"Shhh! Don't get me thrown in the pen again, man! They don't know that. They got no proof. 'Sides, I'm clean now. Ready to start an actin' career. At the thing where they had a bunch of us local folks try out for parts, I was told by one of those Hollywood types that I might be a great character actor. He mentioned some feller with your first name. Somethin' like Steve Butini."

"Steve Buschemi?"

"Bin-go!" Clark smiled big. "Bet he's one those types that get all the ladies, huh?"

"Well, not exactly, but he's a good actor."

"'Member Steve, you owe me. You fixed up Aim real good, and you need to do the same fer me."

"No, I don't Clark, but let me find out more when I see Amy next time."

"Thanks, cuz!" Clark started to walk down my walkway.

I called out, "Don't get your hopes up too much, okay Clark?"

Clark paused a second and looked back, "Sure, Steve. I know you got my back. This gonna be big for me. I just gotta feeling, you know?" With that he was down the street and starting to try to whistle.

◆ ◆ ◆

"Who'd you say you were working with on this movie thing, Amy?"

"Tito Fuentes and Sid Harmon." Amy sat across from me looking so professional. Shoulder length hair. Pearls. Black skirt, not too short, not too long. White blouse, cut perfectly, showing just a trace of cleavage. Gray sweater. Minimum makeup, dark red lipstick. Man, she'd come a long way. She was now very professional. Even her diction was great. No wonder we were making decent money.

"What'd you say the name of the movie is?"

"They didn't say. Something about a woman who finds

herself in Marfa."

"Hmmm. What was the name of the second guy?"

She checked her file. "Harmon, Sid Harmon." Perfectly manicured red fingernails. She'd come a long way from the chick who cussed me out at every turn and even punched me in the stomach last year!

"That's weird. He with Ramirez and Feldstein Productions?"

"Never heard of them."

"Okay. I think I've met him. He and a guy named Ramirez bought the movie rights to my book. Pretty sure of it. When the publisher decided to pick up my book and publish it, inserted was a provision that they could sell the movie rights for a small cut. At the time, I'd gone to two very poorly attended book signings at Front Street Books and Marfa Book Company. I think I'd sold 100 books, tops. So, I agreed to that. Shortly after that, my publisher asked me to meet with Sid and Ramirez. They were attending some big deal at the Judd Foundation, here in town."

"Yeah Steve, I vaguely remember you telling me about meeting up with them."

I continued, "Sid seemed kind of scattered, sort of a joke."

"Yeah, I'd agree with that assessment," Amy interjected and smiled.

"He was there, but I never met Ramirez. He was on the Board of the foundation or something. I really didn't know if they were for real. I guess I should have figured they might be for real if Ramirez was on the foundation board. That was when I gave you the check to deposit. That was the movie rights."

Amy just looked at me then with almost no expression other than showing a bit of pain. She knew I was still at least a part-time knucklehead. The check was pretty small.

"You sure the movie isn't about a guy, kind of like me, kind of a doofus trying to find his way here and then goes to France? You know, like the book I wrote?"

Amy again just looked at me, "Well, Steve...I'm sorry. I haven't read your book. You gave me a copy, but I just haven't gotten around to reading it yet."

"Damn Aim, you were in it!"

She just looked at me with a blank stare. She was very pretty. Something different.

"Say, you get your teeth straightened? You look different, somehow."

"Those invisible alignment things. Four more months."

"Damn, Amy, you look good."

"Steve, don't we have business to conduct?"

"Shit, look at you, all business like. I love it!"

She smiled and winked at me. "Ole Aim is still in here. You're still the first boy I ever kissed. Proud it was you. Just glad I was adopted. Now let's get back to business. You ever heard the phrase 'Me Too.'" She smiled.

"Even though you didn't read my book, you read my mind, Amy. As far as the subject of the movie...sure it was about a woman?"

"Yes."

"This Sid guy...50 something, kind of a hipster thing going? Horn-rimmed glasses?"

"No clue. Never seen him. Just goofy phone calls from him."

"Damn, I think they're already fucking up my story!"

"Whadya mean, Steve?"

"I think this Sid son of a bitch bought my novel, for damn near nothing, and then made my character a woman."

"Sorry, Steve, but this is kind of no BFD as far as I'm concerned. Besides, why the hell didn't you tell me you were selling the rights? I could have doubled our money, dumbshit! That check you handed me was hardly worth cashing!"

She was right. I was a dumbshit. I sold the rights before I knew the book was going to be semi-successful...how could I know I could write something that would sell? This was going to be interesting.

◆ ◆ ◆

Being back in Marfa alone allowed me to start writing again and thinking. Pauline had left a couple of weeks after our miraculous meet up in Marathon at the Gage Hotel. She had recovered from her very long, most unpleasant cab ride with Clark from the airport in El Paso. Clark had her thinking I was a real playboy, but I convinced her otherwise during our reunion night in Marathon. After enduring Clark, she had almost left to go back to France without even seeing me.

I was on cloud nine the whole time we were together in West Texas during her visit. I loved sharing the beauty of the Trans Pecos region with her. She had explored Big Bend National Park a little before I tracked her down in Marathon, but I took her back to experience my favorite places. We spent a couple of nights at the Chisos Lodge in the park and hiked many trails. She loved the ranger programs, especially one about night skies.

She was blown away by the old silver mining town of Shafter. She marveled how the Catholic Church there persisted even as the town had more or less become a ghost town. She compared it to how many Catholic Churches in southern France had struggled to survive in villages with declining populations and noted that like the church in Shafter, many had become a once a month or so venue for masses and occasional weddings and funerals.

Pauline found a charm about Presidio, Texas that I hadn't fully appreciated. She loved the eclectic architecture of the little town and read the cultural landscape in a way that I hadn't found accessible until I saw Presidio through her French eyes. She loved the palm trees. She felt that Presidio and its sister city of Ojinaga over the border, also known as "OJ" around the area, were a fascinating hybrid of the United States and Mexico. Pretty much all things Mexico fascinated Pauline. She seemed to feel more alive the closer we were to Mexico.

Sitting alone in my living room that afternoon I was surrounded by the ambiance of my creation: my books, my art, Indian pottery from New Mexico and my reproductions of Mayan and Aztec figures I had picked up in Mexico. I poured myself a tall glass of a very dry but rich red blend. I took a few deep breaths and just reflected on my time with Pauline and how much I missed her. I reflected particularly on a conversation I had with Pauline at the Bean Café in Presidio during her visit. She felt such at ease in Presidio. Maybe it was her Latin roots that put her at ease. France reflected an interesting combination of Latin and maybe Germanic culture. No surprise given the history of the country.

When I was in France, I felt it might be the ideal European culture. It at times evoked the precision and efficiency of Germany and the northern countries, but it also evoked at times the spontaneity, passion, art and freedom of the southern European countries. It also demonstrated a freedom loving population who vigorously insisted on democracy. Given my take on history, I'd link that trait to both England and France. France offered the odd combination of unpredictability and reliability at the same time. One could relax there, but it wasn't boring. It certainly seemed to become more Latin as I traveled south.

Pauline loved the potential of Mexico because it had the hope of being kind of the France of the western hemisphere in that it evoked the artistry and freedom of southern Europe yet added another element at times missing in Europe: a genuine warmth. Mexicans were among the kindest people that Pauline had ever met. She thought Mexico could be incredible, much better than the US, if only the Germans had brought a bit more of their efficiency and precision to the nation and had a bit more of a democratic zeal developed. She regretted France's ham-handed attempt to interfere in Mexico in the 1860s. Mexico definitely had the Latin part down solid. She thought the fact that Mexico also offered numerous indigenous influences made it even more interesting than European cultures because it truly was a blending of so many diverse cultures from many continents and many traditions, some of which were thousands of years in the making.

She felt that France had benefitted greatly from being a crossroads of Europe and being impacted by the north and south. Pauline reflected that the US could have had that potential if only the Puritans would have kept their asses in England. She further opined that racism and slavery were a major impediment to the US achieving its full potential. She wasn't fully convinced that the US was going to be able to overcome that dark legacy.

At the Bean Café, we had the best conversation about United States policy towards Mexico. Pauline was convinced that we owed Mexico a great deal.

She was sitting there in the restaurant bathed in the bright sunlight that was streaming in the front windows. She looked stunning even in her shorts and hiking boots.

She proclaimed, "You know the United States has violated Mexico's sovereignty so many times over the past 150 years or so. I'm amazed that Mexicans are still so warm to Americans."

I tried to keep up with her, though it seemed she likely knew more about Mexico than I, "Yeah, I suspect so, though we Americans prefer not to think about that too much."

"Think about it, Steve, how much has the US spent fighting the Taliban?"

"A lot."

"Uh huh. I wonder how much they spend trying to shut down the cartels in Mexico?"

"Some?"

"Some of the cartels commit acts just as bad as the Taliban. I mean why are little girls in Afghanistan so much more important than little Mexican girls?" What I read about the Mexican cartels in newspapers in France tells me that the cartels do bad stuff just like the Taliban." She was a tad fierce as she spoke.

"I don't know, Pauline."

"Ever think about it? Isn't it weird?"

"Yeah, yes it is."

"Could it be racism?"

"Yeah, maybe."

I was shooting blanks when it came to countering her observations other than to point out that even though Mexico is a wonderful country with great people, corruption in their government has been a persistent challenge. That level of corruption probably helped create an opening for some of the criminal activities and certainly made reacting to it more difficult. She had me soul searching wondering why having a peaceful and prosperous neighbor wouldn't be a much higher priority for the United States.

Part of me wondered if the United States should be more proactive in helping Mexico build stronger and more transparent civic institutions, or would Mexico be better off if we just left them alone and stopped providing a huge market for illegal drugs. There seemed no doubt to either one of us that our market for illicit drugs in the US fueled much of the criminal activity. The US was in effect investing heavily everyday into propping up Mexico's number one threat. Further, had we played a hand in the corruption politically? Mexicans had taken up arms to secure a better government more than once. Had the invisible hand of American interference thwarted their pursuit of better governance?

She ended that conversation with an interesting observation, "Can you imagine the United States without Mexico? No workers to harvest the food you eat, no Mexican art and style, no Mexican food, no Mexican beer, no tequila and none of your precious margaritas, no tacos and enchiladas, no salsa. Shit, you'd just be a big, boring England with better, whiter teeth! Why can't people in the United States see that? The way some of your politicians talk about Mexicans! It's sickening."

Again, I felt I couldn't in good conscience refute Pauline's French perspectives.

As I drifted out of my pensive mood, I refilled my glass and went to sit on my front porch to watch Marfa ease into its evening aura. Sunsets are usually stunning in Marfa. I sat and thought about the likely upcoming movie fiasco and my trip back to see Pauline in a couple of weeks. Pauline and I had a lot of details to sort out about how we could make this work. She wasn't ready to leave France, and I had mixed emotions about leaving the United States. It may be far from perfect, but it was my home. I suspected that's why many people can't make themselves leave the country of their birth…right or wrong, rich or poor, it's home.

I tried to get my mind around the whole movie thing. Amy and I had a meeting with Sid Harmon at 10:30 on Tuesday at the Paisano Hotel. That promised to be interesting. The "movie people" were once again the talk of the town. Apparently, after the auditions, a few locals had a shot at roles. Incredibly, Clark claimed that he was one of a handful of people who had been called back. Fully amused, Amy told me that she had strongly advised Clark to not quit his job as a cab driver quite yet.

4

The next morning, we were waiting in the lobby of the Paisano Hotel for Sid Harmon and the "movie people."

"What? You gotta be kidding!" I looked at Amy in disbelief.

Amy looked up at me with a straight face. "Yep, not a joke." She was sitting down, legs crossed and dressed very professionally in her black jacket and skirt and light grey blouse. She was representing Clive Miles Enterprises very well. She made me feel a tad underdressed in my khakis and black polo shirt, but then again, this was Marfa.

"No way!"

"Yep, Clark claims they are so taken with him that he is seriously being considered for a major role in the movie. The nitwit has already given the cab company notice." Still no expression on her face.

Sid and his entourage noisily entered the lobby.

"Sam, so great to see you again!" Sid was breathless in his enthusiasm. He had gone from the hipster I had met before to being someone right out of the 1970s, including tight pants and a flamboyant pink flowery silk shirt.

"Hi Sid. It's Steve. Steve Miles?"

"Of course, and you must be Amy?"

"Yes sir."

"Guys, this is the world renown, 'Tito Fuentes.'" Tito spied us with an expression that suggested we were already giving him a bit of indigestion.

As Tito very quickly shook our hands, he mumbled something that contained the word, "pleasure."

"Wonderful, you two! So glad we could all get together. Tito and I have been looking forward to meeting you!" Tito's expression suggested otherwise.

Amy tried to conceal a sigh, "Sure, Sid. The Paisano has offered us a small meeting room. That work?"

"Of course, Amy, that work for you Tito?"

Tito just nodded once with a grimace as he darted his eyes about taking in the lobby. Sid looked back at the entourage. There were a couple of "strung-out" kids who looked like they were straight out of the Manson gang, a very heavy balding guy and for some bizarre reason a person who looked exactly like a fatter version of Deputy Dud, the former local Deputy Sheriff I had tangled with in the past. He stared at me, but I don't think he recognized me. I was now sporting a lazy beard and eyeglasses. The beard would go before I left for France. Pauline hated it.

Sid called out, "Gang, we'll see you at Mike's for lunch at noon, okay?"

Deputy Dud glared at me just as he exited. Did he suddenly recognized me, or was it one of his random, non-sensical expressions for which he was known?

A few minutes later, the four of us sat around a small table in the private room. The room was a bit austere, but there were western landscape pictures adorning the walls. Had I known it would only be the four of us, we could have met at our office down the street from where we run the "sprawling" Clive Miles Enterprises.

I sat across from Tito. He was difficult to age, maybe 40, maybe 50. Lots of gold. Kind of balding and had an off-putting habit of briefly glaring at you before he smiled. One or both of them had a lot of cologne, so bad I had to crack open the door to the room pretty quickly.

"Steve! So good to see you again. Thrilled you are getting to meet Tito. He's the brains of the outfit. I'm just a damn good promoter, really."

"So, gentlemen, I take it you've turned my novel into a screenplay and making the movie here, right?"

"The screenplay is done. Finito. No changes!" Tito erupted. The smile would have been so much more sincere without the preceding glare.

Sid smiled and looked at me, "Yes, Steve. You're correct. Now we just need to negotiate all the terms concerning the ranch and maybe the use of your house, if you agree. I understand you have another movie deal for the ranch right now?" Steve peered across at Amy.

"Correct, Sid. Not exclusive though. We can most likely accommodate your production."

"That's great to hear. Forrest Stanley III, he's our attorney, will be in touch. He likes to be called 'The Third.' Not 'Third' but 'The Third.' You have to get that right, understand? He is a bit eccentric, but a damn good lawyer. Just get his name right." Sid looked at Amy quite seriously, then smiled and then peered over at me expectantly.

"So?" he queried, eyebrows lifted.

"What?" I responded.

"May we use your house to give the movie a real organic feel?"

"I don't know Sid. Kind of…invasive."

With that, Tito stood up and put both hands on his head and started violently shaking his head while uttering obscenities in Spanish, I think. He slowly looked to the ceiling and called out some name that had a lot of clicking noises as though he were talking to the movie gods or somebody in outer space.

"Tito, calm down amigo," Sid placed his hand on Tito's arm and said in a soothing voice with an air that he had to regularly perform this role with him.

Tito left the room, quietly shutting the door.

"I'm sorry Steve and Amy. You know the artist temperament. It'll pass."

"Sid, I'm going to have to think about the house thing."

"No worries, Stevo. It's cool, brother. We're partners, we'll make all this work. I got a great feeling about this." He had a huge and insincere-looking smile on his face.

Tito quietly returned in a few minutes. I tried to probe around to get a little information if they had made the protagonist a female or what the deal was with Clark, but neither of them would say a word about those topics. Tito kept talking about the energy that the Marfa landscape was giving him and something about his Mayan ancestors. I didn't really have a problem with the protagonist being a female, but I feared what else they'd change since the movie would likely say based on a novel by yours truly.

In the early evening, Pauline and I finally connected on the phone. It was very late in France. We mainly just caught up with each other and spoke in general terms about my upcoming trip. She concerned me when she said we still have some very important issues to work out. I was so startled I flat out asked if she was getting cold feet about us. She laughed and asked what the hell was I asking that for? It dawned on me that we were speaking French. After I explained, she reminded me that the French idiom was *"ne pas être chaud pour,"* In other words, "to not be warm for something." Episodes like this reminded me of some of the linguistic challenges ahead. Nevertheless, I was pleased to be speaking French and not thinking about it. More importantly, I was pleased to learn she was not "getting cold feet."

I would book my flight to arrive in Paris the following Friday. I couldn't wait to see her, but I did decide to spend a few days in Paris before heading south. I wanted her to come up to join me for a trip to the Normandy American Cemetery. She said no hurry because her job was going to be very intense for a week or two and then she'd have a few days off. That would give us some time to reconnect and address those issues she referenced.

After thinking all this through, I poured myself a beautiful glass of "Lazer Cat" from the local Alta Marfa winery and got my "Cocktail Hour on a Rainy Night, 1969" playlist softly wafting about in the background. I was going to frame out a new novel. I was striving to accomplish some great nature writing wrapped in a novel, and I wanted to capture readers who'd never crack open a book about nature. A passage from page eight of Sigurd Olsen's "Listening Point" kept pulsing through my consciousness.

> *I must leave it as beautiful as I found it. Nothing must ever happen there that might detract in the slightest from what it had now. I would enjoy it and discover all that was to be found there and learn as time went on that here perhaps was all I might ever hope to know. As I sat there on the rock I realized that, in spite of the closeness of civilization and the changes that hemmed it in, this remnant of the old wilderness would speak to me of silence and solitude, of belonging and wonder and beauty.*

Olsen referred to his "special place" as a world where when one is "aware and still, can things be seen and heard" and "someplace of quiet where the universe can be contemplated with awe." This was the Trans Pecos country and Big Bend region for me. It is part of the soul of Texas, really of America in all its frontier-like qualities. There are no dollars valuable enough to trade them for this. There would be no complete Texas without the wildness of the Big Bend. The nightmare that was transforming the "former" Texas Hill Country where Austin, San Marcos and San Antonio were all becoming one huge, almost uninhabitable, "business-friendly" mess, could never be permitted here.

We needed to keep the soulless, power and money-grubbing politicians and their phony ideologies a long way from this place. We owed it to ourselves to preserve a few places, such as Big Bend, the Boundary Waters of Minnesota, Yellowstone or the California Deserts, where we could, as humans, have habitat to really connect with our innermost most thoughts and be truly alone. I've always felt that way, and that was one reason why working in DC was so challenging, even demoralizing: very few politicians could agree with that position because their re-election funds could dry up if they did.

As I took a deep breath to calm down a bit, I had a strong flashback of my final visit with Father Mike, my Buffalo, New York-native friend in Pauline's town, at dusk. I could see him in front of the small *brasserie*, in his horn-rimmed glasses and the small candle-lit tables surrounding him, and hear his words, "Don't let the world distract you from your purpose. The world will blindly extinguish your fire if you give it half a chance." Funny how a chat with a friend in that village was now helping provide me with such clarity. A clarity to enable me to embark on a grand mission on the other side of the planet. Only now did it dawn on me how wise those words were.

Of course, as I was perfectly primed to start saving my heaven on earth with my "keyboard," my cell phone rang. I was in such a mental groove that I should have ignored the call, but I saw it was Pilar calling. She was part of the fabric that helped me see how important this place was.

"I have a bottle of wine and I am about 200 feet from your place," was how she answered.

"I have fairly clean glasses," I replied.

"One minute."

Within a few minutes, I went from saving the Big Bend region to sharing a bottle of wine with a person who represented another aspect of the beauty of the region and the people it produces.

Over the din of cicadas and with the last seconds of an orange glow on the western horizon, we sat across from each other on the patio. I loved how she seemed so connected with herself, completely comfortable in her skin. She was who she was with no pretenses.

"I just wanted us to visit before I go back to Ithaca for my final year."

"Glad you dropped by Pilar. I wanted to talk to you."

She crossed her legs, smiled and looked at me and said, "Uh huh?" She looked beautiful in her cutoffs, sandals and pink t-shirt. Her scent was almost overwhelming...maybe a mix of patchouli and lavender? It was earthy and fresh and extremely interesting.

"Yeah, about last week, at the party..."

"Uh huh?" She was still smiling.

"You know I really care for you, right?"

"Uh huh."

"Well, I'm in love with Pauline, as much as I think you are awesome, and beautiful, and sexy, and funny..."

"You are so full of shit, bro!"

"Huh?"

"I know that! I just wanted to tempt you a little. No bachelor party would be worth a shit without a little temptation!"

"Oh. Okay. So, you were just kidding?" I felt a twinge of disappointment.

"Hell, I don't know. Yeah, mostly. Maybe I was kind of being a little selfish too. Maybe I just wanted one last kiss before...you know. Before you were a married man. You know how it is, there is an electricity between us, or something."

I just sat there listening, kind of enjoying this moment perhaps more than I should. One doesn't have many moments of complete honest complexity like this with another human.

She continued, "You know there's a connection between us, but we ain't gonna happen."

I just sat there with my mind racing on what she was saying. She was right. There was a strong sexual attraction between us. But I knew how Pauline would feel if she witnessed us slipping and doing something stupid. The thought of hurting Pauline was so painful that a few minutes of pleasure wasn't even remotely worth it. Even if Pauline never knew, I would know and that was something I didn't want between us. Somehow, Pauline made me want to be a better person. I never wanted to let her down, ever. A milestone on the road to being a decent human, I guess.

I finally spoke, "Thank you Pilar. You are one of the most attractive women I've ever met. I am strongly drawn to you, always have been from the very first time I laid eyes on you at the gallery. You were working in the back. Stacy had mentioned you to me. You came out of the back room holding a painting. You had on a loose but short black dress, sandals, and not a trace of make-up. Your hair was in a ponytail. You were so stunning. You seemed so young, and I was still in a trance for Stacy at the time, but it's funny how that image of you is burned into my consciousness." Stacy was my old girlfriend in Marfa, someone I thought was "the one."

"I remember the first time I met you too, Steve. I remember thinking I should have worn a little make-up or some other silly thought. I was taken by you, too." She smiled at me a few seconds, and then looked away and sighed. Staring at the sky, she almost whispered, "But it ain't in the cards for us. You know it. I know it. You've met an incredible woman. There's no way I'd take part in screwing that up. I guess I just wanted to connect with you as a human one last time and maybe somehow commemorate our connection."

After a long pause, I said, "We're like that beautiful work of art that you will never be able to afford. But it doesn't stop you from admiring it and thinking of it as part of you somehow. You just can't physically own it."

The conversation was getting deep and maybe drifting off in the wrong direction. The wine was gone. We just sat in silence and kind of pondered as we listened to a train approaching town from the east. We listened as the train blew its horn at the street crossing up the street. As the sound of the train began to fade to a muted clickity clack to the west, we found ourselves looking into each other's eyes.

She broke our gaze by slapping her legs and standing up. I stood up as well.

She looked me in the eye and said, "Well, in some kind of strange, bizarre way, I love you and hope you and Pauline have a fantastic life. I really mean that."

I looked her in the eye, hugged her and told her I loved her too.

"Pilar, you will always remain one of those rare people in my life for whom I'll forever feel a special connection." Pointing to my head and heart, I said, "You will remain in here, always. Thank you for being a part of me; somehow the connection I feel with you goes beyond the time we have spent together."

She just stared at me with moist, beautiful eyes and said, "You are so full of shit, dickhead! Maybe that's what I love about you. I'm going to let this be our last 'pre-marital' moment together and show myself out. It was a beautiful moment, *muchacho*."

With that she wheeled around and walked out. I didn't see her again before she left town for school.

5

"Steve, the Union Pacific said they ain't gonna service us no more!" Chuppy came bounding out of the warehouse onto the dock at my beer distributor across the tracks from the former Godbold Mill. It was in a pretty dilapidated structure. Impractical, but tons of character. That kind of summed up most of Marfa.

"Hold on, Chuppy. What? I mean, how do you know?"

"Bart, over in Marathon, told me."

"Who's Bart?"

"You know? The mining guy, he mines that fluorspar stuff. He's been talking about resuming shipping of it out of Marathon. He talked to you to other day at the cattle growers meeting."

"Oh, that guy. Yeah, I remember."

"He said the UP told him that they were going to stop making local deliveries soon around here. Too much work for the little amount of traffic we have. Really, you and the molasses dealer are it around here. He said others were interested in shipping and he wants to talk to you."

"Why me?"

"He wants to know if you want to be partners."

"On what?"

"He wants to know if you want to start a local rail operation."

"That's interesting."

I'd never thought about that. I agreed to meet up with

Bart before I left for France if possible. This was news I didn't welcome. My beer came up from Mexico by boxcar and was delivered about once a week to my dock at the warehouse. Customs was easy because there wasn't much interchange at the border on the Texas, Mexico and Pacific Railroad in Presidio. The Texas, Mexico and Pacific Railroad handed it over to the Union Pacific Railroad in Alpine. If the UP stopped serving me, we'd have to go to Alpine to pick it up and then have to handle it again to load into the warehouse. Thought I'd better talk to Amy about it, too. She was really the brains of the business, as I'd learned from recent experiences.

Over dinner that night alone at home, I wondered why keeping rail service in Marfa was a big deal to me. It just wouldn't the same for me having to truck the stuff up. Besides, I loved the scene of having boxcars parked at a business in Marfa. Having real organic commerce rather than just image peddling made the town seem more real. To me, having a couple of dirty boxcars parked next to my old distributor at sunset was kind of an art exhibit itself.

The Marfa art scene was a mixed bag for me. Some of the art was sincere and real, and I loved it. Some of it was hype and ostentatious. Some of it was flat out nothing, a couple of scribbles on a page. I had grown in France, though, and was able to appreciate certain aspects of art more than before.

The Minimalism scene was what had really launched Marfa from an art perspective. I'd dismissed it in the past. Some of the folks associated with it in town seemed pretty stuffy. A lot of "the minimalism works" didn't speak to me. Even though I was surrounded by institutions that interpreted minimalism in Marfa, the significance of minimalism didn't really hit me until I was in Europe.

I saw a Kazimir Malevich painting at the Pompidou Center in Paris. It was just a greenish, black cross on a white background. For whatever reason though, it really caught my eye and compelled me to do some research on minimalism. I was interested in how something so simple could say so much. To my surprise, I later learned that the work of Kazimir would influence Marfa's Donald Judd and other adherents to Minimalism.

On a kind of related note, I was struck too how much I relaxed when I visited French homes. I only went into a few of them, but they tended to be relaxingly spare of stuff. There was almost no clutter. People only owned what they needed, partly because places tended to be smaller with less storage, but also because that approach better meshed with French sensibilities.

While abroad, I came to appreciate how much I liked living with fewer items. On the road, everything I owned fit in two suitcases. I was more relaxed and seldom felt a "lacking."

Over an after-dinner beer on the patio under a brilliant orange and purple sunset, I sought to connect what the hell minimalism had to do with beer and railroads. By the end of the beer, I had decided nothing really. I just liked trains and boxcars parked on my siding, dammit. I'd see what I could do to keep my "works of art" on display in Marfa too.

6

Amy and I sat in the pleasant morning air on the small patio at the back of our office. "No. They are not filming in my house," I said.

Sunglasses obscured Amy's eyes. "Tito claims it's a deal breaker," she said with no expression. She was in full-dress, hardcore, businesswoman mode. In my old Army days, I'd say she was in full battle rattle, locked and loaded.

"Then let the deal be broken. Besides, they didn't pay shit for the movie rights."

She sipped her coffee. "True." Still no expression.

"Okay. I guess that settles that."

"You know Steve, they want Clark to play the character of Tom in the movie."

"Who's Tom?"

"Don't know. Clark says he's the guy that goes around honking and shooting the finger at Maria."

"Who's Maria?"

"The main character I take it."

"Shit! I still can't believe they made me, er, I mean my guy a woman in the movie script! And it sounds like Paco, I mean Shiro in my novel, became a man! Crap! Clark has the role of Paco!" Paco was someone that used to honk her horn and shoot the finger at Stacy and me last year after Stacy had me throw Paco out of my art gallery.

"Whatever, Steve. Look, I don't really care if the movie happens or not," Amy said. "Our royalty is so small. It won't mean a great deal. I mean these guys have had one movie make it big a few years ago, but overall, their track record is not that good."

"Like I said, I guess it's settled. If no house means no movie, then no movie. Besides, my house is manly. 'Maria' wouldn't be caught dead living in my place."

"Yeah, well I forget to mention. Tito wants to redo your interior to reflect Maria's tastes."

"You have my answer Aim," and I got up to walk out of the office. Amy followed me out to the front door. As I reached the door, I paused and looked back at her. "I can't believe that these Hollywood clowns are all into my book, but I can't walk across the street to buy it at the Marfa Book Company. Why won't they carry my book?"

"I thought they did, Steve." Amy looked slightly exasperated with me. "Didn't you do a book signing there?"

"Yeah. Poorly attended. They sold five copies and that was it. They never ordered more."

"Sorry Steve. Maybe they'll like the next book better." Amy seemed increasingly short on pity lately. Not much profit in pity, I guess.

"Yeah, maybe."

"Wait Steve. You know, Clark is not going to be happy."

"I know. And he'd been such a great 'Paco!'"

I had only a few days before I left for Europe. I needed to reconnect with the wilderness of the Big Bend region in case I stayed in France awhile. I needed to rekindle that fire that makes my protagonist in my new novel continue his work to save the region. I also needed to deal with my beer-rail issue before I left. Amy was indifferent to it and didn't understand why I cared whether my beer arrived by rail or truck as long as expenses didn't bump up too much. She was almost too business-like at times. Of course, that's just why I needed her to compensate for my impractical proclivities.

After planning out a two-day camping trip at Big Bend Ranch State Park, I hit the road to drive over to Marathon for a business meeting. Amy was busy so I brought along Jim, our attorney-consultant.

Before long, Jim and I were sitting around an outdoor table at the Gage Hotel with the Brewster and Presidio county judges, "Shank" Wilson and Bud Garcia. A few other local businessmen also ringed the table. It was a perfect evening for outdoor dining. I ordered the elk, one of my all-time favorites there. It was usually incredible. It was early yet, so the place was quiet. As dusk began to emerge, a server lit the candles on the tables.

"Sorry, Steve, Frank couldn't make it. He's the guy in Marfa who'd like to ship in some kind of feed, I think," Bart was a fifty something year-old guy who could pass for a "cowboy" version of Joe Mannix from the old 1970s detective television series. I knew it from watching reruns with my dad. My pop, retired now, was a successful electrical engineer who was a connoisseur of 1970s detective series and some 1960s Westerns. So, I grew up steeped in *Mannix*, *Rockford Files*, *Maverick* and all the good ones from that great television era.

"No worries Bart, this is a good turnout," I replied.

Judge Wilson said, "Steve, we 'preciate you comin' out. We need to save rail service in our counties and think we have a proposal we all can get behind. Bud and I have met with the State and they support giving us a grant, part State and part Federal, to put the infrastructure in place."

"Sounds good. Will it work…and save our service around here?" I asked.

Bud Garcia, the Presidio County Judge replied, "We think so. Coupla more people wanna to jump in, guy over in Hot Wells wants to ship talc and another guy over in Valentine wants to ship something. Won't say what. They're too far west of Marfa for now maybe, but we'll see."

I looked around the table. Everyone was staring at me. I

studied Jim's eyes for a cue. He had nothing to offer.

"What? Just where do I fit in? I mean 'sides being a good customer and all." I was slipping into my West Texas drawl to better fit into this crew of movers and shakers, I guess.

Bart now chimed in, "Well, we gonna operate, with the Union Pacific's permission, a line from Marathon to Marfa, least for now. We'd lease track access from the UP. And we'd have just one interchange with the UP maybe in Alpine. The UP is interested. They'd only charge us a small fee for use of their track if we was generating a fair amount of traffic, that is."

"Who's we?"

"Well, technically it'd be a local rail authority and be operated by our two counties, maybe even Hudspeth County in the future."

"Sounds good, I guess. Do we need to sign a contract to ship a certain amount, or what?" They were still looking at me.

"Well, the State and Feds are chipping in on repairing the rail siding and most of the other improvements needed, and our two counties will float a small bond to cover the rest. But Steve, we still need a little help."

"Uh huh…" I was waiting.

Shank blurted out, "Well, Steve, we's wonderin' if you'd buy us a locomotive."

"A what?"

"A locomotive."

I looked at Jim and he slightly shook his head.

"How much?" As I said that, Jim's head shaking grew slightly more pronounced.

"$250,000."

"Huh?"

Bud chimed in, "Bart has talked to a short line operator up in the panhandle. They got a nice…what kind of locomotive is it?"

Bart with a great deal of excitement added, "A recently rebuilt GP-40!"

I just sat there.

"'Course, we'd pay you back...least half."

Jim gave me a stern look.

"What would I get out of this?"

"Well, you'd be saving rail service and help the economy of the region. We're so isolated out here. You know truckin's 'spensive. We need to save rail service to be competitive," Shank replied.

"Well, I'm going to have to think about this."

Bud looked at me, put his hand on my shoulder and said, "Without your help Steve, we's sunk."

"Okay, I'll think about it. $125,000 is a lot of money. I'm fine shipping, I could probably even bring some stuff in for the ranch maybe by rail, but buying a locomotive? Do we really need something as big as a GP-40?" I used to railfan a little, so I knew my locomotives.

Shank looked around at all the men around the table and then looked me in the eye, "Okay, we're counting on you, Steve. We'll let you decide how to paint the locomotive and maybe even name the line. We were thinking, Big Bend Railroad, watcha think?"

Jim and I left shortly after that, with no commitment. Of course, Jim counselled me all the way on the hour drive back to Marfa. I think he used the word liability a hundred times. I suspected Amy would agree with Jim, so I knew this was probably a bad idea.

A little time in the wilderness the next few days was exactly what the doctor ordered.

7

Big Bend Ranch State Park is really a national treasure. It is over 300,000 acres and just upriver of Big Bend National Park. It has some amazing and huge geologic features, one of the most notable being El Solitario. It was likely a huge dome at one time and has partially sunken to create a stunning circular feature visible from space. Huge, jagged rock formations surround the center. As stunning as that and many other features are, that's not why I love the park. I love it because it is the best place I know where I feel freedom and peace and isolation. I have a secret spot I love to camp that disconnects me from anything but the present. Wind and an occasional insect or two are the only noises. Just me, my small tent and a bit of gear. My car was parked just a few hundred feet away close to the two-track road. No fire. Fires were prohibited in the "backcountry" zone.

I think my total disconnection from civilization and my being able to almost sense my blood pressure lowering, helped me connect with things that really mattered to me. I discussed it with Father Mike a few times. Reflecting on my conversations with him and my personal experiences in the wild, I started to further study the concept of wilderness.

In recent weeks, I had stumbled upon some more writings of Sigurd Olsen. In addition to being a gifted nature writer, he played a huge role in establishing the National Wilderness Preservation System. There are about 111,000,000 acres of "designated wilderness" on federal public land in the US, in national parks, forests, and refuges and on Bureau of Land Management lands. A central tenet is that these lands are managed to keep the lands in a natural state and minimize the presence of man.

Sigurd's passage from his book, *Reflections from the North Country*, resonated so deeply with me when I first read it, "We cannot all live in the wilderness, or even close to it, but we can, no matter where we spend our lives, remember the background which shaped this sense of the eternal rhythm, remember that days, no matter how frenzied their pace, can be calmed and un-hurried." The wilderness before me was not part of the federal wilderness system, but the benefits were the same. Even had I never seen this stunning landscape and was trapped in an 8 to 5 job in Brooklyn, or Dallas for that matter, just knowing a moun-tain lion was crossing this country on any given moon-lit night, could bring solace to me and help me connect with the rhythms in which we evolved as a species. Just knowing it is out there has great value.

A bright shooting star suddenly pulled me back to some of the "rhythms of civilization." I was about to board a flight to perhaps finalize my marriage plans to Pauline. Before I left, I had to also try to settle the movie and railroad issues at hand.

Another shooting star told me it was time to go to sleep. In the absence of cell phone service and in the light of a jillion stars, I drifted off to sleep in my sleeping bag grateful for hav-ing an experience so elusive to most Americans, just me and the stars.

8

My wilderness relaxation mojo quickly faded as I shared coffee with Amy Monday morning.

"Sid and Tito got back with me. They want to sweeten the pot."

"How, Amy?"

Amy sat there studying my eyes with a blank stare. "Well, it's complicated."

"Uh huh."

"You might like it."

"Go on…"

"They are willing to give you 1.25% of gross receipts and a $75,000 inconvenience payment, but they want to film in your house and the ranch house too. Apparently, the scene where you described your real encounter with those crazy chicks renting the place takes on a new 'significance' in the movie."

"Don't like it."

Amy sat patiently, waiting for me to vent my spleen. She re-crossed her legs and peered out the screen into the breezy, overcast Marfa morning, tapping her pen against her notebook.

"So, are you turning this down, Steve?" She was growing a bit less patient.

I just sat there.

"Okay, their last picture was a joke, but a few years ago, a picture of theirs grossed well into the millions, like almost $100 million. That'd be like $1.25 million for us."

"Crap! I don't want them in my house!"

"Okay, I figured you'd say that, so I negotiated a plan B. Tito and Sid can tour your house, but they will not film in it. They will recreate it. But they are insistent on getting in the ranch house and extending their access until the spring. They are to be off the place by November. They will pay us $25,000 for that and 1.15% gross. That's still good money."

"Okay, but I want you there to keep an eye on them if I am not there! And no modifications to the ranch house or interior!"

"I'll see if I can insert that. I already signed off on the deal for you."

I just looked at her with a frown.

With a slightly seductive smile, she added, "Sometimes, I have to save you from yourself. You know that don't you?"

I sheepishly said, "Thank you," as I eased out the door.

Amy called out, "Clark will be thrilled!"

◆ ◆ ◆

I had an 11:00 meeting with the County Judge, Bud Garcia, so I slowly walked over to the courthouse since I was about 20 minutes early. It was a glorious Marfa morning, dry as usual, overcast lifting and brilliant blue replacing it. A cool breeze blew through occasionally, but a hot day was building—hot, but not humid, fortunately. I did not miss the humidity of my boyhood home of Houston, not one bit.

Bud's secretary Dorene was on the phone.

"Now, Ms. Parker, you know Judge Garcia just loves them animals." She looked up at me and winked. She was about sixty and one of those people who could pass for being thirty years younger if you didn't look at their facial features too closely. Almost always bright red lipstick and short skirts. She was an institution in Marfa and had survived five County Judges.

"Okay Ms. Parker, you know I'll tell the judge raht now, or when he comes outta session." Another wink. She was a flirter. "Bye-bye Ms. Parker."

Dorene gave me her biggest smile. "Okay big boy, watcha got this time?"

"I have an appointment this time. We're talking trains."

"That's right. He'll be back in a few. He is making a coffee run."

"Y'all don't have an old decrepit, bitter coffee pot here?'

"We do, sugar, but on Fridays, the Judge treats me to somethin' special. Speakin' of special, how's that nimrod cousin of yours, Clark?"

"He's fine."

"Stayin' outta jail for once?"

"Yeah, he's gotten better. He's driving a cab, or he was. Not sure now. But I think he's staying out of trouble."

"Uh huh, best he stays over there in Brewster County. Let's just say Judge Garcia ain't a fan."

"Few are, Dorene, few are. But he ain't all bad."

"Yeah, well, just sayin' what's best for your cuz."

"Understood." I heard the Judge coming.

Judge Garcia came bounding in with a big smile. "Amigo!" The Judge did not have a single hair left on his head. He was very slender, but somehow had a presence, like a guy in charge. He'd been a builder before being elected and seemed comfortable bossing people around.

"Judge, sir, reporting here to save our economy!"

"Damn straight, Steve! C'mon in."

The judge's office was adorned with a lot of West Texas trappings. On the wall behind his desk was the head of a big longhorn cow looming over him. There were pictures of the Marfa High School football team, pictures of Bud shaking hands with a couple of former presidents. He was very proud of a picture of him as a teenager with LBJ when LBJ made a whistle stop in Marfa long ago while campaigning.

My favorite photograph was an old black and white of him trying to stay on a wild horse as a young man. He'd spent some time as a ranch hand on a few ranches in the area. Bud had lots of stories and loved telling them.

"Steve, you played some football, huh? Safety, receiver?"

"Some, played high school varsity all four years."

"No college?"

"Not much, tore a ligament my first year at Texas A&M and I was done. Made it in a few games on special teams though that year. I tried to rehab, but lost interest and kind of just started focusing on my studying. I'd lost a step or two, and at A&M, that was too much. Love the game though."

"Watcha study?"

"Forestry, believe it or not."

"You ever do anything with it?"

"Kind of, I guess. After I came out of the Army, I worked for a Senator in DC a few years on related issues."

"Oh yeah? Who'd you work for?"

"She was a dinosaur from Nebraska. Bad memories, really."

"Nebraska, they ain't got no forests up there!"

"Not much, but they do have some pretty country."

"Well, I'm glad you're back home and doing great things here. Speakin' of great things, how 'bout that locomotive?"

"I'm in, but I want to do it a certain way. I'll lease us a locomotive for two years. Company out of Midland. Amy found them. They will provide all the maintenance and inspections. Good company. People around Midland and Odessa speak highly of them. After two years, the county, or whoever, will have to pay the lease if you want it still. There'd be an option in the lease for you."

"That works for me! That's great news!"

"Amy will have to help you on this. I head out for France in a couple of days."

The judge gave me a sneaky grin, "I hear you got a sweetheart over there.".

"I do."

"Well, you go have some fun over there, and we'll get a railroad a running here. Can we paint it? Put a name on it?"

"Can't paint it. It's a lease, but we can put a sign on it.

I knew you would want to know. It's black with yellow safety stripes. I'll send you a picture of it. They can bring it down here on a few weeks' notice."

As I got up to walk out, I noticed a picture on the wall.

"Who's that a photo of, Judge? I pointed to a very old photo of a young man.

"That's Jose Garcia. My great grandfather."

"Handsome man."

"Well, he was until the Texas Rangers gotta holt of him."

"What happened?"

"You ever hear of the Porvenir Massacre?"

"No."

"My great grandfather got gunned down by the Texas Rangers and the US Army about a hundred years ago for no reason. He was working on a ranch out near Porvenir. It's way out there, south of Valentine on the Rio Grande. Well, anyway, he and a bunch of other Mexican men were gunned down in retaliation for a raid on the Nevill Place. He had nothing to do with the raid. He'd worked for the Nevill family and had good relations. That's how it was back then. Somethin' happen, go find a Mexican to pin it on, any one of them will do. My poor great grandmother had to provide for three kids from then on by herself."

"I'm sorry to hear that."

"Things a little better now, I guess. But this anti-Mexican talk I hear outta the mouth of some of our politicians, kinda makes my blood boil."

"I know. Don't much care for it myself. You have a great day, Judge."

The judge took a deep sigh and smiled. He got up and walked me to the door.

"Thanks for the locomotive, Steve! You gonna have the best service ever. I promise!"

◆ ◆ ◆

As I entered the white, bright sunshine, outside the courthouse, I saw Clark standing near the street in a Hawaiian shirt, jeans and flip flops.

He waved at me. "Steve! Amy said you'd be over here." He was grinning big and wearing sunglasses.

"Hi Clark. You might want to walk on down the street with me. I heard Judge Garcia gets a little anxious when you're around."

"Damn that guy's got a memory! It's been years since I sold his niece pot. She screwed me on it too! She never paid. He still bitch'in 'bout that? Talk 'bout someone holding a grudge."

"Yeah, well, probably best you don't be too visible over here in Presidio County. Not sure presumption of innocence would hold for you here."

"Huh?"

"Never mind. What's up, Clark?"

"I just wanted to thank you for making me a movie star, *muchacho*!"

"Oh, yeah. The movie thing."

"I figur' I'll stay over here for a while before I move out to LA. You know, since we're filming here and all?"

"Probably smart Clark. See how things work out."

"Yeah, I don't want to go all Hollywood, you know? The movie people said they love how 'organic' I am!"

"Yep. You wouldn't want to mess that up, for sure."

"I hope I get to kiss some famous movie star in the picture!"

"Well, it will be interesting regardless, Clark."

"The movie people said not to count on that though. They said they wanted me for a 'neesh' role whatever that is. They said they want me to play the role of an older college student who goes 'round town flipping off everyone. That don't sound too exciting. I mean I know how to flip the bird as good as the next guy I guess, but I figur' once they see me in action, they'll give me a bigger part, much bigger. Rah't now, I only got a few lines."

"Well, do your best Clark and see what happens." By now we were getting near my house. I mainly wanted to make a big sandwich, crack open a beer and get to packing.

"They have me saying, 'I'm just here to see all the fine art you got in this place.' What kind of line is that, Steve?"

"Clark, just be glad you're in the movie at all."

"Shit, I'm getting' mad just thinking 'bout it, Steve! That and couple other lines, that's all I got. How am I gonna break through with pissant lines like that?"

"Clark, don't look a gift horse in the mouth!"

"What's horses gotta do with this, Steve? You even listening to me?"

"Look Clark, I gotta go. I got some stuff to take care of. You still going to be able to give me a ride to the airport?"

"Yeah, I got the cab that day. I ain't quit yet. It's 'barrassing though, being a cabbie, you know, while bein' a movie star and all."

"Ain't nothing wrong with being a cab driver, Clark, and you know it. It's an important service."

"Yeah, guess so," I heard along with his flip flops flopping down the street.

9

It was a cold and rainy morning at Charles de Gaulle airport as the plane taxied to the gate. Though thrilled to be back in France and even just hearing French spoken on the plane, I found coming into Paris in the early morning hours distinctly depressing. I dreaded the cab ride to my hotel. The scenery between the airport and my hotel near the Arc de Triomphe was pretty awful, actually reminiscent of the gray landscape off the 610 Loop in Houston, lots of graffiti, warehouses and cement. Fortunately, my spirits lifted as we exited the express and entered the Paris I love—beautiful, beige, old limestone buildings, lots of grass and flowers and statues scattered about. A few people were out exercising and shopping, but most Parisians were enjoying a long Saturday morning at home.

Given her hectic week or so, I decided to stay over in Paris a week before heading down to stay with Pauline. I had started a short story about two ill-fated lovers in Paris and wanted to do a spot of writing *in situ*. I wanted Paris to feed my soul as I captured a scene of their final farewell, maybe in the *Jardin du Luxembourg*. I hadn't decided.

I was also toying with the idea of going over to Normandy a couple of days to see the Normandy American Cemetery and D-Day landing beaches. It was something I'd always wanted to do. I was slated to go there during my time in the Army, but my unit's participation in a ceremony got nixed at the last minute. I was conflicted because I wanted to see Pauline as soon as possible, but she said she didn't want to go there, and she had a stressful week at work. I'd hoped we could go together later, but she'd been twice and said she'd left very depressed both times. I wanted to understand why she didn't want to come up to Paris at least but figured I'd have that chat in person with her.

I also wanted to get my French mojo back on before I met Pauline. I wanted to be well rested and ready to speak French with her if she so chose. Pauline's English was perfect, but somehow it just seemed right to speak French with her in her native country. I guess I just wanted to be acclimated. I knew just being in Paris a few days would rev me up to see her. My suspicions were right. I felt a mojo almost right away that was distinctly Parisian.

After dropping my bags at the desk, I hit my favorite café. Even jet lagging a bit, the taste of a *pain au chocolat* and a spot of coffee after such a long absence only heightened that feeling of a new energy, a French energy. I had reservations for Victor's on Rue Lauriston and could already taste the duck and the red wine that I always got. This was going to be great. My only question was should I contact any of my old acquaintances while here. With that, I struggled.

After a long nap, I decided to call Chester just for the hell of it. His number was still in my phone. The person who answered was obviously not Chester, or even French. I hung up. A few minutes later my phone rang.

"Steve, old boy?"

"Chester?"

"Indeed, dear chap, indeed."

"I just called your number. Thought it belonged to someone else now."

"That was Yelena. She's my roommate, kind of."

"Okay...well I'm in town and..."

Chester cut me off, and said, "And you missed your old

buddy Chester, eh?"

"Yeah…something like that."

"Well, the gang is going out tonight. Yelena and I may join them. You are welcome as always."

"Yeah, maybe so. Where?'

"Beth hasn't decided."

"Still hanging around Beth?"

"Why wouldn't I be?"

"Dunno, been awhile. That's all."

"Where the hell have you been, mate?"

"Here and there."

"Radio silence for months from you, old chap."

"I know."

"I'll text with our rendezvous spot later. Sound good?"

"*Bien sûr.*"

After a short nap, I was ready to reconnect with my Paris. Everyone who has spent time here has their own little Paris. Paris is not as much a city but a life-changing experience. Like the sunsets of Marfa, it is something you feel, you absorb. Crazily enough, like West Texas for me, it is a place that becomes part of you, almost like a DNA alteration. You absolutely are changed. If you ever meet someone who claims they spent a few weeks in Paris and didn't feel it, don't walk away from them, run! They are probably soulless.

Post nap, I got tickets on a train to Caen in a couple of days. Rental car reserved as well. I had never been to that part of France and was excited. In the Army I was in the Second Infantry Division and wanted to connect with a little "2nd ID" history across the region, to follow their path in June of 1944. I was thrilled to be finally getting to Normandy.

Victor's on Rue Lauriston was one of my favorite restaurants in Paris. The place has maybe ten or twelve tables. Belle Époque, vintage posters, old maps and ornate mirrors are scattered about. Just the right level of lighting. I loved the way they use a tall, wide decanter to serve your red wine.

I had made the mistake of bringing Chester here once. He was in one of his pouty funks and he almost ruined the meal. I decided on this night, as one of my Marine Corps buddies once told me, "It is better to be alone than wishing you were alone." I would enjoy Victor's *tout seul.*

As I savored the entrée, a fresh tuna avocado soufflé, I thought about with this kind of food, I could savor it alone and have a damn good time enjoying my own company. The duck was so good it overwhelmed the senses. The cute waitress seemed a tad confused by my aloneness and chatted with me a few times. As is often the case, she assumed I was British due to my eccentric behavior of dining alone and being able to speak French. I often enjoyed seeing French people's surprise at meeting a bilingual American. My French was coming back nicely.

As I focused on the pleasure of the meal, I couldn't completely shut out a thought that kept nagging at me. I was picking up just a slightly negative vibe from Pauline over our last chats. I wondered if my staying in Paris a few days and my trip to Normandy was my avoiding confronting whatever was bothering her. Or was it passive aggression on my part? I was completely sold on Pauline. She still appeared to have a few reservations. I wondered if I was overreacting. I resolved to see her as soon as possible and stop delaying. If there was a funk emerging, I wanted to nip it right away. I'd book the TGV to Nîmes to leave as soon as possible after my trip to Normandy.

As I slowly savored the final bites of my strawberry tarte and coffee, I got a text.

"Sir Winston, 5 rue de Presbourg, 21:00."

Ugh. I hated that place. Shortly after arriving in Paris the last trip, I tried to go there. A horrible French woman physically stopped me from going in. She pointed down at my shoes and shook her head. I was wearing regular brown shoes that had a bit of a tread like hiking boots. It was there I learned the meaning of "*faire une randonée,*" to take a hike. Being fresh in France, language a bit rusty and having had a few drinks, I responded by "conjugating an English word, "Fuckez-vous" as I drifted away. Fortunately, she just appeared confused. That was my only real unpleasant encounter during my previous lengthy stay in Paris.

I texted back, "Chester, not my bag. Can we meet somewhere else?"

"No. Everyone has been notified."

"I'm out then. *Bonne soirée.*"

I paid and walked out into a shiny, misty Paris twilight. Couples huddled close as they dashed about. Here I was alone, all alone, in Paris. I yearned for Pauline. I wanted her to show me "her" Paris. She had attended college here though she had lived in southern France for much of her life. Like most non-Parisian French people, she had mixed emotions about Paris. Jokes abounded in southern France about the snooty Parisians.

As I slowly walked up Avenue Kléber towards my hotel, I consciously soaked in Paris one step at a time. It was almost dark. Even in the mist, it was beautiful. I heard a person speaking very excitedly as I passed closed shutters. I saw a couple making out at a bus stop. I saw people walking their small dogs. Typical Paris life.

Two new texts.

"You win. Honest Lawyer, rue de la Pompe. You know it. 22:00. The gang wants to see you."

"Copy that, Chester. *À bientôt.*"

Text two was the disturbing one.

"I hate to do this, but I have to go out of town two weeks, a little more. I am livid, but I can't get out of it. It's a trip to Réunion Island. My partner was supposed to take it. Will mean huge business for my job. Can't get out of it. I tried! I am so so so sorry love. I will make it up to you I promise. You can come down and stay in my place or stay in Paris longer. I love you and

I am so sorry!!!"

That was a gut shot. I mean I trusted her, but it still really worried me. Was she pulling away? Crap. I decided then that I'd just spend a couple more weeks in Paris. I'd make the best of it, and maybe get some writing in, even if I was a bit worried about Pauline. Okay, well a few drinks with the *nouvelle* lost generation would get my mind off of it! Wow, Réunion Island! Lucky Pauline.

I changed the course of my walk to head to Place Victor Hugo, where ten streets came together. There was once a beautiful statue of Victor Hugo here, but the Nazis melted it down during their occupation. I wish the statue had been recreated. It was stunning. There is now a somewhat nondescript fountain in the center of the Place.

As I rounded the Place, I passed by Église Saint-Honoré-d'Éylau. I recalled from my previous stay that Hemingway married Pauline Pfeiffer at this church in 1927. He was previously married to Hadley Richardson and they had a son. But since it was not a Catholic wedding, the Church deemed it a non-event, clearing the way for Ernest to marry Pauline, who came from a wealthy Catholic family. Ernest converted to Catholicism before the marriage.

Ernest and Pauline honeymooned near Aigues-Mortes in the South of France, a short drive from my Pauline's home in Sommières. Even though the marriage was somewhat ill-fated —Ernest left Pauline for Martha Gellhorn in 1940—it had profound literary consequences. Pauline wanted to return to the States and their friend and novelist, John Dos Passos, recommended Key West. She and Ernest would leave Paris in March of 1928. Also, their wild honeymoon in the South of France inspired his novel, *The Garden of Eden*. Not published until 1986, it was one of my favorites, not for style since it's rough, but rather how he tackled a very complex topic regarding human sexuality and gender roles. He worked on that novel for 15 years.

That novel was one of those I liked to consider as I

explored my writing. He broached a subject area, many years before anyone in "polite" American society would discuss publicly, non-binary sexual identities. Writers can help enhance the public's understanding of difficult topics and hopefully lead to a more thoughtful and accepting world. Likewise, Rachel Carlson's *Silent Spring* is often credited with helping society understand that the perceived gains of pesticide use can be offset by many negative impacts that may be hard to immediately discern. For me, that was what made writing so appealing. Writers can help lead us to live more thoughtfully. In that sense, writers can change the world.

10

The drizzle had picked up just as I arrived at The Honest Lawyer on the corner of Rue de Sontay and Rue de la Pompe. The wood paneled, well-lit interior was quite a contrast from the now dark, wet streets of Paris. I scanned the long bar to the left as I walked in and then proceeded to look at the rows of tables to the right. No one I recognized.

I had visited this bar a few times on my past stay. I recalled a fairly international clientele, lots of Americans because the US Embassy had housing in the area. It was a nice place, the Guinness on tap was modestly priced relative to other bars in the area and the food was pretty decent.

I looked at my watch, 10:15. No one. No one I knew anyway.

I nursed a Guinness and waited. I noticed an attractive woman with short blond hair sitting at a table across from me near a window. She too appeared alone. She was looking at her watch as well. We smiled at each other a couple of times. I rechecked my phone to re-read the text. Yes, Honest Lawyer, 22:00. At 10:30, I texted Chester.

After coming back from the restroom, there was still no one I recognized and even the cute blond had left. About 10:40 I called Chester. I left a message.

"Looks like we were both stood up." Woman's voice, flat English. I turned around to see the blond sitting at a table behind me now.

"Mind if I join you while we wait?" She had a beautiful

smile. I couldn't place her nationality. Not French.

"Sure. Please do."

"Sofia."

"Steve."

"Nice to meet you, Steve."

"Likewise, Sofia."

"What's your story Steve? How did you wind up in the bar on a rainy Saturday night in Paris apparently alone? American, right?"

"Yes. Long story."

"Looks like we have time. My date got cold feet apparently."

"How could anyone stand you up?" She was very attractive. 5' 9" or so, slender, very pretty blue eyes. Modest dress but just short enough to be demurely sexy.

"That is an excellent question." She smiled in a way that awakened me that she might be trying to pick me up.

"Well, I am not officially stood up yet. My friends could still arrive."

"Friends?"

"Yes, I was meeting a group of friends."

"I see." With that she excused herself for a moment.

I checked my phone. Still nothing. That little rat Chester probably purposely threw me off track. He was a jealous guy. So afraid I'd get some attention at his expense. Within the circle, there was a young lady named Sarah that might have had a bit of a thing for me, and it drove him nuts last go around. I started to ask myself why I was still here just as Sofia returned. Fresh lipstick. Pretty smile again. She apparently had a large supply of smiles.

"So, Sofia, why are you here in Paris?"

"I'm Danish. I work for the embassy here."

"Interesting. What do you do there?"

"This and that. Mostly administration."

Long pause. Clearly, she didn't want to elaborate. It added a sense of mystery to Sofia. She could really be an accountant, or she may work in intelligence. One never knew when one met a foreigner in Paris.

"And you? Why are you here?"

I stumbled here just a bit.

"I am a writer..." just then I got a glimpse of a pale skinned, soaked red head walking by the bar outside.

"...and I'm here to meet up with my fiancée."

For over a year, I'd been seeing a mysterious redhead woman at strange yet pivotal chapters in my life. I initially "met" her on the streets on Marfa. I had just about decided it was my imagination, yet there she was again, I think. She went by so fast. It was dark. I'd nick-named her "The Red Angel." Maybe she was my guardian angel. Maybe I was crazy.

"Oh, so you are engaged?"

Sofia was very pretty but I knew what my answer needed to be. I guess the Red Angel didn't trust me and thought I needed a wake-up call.

"Yes."

"And where is your fiancée now?"

She was getting a bit nosy. "Actually, I'm heading south to meet her."

"So, you are free for tonight?" One blondish eyebrow lifted.

"Not exactly."

"Suit yourself, Steve. I'm not looking to "hook up" as you Americans say. I just got out of a long-term relationship that ended rather poorly. I'm just looking for someone to have a couple of drinks with and enjoy a bit of Paris on a rainy night. I'm pretty harmless. I think it is great that you have found your special person." She again smiled and tilted her head, "Ever known someone from Denmark? We are serviceable company. We are quite civil and tell the best stories."

"Well, I meant I'm supposed to meet some friends here."

"Uh huh." She opened her eyes big and looked around the bar and smiled. "C'mon, there's a bar around the corner I want to try. It is called something like 'Le Tiki-Paris Bar.' Sounds like it might be fun."

I paused and just tried to size her up. Was she just looking to hang out? Maybe even she didn't know for sure. Before I caught myself, I blurted out, "A tiki Bar? Sure. Sounds fun."

Just as we started to walk down Rue de la Pompe, I peered over across the street and saw Chester and a woman, maybe the Yelena he mentioned earlier, hanging on to him waiting to cross the street. He didn't see me. I was under Sofia's umbrella and besides, I didn't feel the need to be seen, particularly by him. Just seeing him kind of awakened an animosity, and I kept on walking. He'd grown a beard. It looked good on him. A pang of guilt crossed over me, but Sofia and I kept walking, her modest heels clicking on the soaked sidewalk.

◆ ◆ ◆

Sofia was right. Danes are rather serviceable company. Once we got to the tiki bar, the Mai Tais and Zombies flowed a little too easily. I found my smiles coming often as well. The interior of the bar did reflect an exotic South Pacific ambiance that was relaxing and seductive. The music was a strange blend of island music with an electronica bass, very distinctive. Strategically placed huge monitors designed to look like windows conveyed the impression of one actually being in the islands. Somehow the climate control system imitated ocean breezes. One corner replicated a storm coming in off the ocean.

As Sofia and I enjoyed something orange and sweet she ordered us, a tall guy walked up to us from behind the bar.

"Hey folks, you from around here?" He had a recognizable slight drawl. His smile made me feel a sense of comfort and familiarity. I studied him a second and started to reply, but Sofia beat me.

"We're from the Netherlands."

I looked at her a second and started to play along until the guy spoke again.

"Well, welcome folks to what I think is the best Tiki bar

in Paris."

I blurted out, "Wait, are you from Texas?"

"Damn straight. The name is Beach, pleasure to meet you." He stuck is hand out and looked at me a second and slowly smiled. "You from Texas too, aren't you?"

"Well, like we say in Texas, never ask a man if he's from Texas. If he is, he'll tell you within minutes of meeting him. If his isn't, you'll just embarrass him when he must acknowledge otherwise.

"I like you, Tex."

"The name's Steve."

"Guess what Tex? You gonna have a good time tonight." He just smiled and strolled away.

"Beach" returned in a bit. Over the increasingly loud music, some kind of strange retro surfing music, he said, "Say, you're the first Texan I've met here. It's been a long time. Look, here's my card. Text me. Let's get lunch this week. You name the day." The drinks kept arriving on the house until Sofia and I said, "No More!"

"When I finally convinced the waitress to cease the flow, I asked her what is this last round? She said something over the music I didn't understand.

"Blushok"

"*Comment?*"

"Blushok"

"*Comment?*"

"*Requin bleu!*"

I turned to Sofia. "Hey Sofia, the waitress told me that these are Blue Sharks. One-third tequila, vodka and curaçao!"

I was rather friendly with Sofia by this time. I noticed my face was rather close to hers. The music was loud. Her lipstick was quite shiny. Alarms were going off in my head which I'd apparently been dutifully ignoring for a while.

"No wonder I'm buzzing, Steve!" Sofia gave me a droopy-eyed smile and drifted off to the dance floor and started dancing with a group of younger people awhile. She was clearly having a good time.

It really wouldn't have been difficult to get in trouble with Sofia, especially after one too many Blue Sharks. She was stunning. What was maybe even more seductive about her was the fact that she was also funny as hell as she drank. Towards the end of the evening, she confessed that she was really just mad at her boyfriend and that they weren't exactly completely broken up. They were arguing by text as she waited at the Honest Lawyer.

We shared way more than we should have with each other about our respective relationships, but sometimes you find yourself sharing with a stranger when you really have no one else in your life to talk to about such things. Her boyfriend was French, and like my experiences with Pauline, there was a wall at times. I noted that I laughed so easily with Sofia, something I seldom did with Pauline. I ended up having a "98% platonic" few hour fling with Sofia because we connected on many levels.

After a couple of hours in the exotic surroundings of the tiki bar and way too much to drink, I walked her home. She had removed her shoes and was walking on the streets of Paris in bare feet. Not a great idea, but at least the sidewalks had been washed with rain a few hours before. Though much improved as I understand it, dog turds were still threat on the sidewalks of Paris, so I tried to watch closely before us. She sang a song in Danish.

It started pouring just as we arrived at her building, so I dashed inside the kind of shabby *rez de chaussée* of her building.

"Steve, you are welcome to come up a little while to wait for the rain to stop."

I just looked at her.

"I know, Steve. I shouldn't have said that, but I'm drunk and I don't think you'll try anything. You're in love with a beautiful French woman! I don't blame her. You're a good kisser!"

"What! I didn't kiss you!"

"Nice try." She smiled from ear to ear.

"Say, why'd you try to pass us off as Dutch in the bar?"

"I always say that. Everyone in Paris expects people from the Netherlands to be everywhere. It avoids questions."

"Huh?"

"When I say I'm Danish, it prompts more questions. When I say, I'm from the Netherlands, I never get another question."

"You're kind of secretive."

"I just don't like answering a lot of questions. I guess it's my training."

She was very pretty. Just then the image of the Red Angel walking in front of the Honest Lawyer flashed in my head.

"I better go. I had a great time, Sofia. I hope you and your boyfriend can work through your issues."

"And likewise, for you Steve." After a gigantic yawn, she kissed my cheek and hung on to me a second as she lost her balance. I eased away once I was sure she was steady.

"Maybe I'll see you at the Honest Lawyer sometime again."

"Hope so, Steve," as she pushed the elevator button. "You know Steve, it is rare I have this kind of connection with a stranger. Feels so weird, you just walking out of my life after all we shared over a sum total of what? Less than four hours? Somehow it feels like I have known you a long time." She smiled as she stood in the entrance to the elevator.

Just as I walked outside, the rain began to pour like never before. Sofia suddenly reached out of the door, pulled mc in and said, "C'mon up. Wait it out, idiot."

We climbed into her tiny elevator and I was very conscious of how closely we stood together. That was fortunately as close as we got the rest of the evening. I woke up on her sofa about 8:00 am feeling pretty hung over. We shared Tylenol, a bit of a hard baguette and coffee and I was on my way.

I was pretty sure I'd never see her again, but again I was struck how she affected me in a couple of ways. After hanging out with Sophie, I was determined to go to Chateau-Thierry instead of Normandy for now. She made me wonder why Pauline and I seldom share laughs together. Why was our relationship so serious much of the time? I was tempted to meet Sophie again to talk about the plight of having a French lover, but I wasn't completely sure I had the purest of motives.

◆ ◆ ◆

Late morning the next day, my cellphone vibrated.

"American asshole."

I replied, "British bastard."

"I'm American. I just speak as though I'm educated."

"Hungover. Fuck off, Chester." Actually, I was feeling pretty decent considering how much I had drank the previous evening.

"Later."

◆ ◆ ◆

I finally got out of bed around 2:00. I was starving but feeling so much better. Against my better judgement I texted Chester again.

"Sorry about last night."

"No worries, mate. You can make it up Tuesday."

"It's a workday."

"Uh huh. It's our dance night. Don't you remember anything? Besides, none of us work, you silly bastard."

"Silly me. I had forgotten."

"All good."

"What the hell you talking about Chester?"

"Maybe this started after you hauled ass on us as you Americans like to say."

"Do you like stewed tomatoes?"

"Huh?"

"Did you fancy some marmite today?"

"Okay, touché. I'm conflicted. I've been around Brits a bit

too long I suppose."

"What's this dance business, Chester?"

"It's ritual. Beth and Sarah love it. Of course we hit L'As du Fallafel before going."

At this point, I actually called him.

"Chester, I want to see you guys but shouting over loud music, I dunno. "

"Look, Beth wants you there. I don't give a shit really. I mean, you know, I'd like to see you. I guess. No, I would."

"Okay, I'll see you guys at L'As du Fallafel. Fallafel sounds good. Probably not up for the dancing. What time?"

"I'll text you the time."

"Hey, Steve, good to hear your voice. I mean it. Mostly."

"Fuck off. I mean it mostly."

I wasn't sure what to think of Chester. He was one of those "friends" that one never knows about. I didn't trust him, yet I kind of liked him. He was important, sort of, during my first stay in Paris. I had mixed emotions about seeing Sarah. She and I came pretty close to having a thing on my last visit. I came to have feelings for her, but I never acted on it. I think she felt likewise. Not sure I needed any sort of repeats after last night.

I decided to drink a lot of water and crash again.

11

"I can't hear a word that you're saying." Once again, my lips were within the inches of another woman. Sarah was shouting for me to hear her. Her voice was a tad hoarse which made her somehow sexier. It all started innocently enough.

I met the gang a L'As du Fallafel. We had the best falafel Paris had to offer per Lenny Kravitz. Actually, I'd been here many times. The falafel was very good. Being kind of nervous hanging out with these people, I had three Maccabee beers. I had no idea they were about 8% alcohol. I also used copious quantities of the red sauce which reeked of garlic. I thought that might have retardant qualities. Both Beth and Sarah seemed rather happy to see me. Beth's *la bise* actually grazed my lip which was a serious *faux pas* in France. Damn near prosecutable by law. One is not supposed to touch lips to cheek even during the French greeting ritual. That might get you thrown into French social timeout, at least banned from the next dinner party. We are talking serious offense. Of course, Beth was British and rather drunk.

It was about half of the same *nouvelle* lost generation I had known from my first time in Paris. I called them that because there was something very reminiscent of Hemingway's novel, *The Sun Also Rises,* about these people. They used the words "rather" or "splendid" a great deal. Chester was the only American in the group though he seemed to want to pass for British or at least as he proudly termed it, "transatlantic." Think Cary Grant's accent.

Against my better judgement, I went to the UFO bar. We had one drink and then somehow, Sarah and I spent practically the whole night on the dance floor together. I kept waiting for the Red Angel to show up to get me to straighten out. I was engaged! She never showed. I wondered if maybe she had given up on me. We mainly danced but a few times she collapsed into my arms. She was sweaty, but that didn't bother me in the slightest. Pauline hauling ass to the Réunion Island entered my mind a few times. Especially when Sarah was in my arms. She was in a slinky short dress. Bare wet shoulders. I was a sucker for her English accent. I was pondering things I knew I shouldn't. When I looked into her eyes, I felt that awareness of a human-to-human connection I had experienced with her before on my previous stay in Paris.

While I was waiting for her to go to the bathroom, I realized I was about to really screw up. I was committed to Pauline and I needed to own that. Maybe it was the woman dancing next to us with red hair. Not the Red Angel, but now, maybe just red hair had that needed effect!

I said goodbye to the gang and led Sarah outside onto the street in front of the club. Chester looked very confused.

We paused under a greenish streetlight. I took her hands and looked her in the eyes.

"Sarah, you're special. If I wasn't engaged, I'd be very interested in you. It was great seeing you again. I've always felt a connection with you. I don't know what it is. I don't understand it. I had the best time tonight. I lit up when I saw you. I am headed down to the South of France to meet my fiancé. I didn't intend to go dancing with the gang, but I did. I think…"

"Steve, you don't have to explain. You're a great guy. I feel that connection too. I seriously do. But if you feel that your fiancé is the one, by all means, go get her. Make it work. You're a great guy. Many guys would enjoy shagging a girl before getting married. Who'd know?"

"I would."

"That's what I mean. You're special."

"I don't feel too special, getting myself into a situation I shouldn't."

We just looked into each other's eyes. We were experiencing some kind of profound connection with no bodily contact.

"Steve, get the hell out of here! Stop putting yourself in these situations. You're about to get married for crying out loud!" She laughed and pushed me away.

"Okay." I slowly walked away. I looked back and said, "Hey Sarah, you're pretty damn special, too!"

"Hurry back if you get dumped. I know you won't." She smiled, blew me a kiss and headed back in the bar.

About 10:00 o'clock the next morning, my phone rang.

"Steve, I love you." A beautiful French accent.

"I love you too, Pauline."

"I miss you, Steve."

"I miss you so much."

"Leaving for airport. I'll be back very soon."

"Let me know when I can come. I need so much to see you!"

"I must see you, too! I detest this came up."

"Yeah sure. Two weeks at Réunion Island?"

"Well, that part is good at least."

"I love you. Talk soon."

Right afterwards, my phone rang again.

"Hi angel."

"Hi, you getting frisky with me, Steve?"

"Oh, hi Chester. In your wildest dreams."

"P'raps in my wildest nightmares, eh? Lunch?"

"Sure."

I had a couple of weeks on my hands in Paris. Never a bad

thing I suppose. That morning I moved to a hotel that offered the chance to write outside on mild days. I moved to the Hotel Foch on Rue Marbeau, close to the leafy park all along Avenue Foch. A few benches waited for me and my laptop. It was a slightly lengthy but pleasant stroll to Restaurant Victor and a number of other places, including the Honest Lawyer. There was a small "garden" at the hotel where I could sit outside, but it was small enough that sharing it with a few smokers wasn't my preference.

Chester wanted a burger. We met at Schwartz's Deli near Trocadéro. He was already there with Yelena in a corner booth. She really was gorgeous. Like too gorgeous for Chester to land. I mean Chester C. Coolidge III was handsome enough I suppose. He was about 30, tall. Dressed kind of preppy. Light brown-blond hair. I guess he favored F. Scott Fitzgerald from the pictures I had seen. But she was a knockout in the light of day. Tall, slender, blond hair, eastern European accent?

"Steve my man! Looks like life is treating you well!"

"Can't complain."

"Meet Yelena."

"Hi. Pleasure."

"Nice to meet you Steve." Good English, just a heavy accent. She had that "model" look.

"Yelena has to run. She's meeting friends nearby." Yelena stood. She must have been near six feet tall.

"So nice to meet you, Steve."

"Likewise, Yelena, likewise."

Chester attentively watched her walk out the door.

"What do you think, mate?"

"She's incredible, Chester. Where'd you meet her?"

"British embassy."

"Really?"

"Yeah, she thinks I work for our embassy." He had a sneaky look on his tanned face.

"And why would she think that?"

"Well, I had no choice. She loves the glamour of the diplomatic life."

"Tell me more, Chester."

"Well, she wasn't interested in me until she thought I worked in the embassy."

"She Russian?"

"Ukrainian. I know what you are thinking Steve. She's a spy. There's no way Chester could land her otherwise. I read your wicked little mind, my friend."

"Uh huh. Just be careful."

"She damn near lives with me, old chap!"

"Uh huh. Does she ever ask you questions about your so-called embassy job?"

"Well, yeah."

"What do you tell her?"

"I wing it man. I think she's really falling for me."

"I think you need to level with her. That will be clarifying for the both of you."

"Maybe, but I think she digs dating a diplomat."

"One way to find out." Chester looked a bit worried. He looked around the restaurant like he really wanted to be away from me, from this discussion.

"So enough about me. What about you?"

"Did I mention Pauline to you?"

"Who?"

"My *fiancée*."

"What!? You finally found someone who'd have you?" The cocky Chester was returning.

"Yeah, she's beautiful and smart and just incredible to be around."

"American?"

"French."

"Uh huh."

"What?"

"Tell me, does she know you are pretty wealthy?"

"Oh bullshit, Chester! Don't give me that!"

"Uh huh. No one could love the real Chester, but this

beautiful French woman is ready to marry you?"

"Yep. That's about it." I smiled at Chester. It was coming back to me all the things I despised about him.

All of a sudden, Chester looked very worried. He looked deep in thought. He leaned back took a deep breath and said, "I need help."

"Yes?"

"It ain't money. My dad's stocks have exploded. He has greatly increased my allocation." Really, he meant his allowance, but he never called it that. Kind of embarrassing.

"Your dad still doing well? Still in Baltimore?"

"Yes, look, I have a problem. I have diplomatic plates on my car. The dude I got them from has demanded I return them."

"What? You have dip plates?!! Are you fucking nuts???"

"Yeah, I know. Could get me in a little hot water."

"Hot water hell! Deported and jailed stateside my friend."

"No way!"

"Impersonating a US diplomat? Good luck with that, buddy."

"Well, yeah, if you put it that way. Maybe." Chester's eyebrows furrowed as though he was suddenly realizing his profound stupidity.

"No maybe about it. Get rid of them n-o-w."

"What will Yelena think?"

"Shit, that's your least problem. Look you got to dump those plates and tell her the truth!"

"Yeah. I will, but we were supposed to go out of town this weekend. I want her to really fall for me before I tell her."

"Look, tell her the embassy advised the employees that it was too risky to have dip plates. You had to change them. But you must tell her right away you aren't a diplomat. She really could be a spy. That way you'll know."

"Yeah, yeah. Soon enough," he looked really relieved. "You're brilliant Steve! I knew you could help me! I gotta run! I need to get those plates back. Some strange chap has been following me, I think. You can take care of this can't you?" as he shoved the last part of the burger in his mouth.

"Sure, Chester," but he was already almost out the door.

I knew I needed new friends. Living as a hermit and writing was starting to sound irresistible.

◆ ◆ ◆

I committed myself to two solid days of writing. I'd reward myself at the end of each day with a long leisurely meal accompanied by a *cinquante,* pretty much two-thirds of a bottle of wine. I had committed to meet "Beach," the owner of the tiki bar Friday for a late lunch. That meant I had a couple of whole days to write. Problem was, I wanted to write four or so different books at once. I'd stalled on my short story about my lovers in Paris.

The leading contender now was about an African-American World War I doughboy who stayed behind after the war to escape the racism of America. I also wanted to write a natural history of the Big Bend region with a signal as to how we can work with everyone--ranchers, activists, residents, state and feds to protect this region. It's too important to just hope for the best. It's a national treasure, really a worldwide treasure. It must be respectfully conserved in a way that respects private property but saves its beauty. I didn't want it to change. I was also toying with something to help people understand what it's like to fall in love with someone from another culture.

The first day went well and fairly productive. The second day started well. I went to the park along Avenue Foch and claimed a great park bench. The flowers surrounding it were beautiful. The temperatures were mild, sunny, but hints of fall were present. Lots of beautiful people strolling down the sidewalk. I got distracted that afternoon by a couple of texts. Chester tried to reach me with a sense of urgency. I texted him back but no response.

About 4:00, I got a text from my Danish friend. I was surprised because I didn't remember giving her my number.

"Hey Steve, Sofia here. Can you meet me at the Honest Lawyer? I need your advice. French relationship stuff."

I didn't reply. I knew it was too easy to pick up where we left off. She was just a little too cute, too sexy.

I was able to knock out another couple of hours but as the evening rush hour started, it was time to stop. I went to the hotel and took what I thought would be a short nap. I conked out and slept three hours. Wide awake at 8:00 pm. I didn't feel like going out, so I grabbed a pizza and a bottle of red and went back to the room. A funk seized me, and I suddenly felt extremely lonely and doubts about Pauline started to grow. When I recalled the day's events, I was startled that I still hadn't heard from Chester. I texted him again.

About three glasses of red and three slices into my meal, a profound depression hit me out of the blue. I had also gotten some e-mails about what pricks the movie guys had been to Amy back in Marfa and how my railroad efforts to help Marfa's economy were falling apart because the Union Pacific Railroad was getting cold feet, and of course, there were problems securing a locomotive. I felt like I needed to go back to Marfa, but I was stranded in Europe and still hadn't seen Pauline.

I never thought I could be wealthy and be so stressed. It made me reflect on Jim Carrey's words, "I think everybody should get rich and famous and do everything they ever dreamed of so they can see that it's not the answer."

That struck me as so true. So many people think all their problems would disappear if only they had enough money. While it's true that money removes some daily concerns, concerns remain, and actually a number of new ones can surface. I was still grateful that my uncle had left me a ton of money and rescued me from the soul crushing job I had in Congress.

I worked very hard to stay centered and never flaunt wealth or let it define who I am, but I found it created a host of new considerations. One of many things that attracted to me to Pauline was that she really didn't give a damn about my money.

It just wasn't a thing for her. It was enormously attractive. I knew if I succeeded with her, it was because of who we are, not because I had money. She genuinely had little interest in my finances.

My phone buzzed.

"Steve, all is well, sort of. I ditched the plates. I'll tell Yelena this weekend while we're out of town. I'm sure she'll be cool with it. Thanks for your help."

Damn, I guess Chester could be decent for brief spells at least. Sadly, I knew it wouldn't last. I also knew I needed to do something to bust out of the funk. I grabbed my last glass of wine from the bottle and headed down to the *jardin* of the hotel. It was a small, kind of leafy outdoor deck with a few tables, but there were no smokers that night and I was good. I sat down and pondered the world. I was tempted to bolt and go for a walk, but I wasn't sure where I'd go. I guess the beauty of Paris is that there is always some where to go. I could go to Trocadéro and the Eiffel Tower and people watch. Normally, that was appealing. Maybe grab a beer at the Frog, an honest to goodness microbrewery near Trocadéro. The funk was such that even that was lackluster.

Before I had a chance to check myself, I found myself texting Sofia. Sometimes, you just do stupid shit because you must.

"Hi Sofia. *Musee d'Art Moderne*, tomorrow? 4:00?"

"At the Honest Lawyer now, with a couple of friends I want to take leave of desperately. Sure you can't meet me?"

"*Pas ce soir. Je suis tellement désolé.*"

"Got it. Meet you tomorrow at the museum. Love that place!"

I have no idea why I responded in French. I guess it was because I had just drunk a bottle of red by myself. At least I had us meet in a cultural site rather than a bar. I loved that museum. I suppose that was my compromise. For some reason, the image of Sofia pulling me back in her building and out of the rain and our close elevator ride invaded my consciousness. Not something I needed to be thinking about. Damn Côtes du Rhône! I felt better though and found my bed.

◆ ◆ ◆

The next day was another good one in terms of productivity. I was able to work on my African-American doughboy story awhile and then shifted gears and started a short story based on my night with Sofia. I made it a bit weirder to make it more interesting. By 2:00, I was way more than ready for a baguette and ham and butter. I sort of looked forward to meeting Sofia but was also concerned what that might lead to. She said she needed advice. That morning, I did get a text from Pauline that I was very happy to get, letting me know all was well.

As I walked down Avenue du President Wilson, I had an internal discussion raging about why I was meeting Sofia. I was still in a funk. I enjoyed her company. I hoped that she could lift my spirits without my having regrets.

I didn't see Sofia as I entered through the tall square columns of the museum. I stood there a minute peering through the trees to see the Seine. It was a nice view. I loved all the statues that were scattered about outside the museum. I spotted her. She was seated at a table looking at her phone. Her back was to me. She wore a short white dress and white sneakers, gray backpack. I plopped down at her table. There was that beautiful smile. Yes, she was just as pretty as I remembered.

"Steve!"

"Hi Sofia," I got up and we did the *la bise* though neither of us were French. It was just something you did when you were in France. I guess it was a sign of culture. It came easy once one got used to it.

"So glad to see you again."

"Me too."

We just awkwardly looked at each other a moment, and I blurted out, "So, you needed advice?"

"Yes…"

"Do you want it pre-art or post-art?"

"Let's ease into it. Let's go see some art." She stood and reached out her hand. I took it and she led us to the entrance. She looked back and smiled and then whispered in my ear, "So great to see you again." A wise man would have been a bit less flattered and taken that as a heads up of what would happen.

12

After Sofia checked her bag, we took in a temporary exhibit. Lots of huge canvases. Bold splotches of dark red and dark green punctuated by ochre orbs. She asked me a few times what I thought about some of the pieces. She really seemed interested in my opinion. Almost like it was a test. I spoke the truth. I didn't care for most of it, but a few works spoke to me.

She abruptly said, "Let's cut the shit." And she wandered off. It was a strange thing to say, but I followed.

In a few minutes we were standing in front of Robert Delauney's *Eiffel Tower*. Sofia said she wanted to start here because it was her favorite. She took my hand and looked at me and said, "Take me to your favorite, right now."

"I thought we were here to discuss your boyfriend, you know, to compare notes on French relationships?"

"Relax, as you American's say, it's all good. Pauline is secure. No worries!" Crap! I'd even told her my fiancées' name? I didn't have to think about which one was my favorite. I immediately took her to *Le Sphinx* by Kees Van Dongen. I would have taken her to Van Dongen's *The Bowl of Flowers*, my real favorite, but it was a tad racy. And I kind of wanted to cool things down.

She stood there in her short white dress, red lipstick and short blond hair admiring Van Dongen's work. I knew I shouldn't have come. She caught me at a vulnerable time.

"I'm impressed. That French asshole I'm supposedly dating would have blown me off."

"Huh? What do you mean?"

"I need to talk to you about that. I need advice. You know the French. Follow me."

"I'm certainly no expert on that and…tell me what we are doing."

"Standby. Be patient." She laughed, "I might hold your hand again if you don't straighten up."

I just stared at her. She nodded to the door and in a moment, we were retrieving her backpack.

She gently shoved me towards the door.

"Where are we going?"

"We are getting high. Here, carry this." She handed me her backpack in a most business-like manner.

"This is a little heavy. What's in it?"

"Walk, let's go."

"Why do you want to get high?"

"Steve, you need to be honest. You're only honest when drunk. I know you; we go way back. Remember, …the tiki bar?"

"I give better advice when I am sober."

"I get stressed when I talk about my boyfriend."

A few minutes later, we were walking along the Seine. Twilight was beginning to emerge. The breeze was cool. The Eiffel Tower shimmered across the river.

"Where are we going, Sofia?"

"Follow me."

In a minute, we were crossing the Seine. Quite romantic. I longed for Pauline to be here. Great place for a long sultry kiss—the reflections of the Seine, smelling the river, the Eiffel Tower as the backdrop, might really melt Pauline's heart. We paused over the river a few seconds. Sofia studied me just a second, looking back at me. Maybe she was thinking the same thing. She thought better of it. I was grateful, but it was such a human moment.

We walked along the pool at the Fountaine du Jardins du Trocadéro and then she cut to the left to the walk up into the nearby wooded area. I didn't follow. She looked back at me and motioned for me to follow her.

"C'mon. Let's find a place to sit. I want to talk. That's why I called you."

"What are we doing?"

"I just want to sit up there and talk. We'll have a good view still."

"What's wrong with here?"

"I get super stressed when I talk about my boyfriend. I need to smoke just a little pot. I can't do that in the open."

"Sofia, I think I better go."

She looked back at me with such a sad look.

"Let's just talk out here or I might should go."

She actually looked a tad pathetic, "Steve, I really just need some advice. Can we just sit off the public area just a bit? You don't want me to get arrested do you?"

I reluctantly and against my better judgement, followed her.

We took a few steps, and I said, "How about here?" It was still semi-public but away from the sidewalk.

"All right. You are sure making this difficult, Steve."

"I just need to get a little high. Take the edge off."

"Okay."

"Steve, in the backpack, you are holding your wine. There is a plastic glass and my favorite red. Screw top. Start drinking."

"What about you?"

"I like alcohol but really prefer pot." She had perked up. "Unless you want some pot, grab a glass of wine while I go take a few hits over there in the dark. This is still too public here. I'll be right back."

I decided I might as well have a glass and opened a bottle. I reflected on why I let myself get in this position. I was mainly curious where this was going. Situations like this fascinated me from a writing standpoint. Plight of humanity in general always fascinated me. I was interested in seeing what humans will do to and for each other and even themselves. That's the stuff of the best writing, I thought, just like Hemingway and Fitzgerald would say if they were here with me in this situation. Of course, they would probably go with the flow more than I was, at least Hemingway would. Sofia would make an interesting character for sure.

The Eiffel Tower illuminated and shimmered from top to bottom. It would have been intensely romantic were Pauline with me.

In a minute, Sofia returned smelling like an odd mix of pot and perfume and she sat next to me.

"So, what do you want to discuss, Sofia? Do you just find a wall at times between you two?"

"Wall? You kidding? Drink your wine. I need to de-stress a minute. Take a few deep breaths. Standby."

We just sat there. And sat there. And sat there. This was becoming a little less fascinating. It was getting dark, and it wasn't just the approaching evening.

She finally broke the silence, "You buzzing?"

"I'm good. Like I said, I give better advice the more sober I am."

She reached towards me and took both of my hands and stared into my eyes. I pulled back gently. She asked, "Does that bother you?"

"I probably need to go, Sofia. I thought we were going to discuss your boyfriend."

"You might need to drink a little more."

"I think I've had enough to drink. I need to go."

"I'm not seducing you the way you think."

"Huh?"

"Just drink, Steve. Don't be so presumptuous, so American."

"Sorry for being such a bore."

"You, my friend, are not a bore."

"Glad to hear."

"I'm just seducing you in a different kind of way."

"I don't understand."

"You're American."

"Huh?" I stood up. The common-sense side of me said run. The writer in me said see what happens next! Keep turning the pages!

"Don't leave. I do need help. She kind of laughed and said, "You could have stared back at least a little, like you did in the tiki bar. You even kissed me."

She just kind of shrugged. I still didn't remember us kissing, but I'd never drunk unlimited tiki cocktails before either. Of course, it may not have happened. I was starting to question her mental stability along with mine for agreeing to meet her, that is.

"Sorry Steve, I know you're engaged. It was stupid to call you, maybe. I do need some help."

The Eiffel Tower went off again. Sparkles all over it from bottom to top.

"Okay, Steve, I want us to have an honest moment. A moment people seldom have."

"Okay."

"Do you ever feel alone, all alone?"

I sat back down a little further away on the ground. "Yeah. Sometimes."

"I fucking hate it, because I sometimes feel all alone right after Gerard and I make love. I cry sometimes. Why?"

"I don't know. That isn't good."

"I feel like I could make love to someone like you and not feel that way."

"Well, find someone like me then. I'm not that special. There's lots of guys like me out there."

"I need your advice."

"Uh huh…"

"I do."

"I'm here."

"That's it."

"Huh?"

"That's it."

She was stoned, I think. She had at least accomplished

that goal. I needed to get out of here.

"Why do I feel that Steve?"

"I don't know."

"Do you feel what I do, Steve?"

"What do you mean?"

"Look, I learned what I needed to learn. My goal was to kind of seduce you and get you to be honest. You were."

"I don't follow."

"I need to find a different boyfriend."

"I think so. Yes, you definitely do if that's the way you feel about making love with him."

"I just wanted to know how committed you were to Pauline. It is obvious to me now that you are in love and that is beautiful. I am not going to mess that up."

"Okay."

"Look Steve, you are a good guy. A beautiful soul. I don't think of physical people as much as I do souls."

"I don't understand."

"Look, I want my lover to be beautiful, like me," she lifted her eyebrows, like she knew she was sounding pompous. "Look, I know I'm attractive. But what matters more is your soul. I fear my boyfriend just has a void where his soul should be. He's often nice, and gosh he's beautiful, but something is missing. He's super smart, well read...but we never connect. With you and I, we have almost connected from when we first met."

"Okay, maybe I get it. I'm not sure. But no soul? How could that be?" She just kept staring at the Eiffel Tower. She thought for a while then turned to look in my eyes.

"Don't worry. You're in love with Pauline. That's all you need to know. You are good. I just hope she loves you. You are a mess, but you have so much to offer."

"What advice did you need?"

"You gave it to me."

"Look Sofia, you're great. Funny, fun to be with, smart. Don't stay in a bad relationship."

She started laughing.

"Huh?"

"I am willing to be your friend if you need a friend. We are done sexually. I see your soul is committed to someone else."

"You're complicated, Sofia."

"I know. I wish you and Pauline all the best. Soul-to-soul Steve, I mean it."

She packed up her stuff, stood up, took my hand and stared into my eyes one more time. She then turned and slowly walked away, towards the river. She looked back just a second and started to say something. She started to walk back towards me, but then stopped and stared at me a second. She hesitated, like she was thinking about something. She then rushed back in my direction and grabbed and kissed me like a lover saying goodbye.

She looked at me and said, "Sorry, I needed to do that. Things are not as neat as what I described."

With that, she started to back away from me while still staring at me. She then turned and walked away. That was it. Very soon, she was just a shrinking, dark, lonely profile dwarfed by the Eiffel tower behind her. Who the hell was she? I expected the Red Angel to come tell me what just happened. She didn't. I went in the opposite direction up to the topside of Trocadéro. I wanted to get some distance from this little adventure. I was unsettled and, while I wished her the best, I sincerely hoped our paths would never cross again.

None of this would have ever happened had that damned Chester been on time. Of course, I knew very well where the blame rested in reality. It just helped me feel a bit better somehow implicating Chester, even if I knew better.

13

I had a slow morning. I reflected on the night before. What was all that crazy stuff? Had it really happened? Souls? As strange as the experience was, her talk of souls fascinated me. Was there something to that? Could we possibly connect as souls, stripped of our outward manifestations? Our bodies? I knew I wanted to think more about that, maybe even write about it sometime. Maybe I should have a discussion on the topic someday with my "tiki-theologian" friend. Even just the concept of what is a "soul" was fascinating. If there are souls, just where do they reside?

I finally got out of bed when the windows let the sun blast my face. I wandered down to the lobby and grabbed a cup of coffee. I slowly walked around the corner and almost bought a *pain au chocolat* and then thought better of it and just bought a baguette and headed back to my room with a fresh cup of coffee. I had a couple of bananas from the local market next door on hand already.

After a bit of mindless catching up on the internet, I finally started to perk up a bit. I got a text from Chester but wasn't in the mood. I knew I needed to write. Especially after last night. How surreal! I wanted to document that experience while fresh for some reason.

Leaving the hotel, I entered the fresh Paris morning. I

claimed my writing bench along Avenue Foch. I could lean over and see the Arc de Triomphe down towards l'Étoile. The sun was starting to peek out, a fresh breeze was making me feel better. I wrote a few words, then found myself reflecting on my outing with Sofia last night. I never dreamt of something like that happening to me. I thought to myself that the good writer reads a lot of books. The great writer travels and experiences. For travelling and living is like reading an unpredictable book that is three dimensional and that you can smell, hear, feel, and taste the words as well.

Even though it made me feel weird to reflect on the incident, I remembered how I could see the shimmer of the Eiffel tower in Sofia's eyes, smell her perfume and pot, and taste her kiss. I can write that scene so much more powerfully because I experienced it with my own senses. A great writer lives and captures those magical moments and lets readers experience life beyond the reader's personal experiences. A genuinely great writer can make those experiences so real, so searing, that readers feel they experienced it personally, with their own senses.

Lofty writers can also help us to realize that maybe there is more to life than material stuff and fleeting "prestige." Our spirit matters. Our souls matter. I kept striving to understand what Sofia was saying. Was she pretty much nuts or could she see things most people couldn't? I wondered how many people we deem to be insane can actually see things most of us can't. I suppose that could even drive a person insane, to be able to see or perceive things that everyone else is telling you that you can't or shouldn't be able to see or hear. In a way, that was probably the Red Angel for me.

I reflected on how grateful I should be it didn't work out with Stacy, who I initially thought was "the one." I would have never become the person I am today. Not that I was a finished project...we are never complete, after all. It was just that I had grown so much since the time I shared with Stacy in Marfa. I wouldn't have stood a chance with Pauline. I wasn't one hundred percent sure I did now, but I was going to give it my all. That much I knew.

I was so lost in thought that it almost startled me when my phone vibrated with a text message.

"Hi, Steve. We still on?" I had forgotten about lunch with the tiki bar owner!

I called him and apologized and told him to wait there. We were meeting at the Sushi Man restaurant not too far away. I packed my stuff and headed over the hotel to dump my laptop and grab a light rain jacket. The weather was starting to shift. I smelled rain.

As I walked down Rue de la Pompe, I was starting to feel revived. Just seeing Parisians out and about, many of them dressed to the nines as we say in the States. Sushi Man was on Rue des Belle Feuilles. I'd never eaten there but wondered about it the couple of times as I had bought roasted chicken across the street at Fillions. They had the best chicken.

As I walked into the restaurant, I immediately spotted Jim.

"Steve, my man!"

"Hey Jim. How'ya doing?"

"It's Beach. Remember? I know, it's kind of silly, but I've kind of gotten used to it."

"No worries, Beach."

"Sorry, it's just that Jim was like another person or something. I've moved on, I guess. I'm Beach now. Get the, … do you like sushi?"

"Yes."

"Get the sashimi bowl and a *vingt-cinq* of their rosé. You won't be disappointed. I love it so much; I often have to order another round of both."

"Works for me."

Beach spoke French flawlessly and he ordered for us.

"Tell me, Beach, how'd you get here? What's the deal with a tiki bar?"

"What do you know about the tiki scene? By the way,

there's another great tiki bar in Paris, more old school, Dirty Dick. It's on Rue Frochot. Started by a guy from Southern California. We should go. You'd like the guy who started it."

"I don't know much about the whole tiki thing. I'd like to know more."

"Well, how much time ya got?"

"I got all day and night for that matter."

"Really? Well, let's see how it goes. I'm up for going into overtime too. My manager is slated to cover tonight." He smiled as he gathered his thoughts. I instantly liked this man.

"My dad was in the military. Somehow, he was posted in French Polynesia, some kind of liaison or something. My mom was the daughter of a French Administrative official. He fell in love with her and the local culture. This is where it gets a bit strange. My dad was a great nephew of another Texan…he might have been born in New Orleans…named Ernest Beaumont-Gantt. He graduated from high school in Texas I know at least. In Mexia to be exact. Ever heard of him?"

"No."

"Ever heard of Don the Beachcomber?"

"Sounds vaguely familiar."

"He opened Don's Beachcomber in Hollywood in 1933. It's a long story. He had apparently sailed around the South Pacific in his youth and somehow that inspired him to open his place that was so different with its Polynesian theme, that people just fell in love with it. In the next decade, a lot of military personnel came home after having experienced exotic pacific cultures. Tiki spoke to them somehow. Anyway, Don changed his name to Donn Beach. He went all in on this. From there, tiki bars spread across California and gradually east."

Beach paused so I chimed in, "Funny how things can become so popular for a while and fade away, kind of like fondue restaurants."

Beach continued, "True, but not the best parallel. Tiki influence was pervasive. It led to tiki fashions, food, music and even a kind of culture. There were even tiki-themed hotels and apartments." Beach sipped his rosé and peered out the window onto the narrow, busy street to collect his thoughts.

"Believe me Steve, I've studied it. It was a big deal in the American experience. It affected American culture in a lot of ways, but we have sometimes forgotten the source. It was even fused with Jazz to create "exotic escapism." I could go on and on. Sadly, in the 1970s, tiki faded. Many of the iconic bars were closed and demolished. A few hung on like the Tonga Room, Tiki Ti, Mai-Kai and a few others. I blame that fucker Jimmy Buffet for kind of stealing the tiki culture and morphing it into some damn Florida shit. Like those damn crackers would get the esthetic of tiki!"

"Wow, you're invested."

"Yeah, I guess I am. I even studied it in college. I have an undergrad in History from UT, University of Texas. I'm a damn retroist, tiki culture, Atomic culture, you name it. Kind of a curse."

"This is fascinating. Atomic culture? I'm an Aggie by the way. What's a retroist?"

"I'll try not to hold that against you. We can talk retroism next time."

"So, did most of your fascination come from you hearing stories about your Uncle Donn?"

"Well, yes, but I guess it comes from a variety of sources. I was inspired by stories of my great uncle Ernest, or Donn the Beachcomber as he came to be known. But, I was influenced by my parents I'm sure as well. Remember, they lived in the South Pacific for quite a while and loved it. My mom lived there from age 7 to 21. Even though she's French, she passed on a lot of Polynesian culture and perspectives to me."

"I could see that. What an interesting life story, Beach."

Beach smiled, "There's more. Then, I guess inspired by all that, when I started grad school at Tulane, I worked at the Tiki Tolteca bar in the French Quarter in New Orleans. While my dad was alive, I stayed on campus. When he died, our finances got tight, so I lived with some old family friends in the Garden District who still spoke French at home! They weren't Cajun. Some of their family dated back to being in Louisiana since the early 1700s. Crazy huh?"

"That's amazing. How'd you wind up here?" We'd finished our food, and he signaled to the waiter, and out came another *pichet* of rosé for each of us and soon thereafter another couple of Sashimi bowls.

"Okay. I spoke French at home since I was a baby. Then I spoke French 'at home' when I moved in with the Leger's, the family I lived with at Tulane. I was able to complete my master's in history at Tulane and then my mom passed away. I didn't know it, but my parents were actually loaded. I guess my mom freaked out after his death. I didn't really need to move off campus. No worries. The Legers were awesome. Long story short, once the inheritance, which incredibly included a flat in Paris, was split between me and my sister, I was pretty well off. The flat here had been in my family for decades. My mom's dad left it to her. On a lark, I decided, instead of teaching, I'm moving to Paris to open a tiki bar. It's really that simple."

"Unreal!"

"Yep. It was a dream of mine to move to France and honor my relative's legacy by opening a tiki bar."

"Beach, you're a wild man. I like you."

"Thank you, Steve."

"How has it gone? I mean you sank some money into that place. It's amazing."

"Thank you. Yes, to be honest. I break even most months. I mean sometimes I have a good month. But really that's enough. I mainly just want to meet the '*Mademoiselle correct*' and I will start a family here."

"This is so cool."

"I just want a normal French life. No worries about health care or getting the kids through college. None that heavy shit that Americans have to worry their asses off about. Work hard 11 months out of the year and then a month in '*Le Sud de la France*.' I love it down there."

"I do too. My fiancée lives down there."

"Huh? I thought you were connected to that Danish chick."

"No. Why?"

"Well, let's just say you guys seemed quite familiar with each other at the bar."

"Oh, shit. Okay. Well, that was a fuck-up."

Beach just raised his eyebrows and smiled.

"We'd just met that night. Nothing happened. It was those damn Blue Sharks you kept giving us."

"They are kind of ass kickers, aren't they?"

"Well, yeah! Damn near got me in trouble."

"She was a cutie!"

"Yes, she was. But my love lives in Sommières."

"Awesome town. Hey, we've exhausted all the goodness this place has to offer. What say you and I go get a Blue Shark at my place?"

"Thought you'd never ask."

Within minutes of entering *Le Tiki-Paris Bar*, Beach handed me a Blue Shark. He nodded for me to follow him and he took me to his office. Even his office reflected tiki trappings. He really was all in.

"Have a seat, Steve."

I sat on a long off-white sofa. He plopped on a love seat to my side that made an L-shape between the two.

"You let me know when you need a reload. Françoise will make drink runs up here."

"Great."

"Tell me about yourself Steve. How the hell did you get engaged to a woman in paradise?"

"Well, I, kind of like you, inherited some money. I decided to become a writer. Well, I dabble in a few business enterprises in West Texas and write."

"West Texas?"

"Marfa. Ever heard of it?"

"Of course. That's a kind of an artist colony, or something?"

"Yeah, well, it's more than that, but yeah, there's a lot of art, too."

"The New York Times article I read on it made it sound pretty cool."

"Yeah, it's pretty nice. I mean it's very small, but definitely has some positive qualities. I'm just as attracted to the Hispanic and ranching cultures, history and rugged beauty as to the art and pop culture side of Marfa. A lot of media coverage, neglects the total richness of the region."

"What kind of businesses?"

"I have an art gallery, a ranch, a beer distributorship and might be involved in a railroad if I can get back there to help keep that moving along."

"Wow! That's impressive!"

"Yeah, well, it kind of is, but really, most of the businesses break even or make a modest profit at best. Some months we lose on the gallery. Fortunately, I have other investments."

"You have partners?"

"My cousin Amy actually manages most of the businesses."

"Cool."

"In fact, she is working with a production company right now on a film that's using my ranch. There's been two films that have used the ranch. The latest is based on a book I wrote. Believe that shit?"

"Wow! That's great!"

"Well, it could be, if the production company wasn't run by a couple of pricks."

"I've heard horror stories about Hollywood."

"I wish I could go back to Marfa for a few weeks to help Amy out. I know she's stressed. I feel bad I'm not helping more."

"Why don't you?"

"I am here to see if my fiancée and I are able to make this work. That's really the only thing I am focused on right now."

"Why are you here then, in Paris?"

"She had an unexpected business trip out of the country.

"Oh. Got it. That's kind of rough."

We just sat there a minute.

"Say, want another?"

"What else you got? What's a quintessential tiki drink?"

"Most would say a Mai Tai. My great uncle kind of invented it, but I have some other favorites."

"And?"

"I think you need a Castaway."

"What is it?"

"Two parts rum, one-part banana liqueur and one-part cream of coconut."

"Okay."

Beach texted his manager for another round.

"Tell me about this writing thing, Steve."

I filled him in while waiting for our drink to arrive.

In ten minutes, Françoise tapped on the door.

"Come in."

Françoise placed a beautiful mug with carved faces before me.

"Steve, I think you are going to like this." He was right.

"Quite refreshing."

"Good. Get refreshed. Chloé and Adèle will be here soon."

"Who?"

"Our dates."

"Woah…wait a minute. I'm not up for that."

"No worries. Just kind of play along. A few nights ago. I met this pair. I am really intrigued by the one named Chloé. She seemed so reserved, almost tense. I just want to get Chloé to relax. For her to just give me a chance. We'll go have a drink, grab a steak, my treat, and you'll be in bed by 10:00 if you wish."

"I don't know Beach. I'm kind of wiped."

"Hey, for a buddy?"

"By 10:00?"

"If not sooner."

"Can I make it clear I'm engaged, Beach?"

"I guess. Wow you are kind of insecure, huh? Don't trust yourself?"

"Long story."

"Sounds juicy."

"Maybe another time I'll share it."

"Get ready."

"You owe me."

"Hey, I bought you lunch. I said I'll buy dinner, too. How's that?"

He was right. I was in bed by 9:30. For whatever reason, Adèle didn't like me. I didn't work at all to change her mind either. She seemed a bit stuck on herself. No, she was way stuck on herself. She didn't pass a mirror or glass without checking herself out. She was a knockout no doubt, but I had no interest, and she had even less in me. Besides, I was, after the previous evening with Sofia, done with adventure. Sofia had, at least for a while, exhausted my need for any kind of intrigue. I guess Beach was happy though. I bought him enough time with Chloé that they seemed to have formed a bit of a bond. Seems I was a last-minute replacement when his friend bailed on him. Adèle had expected a French guy. For once, I was happy to disappoint.

14

Saturday afternoon, my phone awakened me from a deep nap.

"Yeah?"

"Steve, I need to talk to you."

"Okay."

"Can we meet?"

"Uh…I was kind of resting, Chester."

"Look, it's really important."

"Want to grab dinner later?"

"Can't. Meeting the gang."

"Where?"

"Steve, hate to break it to you but you're out."

"Huh?"

"You've been kind of been disinvited."

"Oh, okay. No worries."

"Don't take it personal."

"Oh, I won't."

"Good man, good man."

"Just curious why."

"Because you kind of led Sarah on, you know?"

"What?"

"Look, Beth says you're out. Nothing I can do about it."

"Whatever."

"Can we meet for drinks? I really need to talk to someone. Don't be sore at me, Steve."

"Yeah, fine. What time?"

"5:30?"

"Sure.

"Honest Lawyer?"

"No."

"Why not?"

"Long story."

"Romeo's, Place Victor Hugo?"

"Sure."

I didn't really want to go get beers on Place Victor Hugo with the beautiful people, but I wasn't ready to run into Sofia at the Honest Lawyer either.

As I walked up Avenue de Malakoff to meet Chester, I was reflecting on what I want to do with my final week in Paris. Beach wanted us to connect again. More sushi seemed like a no-brainer. I thought about trying to open a bank account but opted to wait until I got to Pauline's. I decided to mainly write and stay out of trouble. There were a couple of museums I'd missed last time that I wanted to check out. I had had a good chat with Pauline in the morning before I drifted back to sleep. I was relieved. She told me, "I can't wait to see you. I miss you so much." I needed that. It felt so good to hear those words.

I looked around for Chester as I approached Romeo's. I walked in when I didn't see him outside. I was about 5 minutes late. Just then I felt my phone buzz.

"I'm in the corner, near the statue."

I looked around and finally recognized him. He had a ballcap and dark sunglasses on.

"I've never seen you wear a ballcap."

"Have a seat."

"You okay? You looked worried."

"I'm fine, just trying to keep a low profile."

"Not that stupid license plate issue is it? I thought you were going out of town."

"Well, it's complicated."

"How so?"

"I took your advice. I started to tell her."

"And…"

"She had such a strange look on her face I chickened out."

"Oh brother, Chester."

"Well, it gets worse."

"I contacted that dude I got the plates from to let him know I needed them a little longer."

"And…"

"He said no can do. He's in a jam and needs to put them back in the Embassy supply. The plates had been assigned to a new person being brought into France."

"Give them back. How stupid can you be Chester?"

"Well, cut me some slack, Steve…hold on!" He paused and looked around again. He whispered, "I lost them."

"What!"

"Pipe down, Steve!"

"It was more like they were stolen."

"What?"

"I removed them, but like a dumbass, I left them on my front seat. I had just run back into my flat for 10 minutes, and boom, they were gone. Someone broke in and took them."

"Shit, Chester!"

"Someone is now following me!"

"Who?"

"I don't know."

"Well, at least you told Yelena, right? Told her the truth."

"Not yet."

"Damn Chester, don't be such a fuck up."

"I don't know where to turn. I can't tell the Embassy, or I'll be in cuffs and deported tomorrow. I can't tell the *Gendarme* because a similar fate would await."

"I don't know, Chester. Did you tell the guy you got the plates from what happened?"

"No, I told him I'll have them back to him soon."

"You got to tell him."

"He said it'd be 20,000 euro if I don't return them. I don't have that kind of money. My allowance, I mean allocation, is only 6,000 euro a month."

"You're just going to have to tell him they were stolen."

"I think he has that thug following me."

After a couple of beers, I was ready to get out of there. I needed air.

"Chester, come take a walk with me."

We claimed a bench along Avenue Foch. Chester kept looking behind him.

"Look Chester, I think I know what's going on."

"Tell me."

"You aren't going to like it."

"Try me."

"Okay, if you tell Yelena and "the license plate dude" the truth, I think all this goes away."

"What? Are you crazy?"

"Hear me out. The thug has nothing to do with the plates. I think your thug is an intelligence operative from whatever country for which Yelena is working."

"No way!"

"What kind of job did you tell her you do?"

"I told her it was classified."

"Shit!"

"She's working for someone. Probably not Russian. They'd have been able to spot you for a fraud right away."

Chester just looked at me and swallowed hard.

"Well, that'd explain why she wanted to talk about my job so much. She seems to raise it just as we are getting intimate almost every time."

"There you go."

"I thought it was because it turned her on so much."

"Well, hate to burst your bubble."

"Shit!" The scales were finally falling from his eyes.

"You tell her the truth; the thug is gone."

"What about the dip plates!!"

"Also tell him the truth. He'll have to stay quiet. He'll lose his job if he says a word."

"He's a rough looking dude."

"You tell him you told some American friends about this and they are to go to the Embassy if anything happens to you."

"Yeah, I guess you're right. Shit, I am kind of a screw-up."

"Yeah, well, you are right about that...this time."

"Thanks, Steve."

"You're welcome."

"Hey, why don't you come tonight?"

"Did you forget? I'm banned from the group."

"Maybe I can talk sense into Beth. Honestly, Sarah was supportive of you. It was Beth. I really think she just doesn't like married people in the group. I think that's it."

"Honestly, Chester. I think she's right. I deserve to be banned. I own it and support it." I smiled like I didn't have a care in the world.

"Let me try, Steve."

"Nope, I gladly accept my punishment." I got up and slowly strode away. I looked back to see Chester just sitting there looking confused. "Chester, have a nice life, my friend. I mean it."

Chester hollered something at me, but I chose not to hear it.

15

The next week went really well except I couldn't write worth a damn. One day sitting on a "my" bench along Avenue Foch, I had a deep inner conversation. I gave up writing the story of the African-American doughboy. I finally conceded I just couldn't adequately get in the head of someone who had been so discriminated against. I reflected on a Hemingway quote concerning writing, "Good writing is true writing. If a man is making a story up it will be true in proportion to the amount of knowledge of life that he has and how conscientious he is; so that when he makes something up it is as it would truly be."

I reflected on this quote in a couple of ways. It really kind of shut the door on my being able make "something up it is as it would truly be." I had never suffered the pain of discrimination over a lifetime. Who was I kidding?

I also wondered if it is was why I sometimes let myself get in such unusual and challenging circumstances. I knew I put myself in situations at times where I'd be tested. Was I seeking of have "the amount of knowledge of life" that Hemingway was talking about? It sounded like such a rationalization.

A good friend of mine once told me that, "An above average pilot avoids situations where above average flying skills are needed." But what if you want to write about certain situations about pushing the envelope? Did I subconsciously seek "Sofia" type situations? Did these situations make me alive, sparking the desire to create prose in a way that I probably never could just sitting around and using my imagination alone?

Would marrying Pauline shut the door on that aspect of my life? Shit! I loved Pauline. I was coming to love writing, I think. Hemingway dealt with this by just going for what he wanted, married or not. He was married four times! I knew that wasn't my bag. But I also didn't want my bag of true-life encounters, my knowledge of life, even the experiences I had that could help others, to stop on my wedding day. Hemingway was right about this, "true in proportion to the amount of knowledge of life."

Of course, I didn't want to be a user and miserable bastard like Hemingway probably was. He was an amazing writer, but how could he honestly feel good about the broken marriages and children he left in his wake? There's nothing amazing about that. Not in a positive sense anyway.

Could I continue to live a life that offered Sofia-type wrinkles and surprises as a married man? A man that respects his vows to his wife? Was it a pipe dream to even consider that? I had balanced it here in Paris during my time here well enough, I guess. I had real human connections with two very interesting women without being disloyal to Pauline, certainly not physically disloyal. Both women would be in my writings at some point. And I could write those pieces with a true "knowledge of life." Could I write well and be a good husband to Pauline?

On the flip side, would I want Pauline to have gone dancing with a man or had a "Sofia" experience with another? Maybe it is something I'd not love but be okay with, if I knew she reserved the physical expression of her love for me alone. Who knows, maybe it would help keep our marriage stronger, help us maintain an edge that keeps our relationship more vibrant. Upon further thought though, I realized that Hemingway probably engaged in this kind of self-delusion. Who was I kidding? I'd be hurt, maybe even angry to see Pauline do some of the things I had done. I had to be honest with myself if I wanted to be a better man than Hemingway or other self-indulgent people the art world often helped create.

I knew I'd be a better partner to Pauline if I could fulfill my urge to create, if I felt truly alive. I suspect she'd be a better partner to me as well if she felt freer. Who wants to feel constrained? I guess in a beautiful relationship or marriage, the parties love each other to the extent that they willingly impose self-constraints to protect the relationship and each other's feelings.

I doubt Pauline would care if she saw me having a conversation with Sofia or Sarah. But based on her reaction to my Brazilian neighbor's topless sunbathing on my last visit, I think she'd be livid, of course, if she ever saw me kiss another woman. And it would damage our relationship for a long time if not forever. I'd be destroyed to see her be romantic with another man. I had to be honest with myself if I was going to be a good husband to Pauline. I needed to get real. I guess that was a silver lining to my strange encounter with Sofia. It opened my eyes and prompted me to have this internal conversation I should have already had!

Some couples might be okay with their partner being romantic with another. Some couples would never be okay with seeing their partner talk to a member of the opposite sex. This is the dichotomy of building relationships, I suppose. One must find a partner with a similar sensibility on these issues. With Pauline's self-assuredness, I think we had a good chance to find a balance that worked for us.

This was an issue. I enjoyed having women as friends. I had women friends in college and even in the military. They were just fun to be around. Not to be sexist, but women bring something "to the table" I typically didn't get from my male friends. I can't really characterize it, but it was important to me and enhanced my quality of life. It's weird how often that ability to have even platonic relationships with members of the opposite sex in many marriages goes away. That wasn't attractive to me. Especially as a writer, I need those insights that only women can bring. My relationships with Amy and even Maurine, the owner of the inn in Marfa, were important to me. I got a great deal out of their company and perspectives. I guess that's why I enjoyed reading some women authors.

Contemplating marriage and all that went with it was so complicated.

Perhaps Pauline would provide the bulk of my "knowledge of life" from now on. If anyone could, it'd probably be her. She kept me on my toes. And I felt an urgency to have her I had never felt. The intensity was far greater, much richer, than my desire for Stacy, my Marfa love, when I looked back over the last couple of years. I think her self-confidence would allow me to have male and female friends provided I knew where to draw the line, how to "avoid situations where above average flying skills were necessary." As a writer, I wanted to be able to gather insights and perspectives from anyone I found of interest.

I impressed myself that I was beginning to think as a more experienced and insightful writer and that I was tackling something that people just accept and don't talk about, though it may stunt many relationships and people across the globe. It may even stunt society perhaps. But I didn't want to think about this anymore. I was getting a headache. I put my laptop away. A long walk then luxurious dinner at Victor's was in order. I felt a bit more *maigret de canard et un bon vin rouge* would sooth my soul. Good duck and wine always had that effect on me. I had more than earned it in my self-indulgent eyes.

16

I decided my last week in Paris was to be filled with writing, museums and another chat with my new friend, Beach. **Early in the week, I made it to the** Musée de l'Orangerie and a return trip to the Centre Pompidou. Both were excellent. The 360-degree Monet painting, Les Nymphéas was stunning. The viewer was surrounded in almost every direction with impressionistic splashes of varying shades of green, blue, pink and indigo that created the effect of standing at dusk before the beautiful pond at his garden at Giverny.

Wednesday late morning, my phone actually rang. I was hoping it was Pauline. It had been a couple of days; I didn't recognize the Paris number.

"*Allô.*"

"Steve?" English accent.

"Yes?"

"Sarah, here." I had never heard her "phone" voice.

"Hi! How are you?"

"Good. Say Steve, I'm near your hotel. You're still in Paris, right?"

"Yes."

"Can we get coffee by any chance?"

"Sure. Say, how'd you get my number and…know where I'm staying?"

"Chester."

"Oh. No worries. I'm happy to meet you."

"Good, there's a Starbucks near Place Victor Hugo. That

work?"

"Sure. When?"

"15 minutes?"

"See you soon."

"See you shortly." My, how I loved her accent. Was it time for a bit more of Hemingway's "knowledge of life?" Or, was it time for me to stop courting stupidity?

As I walked over to the Starbucks, I once again passed by the Église Saint-Honoré-d'Eylau across the street. Again, I reflected on Hemingway's second marriage there. I just couldn't get away from Hemingway it seemed. I said good morning to the *Jeanne d'Arc* statue on the side of the church as I passed her on the other side of the street.

Sarah was sitting at a table in the back. She wore a black skirt and white blouse and black boots, contrasting greatly with the brightly hued murals on the walls. There was a black fedora of sorts on the table. She could have passed for a model. After I got my coffee, I joined her. She smiled so warmly.

"Thanks for meeting me, Steve. Hope you don't mind the venue but somehow Starbucks gets what a lot of cafés around here don't get. Sometimes you want a relaxed, quiet place inside to just have a cup of coffee and be left alone."

"It's perfect. No worries."

"Steve, I wanted to apologize. Chester told me what happened with Beth and what she said." She paused a minute, "You know from the last time you visited I felt a connection with you. I remember you so sweetly getting me home the night I was legless, I mean so drunk. You didn't try to take advantage of me, though I think it crossed your mind for just a second." She winked at me.

"I was..."

"Steve, I was flattered and felt when we looked at each other there was a bond of some sort. It was a connection I didn't understand. It was like we had known each other well in the past, or something crazy like that. It's happened to me a couple of other times in my life. Where I feel an inexplicable connection with a person. The other times it was with women I met." She peered down at her hat on the table a second.

She looked up at me and then said, "Just wondering, do you feel it too? Maybe I'm just crazy."

"No, I feel it too." I just sat there looking at her.

I added, "I've told you that. When our eyes have locked in the past, there was a strange feeling of familiarity. I tried to blow it off. Doesn't make sense. Maybe we're related somehow, way on back!"

"Or maybe we had a torrid love affair in another life," she said in an exaggerated, crazy-eyed, breathless way and laughed.

She quickly added, "That sounds nuts, but it almost is that kind of feeling. Glad to know I'm not the only crazy person at this table."

I smiled at her, wanting her to feel okay. We just stared at each other a minute and then kind of looked away. This was no doubt "knowledge of life." I felt something with her that was unique.

"Well, before this gets so awfully awkward, I will let you go, Steve. I just wanted you to know I care for you, for whatever crazy reason, and for you to not worry about what Beth told Chester. I wasn't angry at you in the slightest. I felt awful when Chester told me what he told you. He can be such a dick, you know?"

"Oh, I'm quite aware of that. As for us, thank you Sarah, for telling me this, all of this, really. I knew you were fine. I knew it was a Beth thing. And as for our connection, it doesn't make sense to me either."

"I know you are heading south soon to join your fiancée. I wish you two all the best, Steve. Please join our group anytime you like. Alone or with your wife. You're always welcome. I'll deal with Beth."

"Again, thank you Sarah for doing this. I hope we see each other again. Perhaps we'll have another torrid affair in our next life."

"Perhaps we shall. I look forward to it, my friend." Warm

smile on her red lips.

We stood and did the *la bise*. She suddenly stopped and looked me in the eye. She put her hand around my neck and kissed me lightly on the lips. She then released me, smiled and said, "That will have to do until the next life." I laughed and said, "Pretty sure I'm going to remember it until then."

She gave me a flirtatious smirk and then grabbed her hat and was out the door. All that remained was the taste of her lipstick on my lips. What a classy farewell.

That afternoon, back on "my" bench, I reflected on a couple of things. I reflected how I perceived Sarah the first time I met her long ago at Au Petit Suisse, across from Le Jardin du Luxembourg. I recall having had a strange feeling the first time our eyes met, but I brushed that away by focusing on a tooth, one single tooth, a bit out of place. I regarded her as the pretty girl "with crooked teeth." It was the only thing I could see, until I hung around her a bit more. Over the time, the tooth became a cute feature. How can we humans be so quick to dismiss each other? Do we really want to go around just finding things to not like about each other?

I do recall feeling a connection to her by the strange greenish light of the streetlamps near her place the first time I walked her home. I had trouble putting the feeling in context until she just articulated it a little while ago. It is as though we were once lovers. So weird. Was I succumbing to the power of suggestions? Or did I really feel it too? I think I felt it too.

I also reflected on my earlier inner conversation on relationships. What if I had blown her off? What if I said I can't meet her because I can't trust myself to do the right thing? I would have missed out on an episode that I will remember for the rest of my life. I have another connection with another person on the planet that I think will last as long as we are alive. I feel like if we met each other 40 years later, we'd both still feel that connection. Yet I am hopelessly in love with Pauline and have no interest in doing anything that would jeopardize our relationship, which I believe is both deeply emotion and physical, and intellectual too. I hope she feels likewise. We still had so much to learn about each other. I was pretty sure that the event of this morning would be featured in my prose one day.

17

"Damn Steve, what did you say to Chloé's friend?"

"Nothing mean that I recall." I'd met up with Beach at his place.

"She wanted no part of you."

"Feelings are kind of mutual."

"Huh? I thought she was amazing."

"She was easy to look at."

"Well, she wanted no part of hanging out with you again."

"I'm devastated, Beach. I told you I'm engaged. Did you forget?"

"I can tell you are so disappointed, Steve."

"What can I say? Some women like me. Others, not so much. It's a thing for me. I've never understood it."

"I know the feeling brother! I hate it when I am down on my luck and I approach a woman who is okay to look at, and even she blows me off. Kind of harsh on the ego."

"Been there, buddy. It's harsh. Good word. Speaking of harsh, where's my drink?"

"Hey, I want you to enjoy my place. Mind if we eat here?"

"Not at all."

"I want you to take in some fine tiki fare."

"I'm ready!"

Within minutes, we were in a private niche within the Le Paris-Tiki Bar. You had to go underneath a couple of faux palm trees to enter a "big hut." You had the sensation of being in a beach hut looking out windows to see a surrounding scene that looked like a Gauguin painting of French Polynesia.

"Steve, this is kind of my indulgence. I wanted a fun but civilized place to be able to entertain, talk business or give other businesses a fun place to meet." An obligatory stone statue looking like the moai heads on Easter Island sat in a corner.

"I'm impressed. I'd have fun doing business in here."

"*Marie, nous sommes prêts*." Marie poked her head in, smiled and said, "*Bonsoir*."

"Steve, you mind if I just order for us? I want to give you a few of our highlights. That okay?"

"Of course. Please."

"Already done. Prepare for a Polynesian orgy of gluttony!"

I liked this man. I just felt good around him.

Marie came in and sat a regular glass in front of us. Golden, brown with a couple of cubes.

"I'm starting you off simple, Steve. Enjoy a Dark n' Stormy."

"Nice."

"Simple, ½ dark rum, ½ ginger beer. Key is quality dark rum. Some like a little lime juice. We spray a little fresh lime on top. Some go less on the rum. I like it half and half."

After a few sips, Beach could tell I was enjoying it. He was smiling.

"Watcha thinking about Steve?"

"Good booze, good food, good company. Just happy to be here."

"Not bad, but I want you to be transformed. I want you ease into tiki land, man." He had a big, relaxed sigh. He closed his eyes as he exhaled and smiled. I could see stresses leave his body as he slowly exhaled a few times.

"Okay."

"With every sip, Steve, you should be whisked away to a white beach, palm trees, beautiful women, hyper-relaxation, the smell of the ocean…"

"Hmm."

"Every sip is a little celebration of freedom, love, paradise, ocean breezes."

"Okay?"

"C'mon, Steve, don't let me down."

"Well, this is my first drink, Beach."

Just then Marie entered with an orange drink in a funnel-like glass and a couple of plates of small ribs and a plate with a pile of some kind of chips.

"Steve, these are kind of messy but worth it. Pork ribs, our special sauce. Taro chips gently showered with curry with a trace of cumin. Oh. And a damn fine Mai Tai. I figured we should get that one out of the way."

"Yum, I'm feeling that ocean breeze, Beach!"

"Good man."

"Tell me Beach, tell me more about tiki culture. What draws you so much?"

"Okay, as I tell you this, take a deep breath and let waves, gentle turquoise waves and refreshing ocean breezes wash over you."

"Okay."

"All right, tiki culture, look, I know my relative Donn launched this and maybe I'm overplaying it, but work with me. I try to keep it simple. The philosophy, if you will, is living moments of a peaceful life. Let the magic of the ocean and the breeze heal you and wash away your cares. Think white sand and the smell of an ocean breeze. It's primal. Maybe we came from the ocean way back…that's what they say, anyway. Let it knock your blood pressure down a notch or two. Take deep breaths. Think relaxing exotic music, drinking a refreshing cocktail, a beautiful woman next to you, and really, really letting yourself feel the warm ocean breeze under the shade of a palm tree. Try to master the art of letting go to those things that bring you pleasure. Don't succumb to the need to feel in control. Surrender to pleasure. I guess I strive to use tropical splendor as a means to get people to connect with the good life, peace and pleasure."

"Whoa, that's some deep shit. I'm liking it."

"Who in their mind wouldn't!"

"You're blowing my mind. In a good way, Beach."

Just then a different waitress showed up and put a pinkish drink in front of us and some egg roll looking things and some kind of chicken with rice.

"A Viequense, Shanghai Lumpia, eggrolls, and Chicken Katsu."

"This is truly a culinary orgy, my friend."

"I told you, feel the breezes, take time for a deep breath and relax. Enjoy the good life."

"I love it. I think I do feel my blood pressure plummeting."

"If you have a pulse, what choice do you have?"

"Good point."

"Tell me, Beach, with your love of this, why didn't you move to the islands? I love hearing the surf intermingled with the music. How do you do that?"

"I do love the islands. I go for a month every other year. I actually go down near Marseille every other year. Other years, I go to Guadeloupe or Réunion Island. Where your sweetie is right now."

"Tell me Beach, is tiki your god, I mean like, is this a religion for you?"

"Well, funny you should ask. I practice a fusion religion. I practice a religion that incorporates tiki culture and, stand by for it...the first four books of the New Testament and a little more."

"Huh?"

"I call it Tiki-Christianity," he paused and studied a barely clad woman in one of the murals. I could tell he wasn't sure whether to proceed. "Look, I'm going to have to know you a lot better or I'm going to have to be even drunker to give you all the details of my religion."

"I'm a writer. You have my attention."

"Someday maybe. Just think of Christ as a loving, caring, Lebanese-looking surfer dude and you get half of it."

"Lebanese? Surfer?"

Beach got a real serious look. He wasn't bullshitting.

"I'm still here, Beach. I like it, tell me more."

"Look, the tiki culture initially was probably more gimmick than not, but it really meant a lot to a bunch of people. I think it offered hope to the American culture. Some folks criticized it as "synthetic exoticism" and exploitative and demeaning. There was some truth to that, but it also offered something else. It offered Americans a chance to maybe escape the hollow materialism that was drilled in our brains after WWII, and maybe even finally cast off that puritanical yoke from our shoulders. Approached correctly, it awakened some Americans that there was more to life than washers and dryers, new Chevrolets, and all that materialistic crap, and that love, and peace, nature and spirituality mattered too. It was a chance for Americans to connect to something inside themselves, something spiritual too, to escape the endless distractions the media and industry threw at us, and of course, that's only gotten worse... way worse."

"Man, this is heavy, but pretty much rings true."

"Well, for me, I went all in. Well actually, after three things happened. Uncle Stu, my working at a New Orleans bar named the Tiki Tolteca, that I already told you about, and my discovery trip. When I was little, my Uncle Stu used to talk to me on his front porch in Texas. After he served in the Navy in the Pacific in WWII, he worked as a young man in Donn's original location in Hollywood. Having lived in the islands during the war, the tiki scene spoke to him. Especially after he had married a Filipino beauty. After a few years, he left Hollywood to open a tiki bar in Houston with a buddy. It had a few good years, but by the mid-1970s, people had lost interest and he retired to the Texas coast. He had a nice little place on the beach. My Aunt Dorrie made the best Filipino foods when I'd come out to visit. He really never lost faith in the significance of tiki in America.

As a kid, hearing my uncle wax poetically about a grand lost culture, while listening to the surf of the Gulf in the last moments of the sunset, it was very impactful."

Beach was looking down at the table. Barely sipping his drink.

"When I went to Tulane, I decided I wanted to experience what my uncle told me about those countless evenings on the front porch. He called it the 'Promise of Tiki' to help Americans see another lifestyle, a more care-free lifestyle. There was something special at the Tiki Tolteca bar. I got to meet some of the most centered, calm people I've ever known. I'm still tight with the owner. I still get back to NOLA as much as I can. Special city. You should go some time. Ever been?"

"No. Almost went awhile back. A hurricane messed that up."

"It has echoes of France, unlike any city in America. The French were really in charge of the place from the early 1700s to the middle 1800s, a few decades after the Louisiana Purchase. Hell, they were still publishing novels in French there up until the Civil War! Go! Got great friends I'll hook you up with. Oh, you gotta meet Drift! He will blow your mind. They got another tiki place there now that's good, too. A guy who has written some amazing books on tiki drinks owns it. Check both of them out if you go."

Beach took a sip and refocused, "Anyway, I did talk some philosophy with folks there at the bar to build on what my Uncle Stu had drilled into me. Most of the customers were just there for good drinks, good food and a good time. But a small, hard core group was there for more. They shared a philosophy that tracked with Uncle Stu's about peace, love, and relaxing. It isn't Zen. It's different. They believed that the ocean could speak to us and transport us to our roots somehow. Anyway, it's complex and I'm starting to buzz."

After a sigh and smile, Beach continued, "And then there was the discovery trip. My Aunt Zelma was a wealthy widow in New Orleans and one day invited me over and asked me if there was one thing she could do for me for graduation, what would it be? She was proud of her nephew doing well at Tulane. She had a gorgeous house in the Garden District, not too far from campus. I initially said help my mom pay the tuition. She waved that off and said that was silly. My folks had plenty of money. I then said I wanted to go the French Polynesia. Boom. She paid for me to go over a long break. It was there I met him."

Beach was staring at me.

"Who?"

"The Tiki-Christ."

"Okay..."

"He was walking out of the ocean carrying a surfboard. He looked Lebanese...Middle Eastern. He just walked in front of me, stopped for a second, smiled the most loving, caring smile I've ever seen. It put me at total peace. I knew he wasn't from this world."

"What'd he say?"

"Nothing. He smiled at me a minute and...just walked on."

"That's it?"

"Well, yeah, but...for me, it was enough. I had met Jesus." He looked me in the eye. He was dead serious.

"That's...cool, weird, but cool." I didn't really know what to say.

"Look, I was brought up Catholic. Much of the Catholic stuff I was taught felt sort of like bullshit until I met him. I mean, some of it still does. But what I clung to that day was Jesus' teachings. I read the Gospels of the New Testament over and over. Anyway, I know you think I'm nuts, but its real to me."

"Were you sober? Not being mean, just curious."

"Absolutely. See, I merged the tiki world my uncle thought was beautiful and the teachings of Christ. The central teaching of Christ is love. Look, I know, the ten commandments and all that. I get it. But if you embrace love, that's where it's at. I mean, I really love most aspects of Catholicism, I just am seeking to infuse more love, less judgment into it. I'm still Catholic, in my eyes at least. I just want them to reconsider some of the medieval teachings, especially on sex, that are dead ends. I want Catholicism to survive and even thrive! It can if the Church follows Christ a little more, Saint Thomas Aquinas a little less. Aquinas was brilliant but talk about wanting to take the sizzle out of sex. God gives us this great gift, and he seemed hell bent on sending some of it back to God."

"Wow! That's deep, man. I wish I was sober so I could really absorb it."

"I know you think I'm crazy. Aw, fuck it. Let's just have a good time. Everyone thinks I'm crazy when I talk about it."

"I don't think you're crazy. I want to try to absorb this."

"Sure, drink up, Steve."

"I look forward to meeting up with you in the Réunion Islands one day and having you enlighten me more. I want to see where this happened."

"I might. But, it's just my take. I don't proselytize. I may be all wrong."

"I look forward to it."

"Meanwhile, just think of Christ as a loving surfer dude. When I read the gospels, I don't get the lily white, capitalist, damn near racist Christ some of America believes in."

"Amen, brother."

"I told you enough to get it. I'll butcher an Aquinas quote, if you get it, no explanation is needed. If you don't, no explanation's possible. Chew on that until we meet in the islands, my friend."

"Damn, Beach. You are an impressive son of a bitch!"

"It isn't about me, it's about us, all of us. Hey, I want to give you something. It is just draft. Just something I've been working on it. Standby." With that, Beach bounded up out of the chair and disappeared.

I just sat there buzzing. Damn, the drinks were strong. I admired the little incredible tiki-world Beach had made. I heard occasional sounds of thunder and hard rains "hitting a tin roof" in the background. His sound system was incredible.

Just then another waitress came in as Beach ducked under the palm fronds and re-entered holding a few of sheets of folded paper.

"Okay, for the grand finale. Steve, this is Camille."

"*Bonsoir*, Camille." She just smiled and put a tall orange drink in front of us and took some of our mess away.

I just took a few deep breaths and tried to let the relaxation Beach described soak in. It was kind of working. Of course, I was getting lit up so why wouldn't it? I just looked at the faux Gauguins. The mural was beautiful and relaxing in a real but retro way. I mean damn retro, actually. I think he painted his paintings in the late 1800s.

Beach eased back in his seat, "You enjoying the Zombie, Steve?"

"Shit, I'm bombed. I'm enjoying all of it."

"Take these pages and put them in your pocket. We can discuss someday. Not now!"

"What is it?"

"Think of it as my fifth and final book of the bible."

"Okay." I just smiled, almost laughed.

"Let's knock off the spiritual shit for now." He had a big grin.

"Yes, Beach, what is it?"

"Steve, I have great news. This is your Paris bachelor party."

"Huh?"

"I got good news and, well, other news."

"I have a date with Chloé tonight. I want you to come."

"Okay…what's next, Beachboy?"

"Well, I polled the crew about who wanted to come with us."

"Shit, Beach, you didn't?"

"Look dude, you are going to be married soon. You'll be off limits. These are your final days of freedom."

I just looked at him in astonishment. My mind was racing and swirling with way too much alcohol and images of

"Gauguin's" half-clad women.

"Look, a few of the crew thought you were cute. About half of them gave me a big thumbs down."

"You fucker! Why'd you do this? And, whaddya mean half rejected me?"

"Warm ocean breezes, white sand, under the shade of a palm tree, fronds rustling. Let the relaxation wave over you."

"Damn, you're different, Beach!"

"Warm ocean breezes, deep breaths, smell of coconut butter, tanned brown flesh."

"Who are you?"

"Think of me as a modern-day prophet. Let go of all that puritan shit you were taught growing up. Evolve. Warm ocean breezes. Sensuality is great when you manage it."

Just then music started playing loudly. I could hear that the bar had started to fill up.

"Look, Beach, I'm grateful. I really am."

"Yep. You right on that! You sure gonna be grateful. Go upstairs and wash up. The closet is full of new toothbrushes. Let's go have a good time. Juliette, Camille et Stéphanie await."

"Who?"

"Our entourage. They know you're getting married. We are just going to party and have fun. They're quite stunning really. Camille is getting some kind of advanced degree from the Sciences Po. Juliette is a theater actress. I think Stéphanie is studying at the Sorbonne. You'll love them!"

"Beach, I can't."

"Yes, you can."

"I'm engaged and thanks to you, really drunk."

"Look this maybe your last chance to just live it up. You aren't married. All the women I thought who'd like you, said you were too *"Americain"* or *"Il est trop ivre."*"

"Yeah, I'm too drunk thanks to you!"

"Deep breaths, refreshing ocean breezes, shade of palm trees, palm fronds rustling in the breeze. What part of warm, turquoise water do you not get?"

"Freak."

"That any way to talk to your new best friend?"

Admittedly, he was an upgrade from Chester, but he was trying to get me in trouble. Sadly, the alcohol was only upping its game in my head.

"Tell me more about this Tiki-Christ."

"Later bro. You need this catharsis. Look, I think I know you. Once you're married, you're done. You are sexually off the market. You're done for anyone but your wife. You just are. You can't help it. Like to think I'll be the same. I very much want to be the same. But meanwhile, enjoy."

"I can't. I'll see my fiancée in a week. Don't you get it?"

"Yeah, I totally get it. Kind of a mayday situation if you ask me. This is the closing days of you being able to sow your oats."

I just looked at him and tried not to wobble.

"Why aren't you drunk, Beach? I'm damn near legless, as my English friend says."

"Well, I drink too much, my friend. I'm working on that."

"Again, tell me about this Tiki-Christ."

"That comes later, after we really know each other. I don't want to tell too much, too fast."

"Is that bogus Beach? All this spirituality stuff?"

"All in due time, Steve, all in due time."

"Okay, where's the toothbrushes?"

"That's the spirit. My good man. Keep it simple, just remember, "Let the ocean transport you to a place of relaxation. Deep breaths."

At some point in the future, five minutes later or five hours hour, we were in a dance club somewhere. I was dancing with Juliette, I think, might have been Camille or it might have been anyone, I wasn't sure. It was foggy and I felt her or someone holding on to me. We were having a good time as far as I recalled but all of a sudden, I had to go pee. I don't know if I had peed that night 12 times or if this was the first. Never go drinking with Beach again was my mantra at that point. He was mercifully making sure I just drank water the rest of the evening.

Gradually, the buzz slowly began to wear off a bit. I was ready to go home.

Moments later, I found myself in front of my hotel. I really don't recollect how I got there. In fact, the last distinct memory of the evening was asking Beach once more to tell me more about his "Tiki-Christ." I think Beach may have walked me to my room. What a weird night. I regretted getting so drunk, being so out of control, especially with people I knew so little. The hangover was bad, being that stupid was worse. I thought I had outgrown getting like that. I wasn't used to drinking those kinds of drinks. Once again it kind of snuck up on me. I thought I'd learned the first time. Obviously not.

Compared to my Marfa "bachelor party," this definitely felt like what a bachelor party should feel like. Finally, for better or worse, I'd had a real bachelor party. I reluctantly felt gratitude to Beach for that, I guess.

The next day, Beach and I spoke by phone. My head was pounding. We made plans to see each other in the Réunion Islands next August. I had no idea if we were serious. I think he was. I definitely had a "knowledge of life" experience the previous evening. Too bad I didn't remember much of it. I noted to add "staying somewhat sober" to the "knowledge of life" playbook. Beach certainly was a fascinating character. He might have had a bit too much edge for us to grow close, but his life philosophy made me want to know more.

18

"Retreat, hell we just got here!"

A few days later, I found myself in an Indian restaurant in the small city of Château-Thierry reflecting on those words. It was getting dark outside and the restaurant was a brightly illuminated relief on its otherwise dark gray and almost foreboding street. The restaurant sat on the edge of the *centreville* near an old hospital that appeared to be abandoned.

As I nursed a *pichet de rosé*, I reflected on the absurdity of life, how one's path can be so altered by just one encounter, maybe an extra 5 minutes somewhere can change everything. I had planned to go to the Normandy American Cemetery and instead I found myself well east of Paris near the site of the Battle of Belleau Wood. As a result of my soiree with Sofia a couple of weeks before, I had shifted gears. Sofia had attended a diplomatic ceremony at the nearby Aisne Marne American Cemetery and told me that it was one of the most beautiful places she had ever visited.

As a result of a little research, I was reminded that the Battle of Belleau Wood was also an epic chapter in the history of my old Army division and decided to head east instead of west this time and see what my 2nd Infantry Division was up to in June of 1918 instead of June of 1944. Over some pretty tasty Tandoori Chicken, I was thinking how I only knew a certain officer's name because the 2nd Infantry Division was sent near here to help the French Army hold the line against the Germans in 1918. The quote about retreating was Marine Corps Captain

Lloyd William's reported reply when ordered to pull back by a French Colonel. How a Marine was part of the US Army 2nd Infantry Division is a long but rather interesting story that would reverberate throughout the US Military for a long time.

After awakening the next morning in my hotel on the edge of Château-Thierry and nibling on the breakfast in the lobby, I was in my rental car heading to the Aisne-Marne American Cemetery. Before I had the "weird" encounter with her, Sofia had suggested I rent a car and maybe make my way down to Sommières by way of Château-Thierry. Not that Château-Thierry was on the way, but I could drop south afterward and see a couple of places, such a Dijon and Montélimar, on the way down to Sommières. I was anxious to see Pauline, but wanted to see more of her country, especially places a little more off the beaten path. Plus, I wanted to give her time to settle back in her place after being gone so long.

Sofia was right. The Aisne Marne American cemetery is stunning. As you enter the gates, you see the crescent of headstones hugging a hill and a beautiful chapel in the center up a bit on the side of the hill. The landscape architecture, the plantings, the trees, the immaculate lawn combined to yield a stunning statement of commemoration. Hard to not to get goose bumps as an American, especially as an American who served in uniform.

"Constant?"

Constant was the cemetery guide employed by the United States to help people find their loved ones and learn the story of the military campaign here. He was French, about 30, clean cut, very formal.

"*Bonjour, oui?*"

"I'm Steve, Steve Miles."

"Oh. Yes. Monsieur Miles. We spoke on the phone yesterday."

Constant gave me a tour of the cemetery and chapel. Knowing my background, he shared many stories of the 2nd Infantry Division, first organized in October 1917 at Haute Marne, France. It was on the hallowed ground just above the cemetery that the famed unit drew its first blood in the hellish landscape of the Battle of Belleau Wood and helped end a four-year standoff between the French and the Germans during the Château-Thierry campaign. Constant shared with me that the division emerged from World War I as the most decorated American Division of the American Expeditionary Forces. During the campaign, two Soldiers, six Marines and six Sailors from the Division received the Medal of Honor. I felt my chest puff out just a bit more hearing this. However, I was disappointed that this was the first time I had learned some of this...seems like this history should have been a part of my orientation to the Division when I served with them.

Constant directed me to the battlefield above the cemetery and suggested I visit the Bulldog fountain across from the cemetery, the nearby Château-Thierry American Monument and head over to Oisne-Aisne American Cemetery before I left the region. Though not a Marine, I sipped from the fountain since we were comrades in arms on this battlefield. A drink from the fountain is supposed to add years to a Jarhead's life. Not sure how it affects soldiers, but my guys fought here too, and I felt entitled.

The American monument overlooking the city of Château-Thierry was huge and beautiful. Statues of two 30-foot tall women, personifying the friendship between France and the US adorns one side of it. An operations map of the campaign was featured on the side facing the city. It was well worth the visit. Oisne-Aisne American Cemetery was beautiful as well, and I paid respects to some of my 2nd Infantry Division comrades there also. I even paid respects to a member of the 42nd Infantry Division, Joyce Kilmer, a famous American poet. He died at Seringes-et-Nesles, north of Château-Thierry.

Being a forestry major in college, I had learned Kilmer's

famous poem, "Trees." Maybe I learned it to convey a nobility to my college major. But the purest sense of his work and its nobility was on display in his poem "Rouge Bouquet." Kilmer wrote it to describe a German artillery attack of an American trench in the vicinity of Rouge Bouquet Wood in March of 1918. The attack killed nineteen Americans. He wrote the poem right after the attack. It was first read over the soldiers' graves. The poem was published in the *Stars and Stripes* newspaper two weeks after Kilmer's own death when he was killed by a sniper's bullet on a nearby battlefield at the age of 31. It gives me goosebumps thinking that it was read over Kilmer's own burial as well.

Here is a part of it that most resonated with me:

> In the soil of the land they fought to free
> And fled away.
> Now over the grave abrupt and clear
> Three volleys ring;
> And perhaps their brave young spirits hear
> The bugle sing:
> Go to sleep!
> Go to sleep!
> Slumber well where the shell screamed and fell.
> Let your rifles rest on the muddy floor,
> You will not need them anymore.
> Danger's past;
> Now at last,
> Go to sleep!

I was humbled to pay respects to this man who last walked the earth and made great art for us over a century ago. Though I never faced combat in the Army, I lost buddies who died in combat. Like all who serve, Kilmer was our comrade-in-arms. In this respect, I appreciated meeting Sofia. I may have never found myself on this hallowed ground before Sergeant Kilmer's grave and all the others were it not for our strange encounter. Life is full of mysteries if you are open to them

The next day I began my journey south. It was time to see Pauline. I had given her a full day to recover from her trip to Réunion Island.

After a bit of a tense call the previous evening, I was feeling the heat to keep moving to see Pauline, but I did walk a few streets in the cool afternoon sun and brilliant blue skies.

Dijon was incredible. Like many iconic places in France, there was a long history to the city, including a settlement here in Roman times. One of the signature features of Dijon is the multicolored glazed roof tiles, called *toit bourguinons*, in rich shades of green, yellow and black that display intricate patterns on the roofs of many historic structures.

I'm sure Montélimar would have been awesome if only I'd stopped. It was almost dusk by the time I reached Montélimar and I only saw a few rooftops and a steeple or two in the fading golden sunset from A7, the highway taking me to Pauline. I still had another couple of hours to go to get to Sommières.

As I headed south the countryside became more arid and beautifully cloaked in the golden-orange rays of the sunset. Certain scenes and the dryer air reminded me a bit of the country around Marfa, though I knew I was so very far from home. As I neared Orange, I kept my eye out for the exit to A9 which would take me west and closer to Pauline. I was puzzled about my feelings of soon being with Pauline. Part of me was ecstatic yet another part of me was filled with ambiguity. Would we click again? It had been a while since we'd see each other. Would she be a little cool like she was at times when we were in Sommières together?

19

I opted to take exit A9 and then D34 up to Sommières. It was a bit out of the way but involved less navigation. Watching for road numbers and turns was not as attractive since it was now dusk. By the time I reached Sommières, it was almost dark. As I waited for the light to cross the Pont du Romain, I was surprised that I had forgotten what a beautiful city Sommières was. The old bridge, originally built by the Romans as part of the Roman road from Nîmes to Toulouse, was regally lit by lights spanning the bridge, bathing it in an orange-golden light against the blue-black sky. As the traffic light changed, I eased onto the bridge and drove towards the *tour de l'horloge*, a gate to the city with a large clock facing the bridge. The interior of the gate was warmly illuminated by the numerous shops along the pedestrian way inside the gate.

Just a few turns and I'd be with Pauline. I was nervous, but mostly in a good way. Crazy thoughts ran through my mind. What if she was getting cold feet? What if the attraction was not as strong? There was nowhere to park, but I remembered where she parks her car around the corner in a small lot. Fortunately, there was a spot, but I had no idea if it was legal. I just needed to see her.

I grabbed a small bag and headed up the street. I had called from near Orange just as I got on A9. She knew I was near. I looked at the buzzer box near the door to her building. I got excited when I saw "Mlle Ferrand" written out in her beautiful cursive. The French have such great penmanship. Funny how something like seeing someone's handwriting can elicit such a response.

"*C'est moi.*"

"C'mon up."

Her door was to the left. She stood there waiting for me. I'll never forget what she looked like as I climbed the stairs. She was in a burgundy short dress and barefooted, glossy black hair framing her beautiful face. I felt the electricity immediately and was enormously reassured as I hit the top steps. We embraced forever and she finally took a step back and looked me in the eye.

"*T'es à moi!*"

"Yes, and you are mine!" Suddenly all seemed right. I tried very hard to really savor that feeling, that moment.

"Have you eaten?"

"No."

"Let's go."

"I have a lot of different hungers right now," as I stared into her eyes.

"Uh-huh. So do I. Let's savor this. Let's go eat at a very romantic spot and work up a proper appetite," she responded with a challenging stare. She was killing me!

"Okay," as I let out an awfully long sigh.

A few blocks away, we walked back across the bridge and around a curve, and there sat the Chez Tibère. Pauline had reserved a table outside overlooking the Vidourle River. She couldn't have picked a better romantic spot for us to celebrate being back together: the river, the cooling fresh air, the dancing candlelight.

I couldn't take my eyes off of her. She was just as beautiful and sexy as I had remembered. We had video chatted, but it wasn't the same as seeing her, touching her, smelling her, just being with her and holding her slender fingers in my hand.

The first taste of the magret de canard followed by a sip of the Cahor, a red from a region far to the west, caused an explosion of that "All is right" feeling in my mind. I was with my beautiful woman surrounded by a river and gently illuminated 2,000-year-old French city eating perhaps the best culinary combination ever created. Most Americans are almost completely ignorant of the magnificence of duck. *Quel dommage.*

This incredible feeling lasted maybe ten minutes before Pauline asked the big question.

"So, we'll live here, in France, no?"

I stupidly hadn't wrestled with that issue. Love conquers all I thought. "Well, let's talk about that."

A trace of concern surfaced on Pauline's face as one of her eyebrows lifted. A look both sexy and of concern for me based on our history. Given her French diplomacy genes, one never knew if that eyebrow was all there was or was there a large iceberg lurking below the surface. I felt that "All is right" feeling starting to flow out of me, down the bank of the river and towards the Mediterranean. Ought to be at Le Grau-du-Roi by daybreak. Had it been a number of decades ago, perhaps I could have "telegraphed" David and Catherine, Hemingway's characters in *The Garden of Eden*, to keep an eye out for it as it flowed into the Mediterranean. The curse of being a writer.

"Steve…Steve?"

I let go of that imagery and snapped back to earth.

"Pauline, I just want us to be together…I just assumed, we'd work that out."

She just looked at me. The eyebrow was cocked again.

"Pauline, we will work this out."

"Well, it is important. I am French. I plan to remain French. I love you so much, but we must figure this out soon. I want to make sure you know who you are in love with. I don't plan on becoming an American."

"*Chère*, can we plan on having a number of discussions on this in the coming days? I am committed to this. It is critical. I agree. But I want us to have a beautiful evening to celebrate us being together finally. Can we talk about this tomorrow? What you have said is not a deal breaker for me," I looked her in the eyes hoping she'd melt a bit.

"D'accord. Mais…c'est très important pour moi."

"Je comprends. Moi aussi."

My acknowledging that it was important in Pauline's native language seemed to be enough, for now at least.

We went on to have a spectacular evening. The intimacy we shared was powerful and true. It was real and clearly affirmed for me I was right to come for her, to seek her being part of my life forever. Unfortunately, there was a weight on my soul I couldn't completely cast off no matter how hard I tried. For some nonsensical reasons I briefly reflected on the lyrics of one of my favorite French songs by Autour de Lucie, *"Je Reviens."*

"Ne sommes-nous comme le sable"

Deux êtes friables

Balayés par le vent?

On est loin dès l'instant"

I had used music lyrics to improve my French long ago, and for some reason these lyrics and music of this beautiful song resurfaced suddenly. "Are we not like sand, two friable beings, swept by the wind, we are far from the now." Those lyrics spoke to me about the fragility of relationships, especially when two people come from different cultures with different value systems. Language is powerful in ways we don't understand. These lyrics spoke so much more powerfully to me in French than English. I wasn't sure how that could be possible, yet it was true for me.

I knew days of complex discussions, maybe even negotiations, awaited us, but I didn't want to let that spoil the reemergence of that "All is well" feeling no matter how brief it might be.

20

The next few days were a bit rainy. Even in the rain, Sommières had its charms. I quickly settled into a French rhythm. I'd make a small pot of *Carte Noire* and go around the corner to get a baguette. I had missed French coffee, bread and butter during my time away. When Pauline remarked that we don't have to eat the same *petit déjeuner* every day, I assured her we did after I vigorously went off on what passes for bread and butter in America. I found myself getting angry about what Americans do to food. Ahh, *nourriture industrielle américain*. I whisked that anger away as quickly as it came. It was time to focus on Pauline and us.

Lazy days of love, walks, reading punctuated by meals, flirting and at times intense conversation. I was grateful she was off from work so that we could just focus on each other. Mostly very enjoyable except when the conversations turned serious. I guess you could say that we were seeing how we'd live together and…and where. A test drive of sorts.

I was surprised how well it was going in some respects. Some of the tensions that had plagued us before were gone or at least muted. But big issues remained. A couple of them came to a head at 3:00 am!

The day had started pleasantly enough. Her friend had invited us to a "*dejeuner de dimanche*." The event was an outdoor dinner party at a house just on the edge of Villevielle, a village next to Sommières. As we drove out to the house, we passed the olive oil cooperative where my temporary next-door neighbor from my earlier visit, Brites, and I tasted *huiles d'olive* during my earlier visit to the area. I briefly wondered what happened to her. I hoped she found happiness back in Brazil. Funny how people can come and be important to you a short period and then, boom, they are gone.

The hosts had already set up two long tables in the yard. White tablecloths in the white Languedoc sunshine of midday. Rather elegant. A few of the guests had already arrived. I just followed Pauline's cues. A host offered me a pastis upon my arrival. There seemed to be a ritual and I wanted to follow as best I could.

After many, many air kisses and greetings, we were seated. A small placard announced where I was to sit. Being a bit out of practice, I was already getting tired after speaking French by the second course. I was quite diligent in ensuring the wine glasses of the women around me were refilled since French etiquette dictated that ladies typically did not serve wine to themselves.

The attractive woman to my left was the head of a small Catholic school in Sommières. The distinguished woman to my right was a retired naval officer. I wish I hadn't been so tired because they were both fascinating people, well read with many interesting stories. I kept an eagle eye on Pauline to ensure I was observing all norms. I had grown to where I was comfortable around French people, but I had never been in this particular social setting. French customs could still occasionally trip me up, and I had no interest in embarrassing Pauline. I was, after all, still trying to woo her. I regretted her meeting my cousin, Clark, or the *"plouc"* as she liked to call him. It seemed a fitting name in reality.

After an incredible six course meal, the host offered a Cognac or Armagnac to close out the experience. As I learned, the *digestif* was to help us digest the culinary debauchery in which we had just participated. I was pretty much wiped out by the end. Not sure if it was the duration, volume of food or alcohol, or having to speak French for five hours. Probably the latter.

I needed to start speaking more French if I was going to spend a significant part of my life here.

After that "wonderful ordeal" I told Pauline I need to crash awhile.

◆ ◆ ◆

"Well, that was delightful but exhausting." I looked over at Pauline as I emerged from the bedroom after a two-hour nap. She was sitting on her small sofa with her legs tucked under her reading a magazine. She looked sexy as she peered at me over her reading glasses.

"*Est-ce que tu es une poule mouillée?*"

"Huh?"

"Wim?"

"Oh, you mean "wimp.""

"Yes, wee-mp." It was funny when she mispronounced her English. Being a French instructor for mostly American business professionals, her English was normally quite good. I guess she didn't use the word "wimp" that often with her clients. Understandable.

"Oh. Well, only when it comes to consuming food and drinking alcohol and speaking French five hours *chouchou!*" I slowly said the *chouchou* part hoping it would soften the edge of what I said.

"Okay, I don't want a low energy guy," with a French pout as she turned a page. "*C'est vrai.*" More pouting.

"Do I strike you as low energy?" I gave her a challenging stare. "Let's go in the bedroom and see how low energy I am. C'mon."

"*Ce ne sera pas necessaire.* I know you aren't low energy that way." She finally smiled.

"I like you in glasses. *Très sexy.*"

She looked at me and puffed up a cheek full of air and made a big production of pushing the air out with her finger.

"I mean it!"

"Okay, get dressed. Let's go for a walk."

We walked along the Vidourle River under a long row of Sycamore trees. Pauline would occasionally wave to someone. She saw her *Ostéopathe* in front of her office. It gave me pause when she introduced me as her friend rather than her *fiancé*. That would trigger intense conversations later.

The sidewalk played out and we continued along the river on the street passing a long row of cars. We continued down the sidewalk along the river until we grabbed a table at Restaurant L'Esplanade. It was a *provençal* yellow two-story structure across the road from the river.

"My cousin owns this place."

"Nice place."

She just caught the eye of the waiter and made a circling motion about our table, and he brought us two robust glasses of rosé.

"Étienne knows me well. I might be related to him. Not sure. Way down the line. You know, Étienne will be your name here. It's Stephen in French."

"Cool, I like it. By the way, excellent rosé. Bold citrusy notes, right amount of acid. Nice."

She looked at me and just pursed her lips which meant she wasn't impressed.

"Okay, sorry. I read an article on rosés recently. I'll cut the shit."

"*Merci.* Remember, part of your appeal is a lack of pretension."

Quiet prevailed while Pauline watched the river flow by through a hedge.

"What are you thinking?"

"Steve, we have a big decision to make."

"Yes, we do. I noticed you didn't introduce me as your fiancé."

"No, I didn't."

"That's okay."

"I can't truly commit to you, to us, until I have some

assurances. I am an independent woman. You are an independent man. I may not have the financial wealth you have, but I am wealthy in other ways. I am not any more willing to give up my wealth than you would be."

I admired her. She was so strong. So smart. She still hadn't looked at me. Étienne brought us another round.

She introduced me to Étienne this time, as her "*petit ami.*"

After he left us, she peered over at me, "*Est-ce que tu préfères ça?*" Eyebrow lifted, mischievous smile.

"Yes, that was better, more hopeful." Boyfriend better than "friend!"

"*Bon.*"

"Okay Pauline, the two of us beating around the bush is not going to help." She looked confused. "I mean Pauline, please tell me what's bothering you."

"Steve, I don't know if we want the same things. When I read your book, I saw so much substance, deep thinking. But you don't always show that. Plus, I don't know what you want out of life."

"Do you know what *you* want Pauline?"

Silence prevailed as a giant Sycamore leaf drifted down between us. Somehow, I strangely hoped it was tearing down the curtain between us. She slowly picked up the leaf, and said, "*feuille de sycamore,*" and smiled at me.

"Sycamore in English too."

"Yes, Steve. I think so. At least as much as anyone does."

"What do you want?"

"This."

"This?"

"Yes, what we are experiencing right now...and earlier today."

"Wealth?"

"Yes."

"I get that. Are you saying you want me to move to France?"

"Yes, I want you to become something you may not want

to become. I have no right to ask that of you."

I watched her study the last vestiges of the sunset as it, to describe it the way the French do, went to bed on the horizon. She was beautiful in the fading light. Her black hair pushed back by her sunglasses resting on her head. Somehow, her lipstick was still red. I so wanted her in my life, but she was making this so complicated. It is as though complexity is a virtue in France.

She looked me in the eye, "I mean, I see how happy and alive you are in Marfa, in West Texas. I have no right to take that from you. I want you to be happy. I want to be happy. I want us both to be happy."

"Look, let's reflect on this conversation awhile and keep this conversation going. I love West Texas, but I love France too. It doesn't have to be either-or, but please know, I will do what it takes to make us work. Let's leave it there for now. I love you so much. And I am now hungry believe it or not."

She smiled, "*D'accord, mon petit ami.*"

After a butter and ham sandwich on the baguette left from breakfast and a quick shower, I was asleep I think before my head hit the pillow. The Sunday dinner ordeal and intense conversation that followed wiped me out. I slept soundly until 3:00 am.

"What did you mean, 'It doesn't have to be either-or?'"

Clearly, Pauline was ready for our discussion to continue. That made one of us.

"Baby, let's talk in the morning. I'm sleeping, my love."

"Well, I'm not sleeping. I want to know."

"Don't you normally sleep at 3:00? You have since I've been here, at least as far as I know. I kind of like to sleep in the wee hours of the morning."

"*Normalement, oui. Mais pas cette nuit.*" Oh, how I hoped she didn't want to argue in French. Maybe I was low energy. I was still drained.

"Look Pauline, I love you. I very much want us to be together. We absolutely will figure this out."

"I want to figure it out now."

"I've been thinking on this. What if we have two homes? Maybe one in Marfa and one here. Could that work?"

"*Je ne veux pas devenir américain!*" She was becoming angry.

"Okay. I get it. You don't have to be American."

"*Es-tu certain?*"

"Yes, I am certain. It's up to you."

"I don't know about this!" With that, she pulled the sheets up over her and flung her body to look away from me. She could make a bed move a lot for someone so light.

Obviously, we had so much more to talk about, but that could wait. Her intensity was becoming a concern for me though. I had much to learn about the person I was sleeping with, the person I thought was my *fiancée*. I was glad to be tired, because sleeping was the only thing going to happen in this bed for the rest of the night.

The next morning, I had the coffee brewed, baguette properly displayed and "*du beurre et de la confiture*" attractively arranged. She came out of the bedroom, grabbed a cup of coffee and headed for the shower. Of course, I took the lack of words as a troubling sign. Clearly, she was still apprehensive, or maybe even pissed.

Thirty minutes later, she came out of the bathroom wearing a short black dress and heels, grabbed a couple of pieces of fruit and headed out the door. She returned a second later and grabbed a scarf only to exit after a cursory, "*Passe une bonne journée.*"

I remembered that she did have work today. Sadly, her week of leave was over, just when we probably needed to be together more than ever. Yes, there was a lot we needed to learn about each other. At least, I knew she deeply cared for me, so I was able to keep it in perspective. I committed to figure out how to peel back another layer of Pauline. There was more she wanted to tell me. More I needed to know. After I tired of struggling through the regional newspaper, I'd work on thinking about Pauline while writing the new story I had started in Paris. Sometimes, I was successful in working on an issue while working on another if I could get my mind to use its "back processor," that part of my mind that thinks about things without my being really conscious of it.

I took my coffee and sat on her sofa, admiring her little world. It was basically two rooms: a smallish living room with a small kitchen and dining table all in the same room. A bedroom with a bathroom carved out in a corner. The bathroom had a long window, almost like a door that led out onto a nice-sized shady patio. White walls throughout with half a dozen original paintings similar to Matisse scattered about most tastefully. Zero clutter other than a lot of books. I loved her style. I loved how small and uncluttered it was and her perception that she was wealthy. Many Americans would have chafed at how small her place was. Yet she appeared to be genuinely happy, other than with the doofus to whom she was engaged, maybe.

The bakery across the street filled her patio with an incredible smell in the morning and many afternoons, though she insisted I go around the corner to another bakery, where the crust was crisper. Her perfume still drifted about since her departure. I knew I loved this woman. I knew I wanted to know how to make her happy.

As I looked around her place, I felt so privileged that she'd given me a chance to win her heart. French people didn't open a door like this often, especially to an outsider. She obviously saw something in me. I knew it wasn't my money. Miraculously, it was something else.

As I sat my cup down on her coffee table, I stared at a small notebook where she had made notes. I even loved her perfect handwriting. The French and their handwriting. Yes, I could become French. But is that what I wanted? I, too, had a lot of thinking to do.

After a morning walk and doing a lot of sitting and thinking, I decided to see if I could get some writing done and energize that back processor in my mind. Her patio was about twelve by ten feet. The large statue of the virgin in the corner was still there, just where I recalled seeing it from my last visit. It was there when Pauline moved in. I walked over to the low stone wall that surrounded the patio and peered over the edge. Down below across the street, the bakery was closing for lunch. It would reopen most evenings but not all. It had an arrangement with the other bakery in the town to try to ensure that there was a bakery open somewhere in town most mornings and evenings. The pleasures of civility.

Seeing the bakery reminded me I was once again hungry. In a little while, I'd open a box of soup and enjoy a bit more of my morning baguette. Might even have a taste of rosé with it. Yes, I was quite sure I'd make a good Frenchman. But, like Pauline, a few doubts nagged me if that was what I truly wanted.

Just as I finally got my laptop set up and I'd had started to get into a little bit of a groove, it hit me. I never read the note that Beach had given me!

I was getting hungry but couldn't wait. I retrieved it out of my suitcase and returned to the patio. I also threw on a long sleeve t-shirt. It was getting cooler. I carefully unfolded Beach's note and began to consume it. As a gentle breeze washed across Pauline's patio, a few leaves fell as I carefully read it, but I didn't pay any mind to that. I was absorbed.

Background on "The Book of Tiki" (Draft 7)

This book of the bible is asserted to be my account of Jesus and considered the final book of the bible at this time. We don't know if Christ is returning today or one million years from now. As such, many more revelations may occur. We don't know. Would God really authorize a handful of men, they were all reported to be men which is problematic, then as much as now, to argue over what should be included? These men probably foisted much of their perspective into the text but finally kind of agreed to what should be in the bible over a few junctures and finally called the book closed in 382 AD or the early 1600s depending on whether you are Catholic or Protestant. We know that priests and preachers often make mistakes from the pulpit, yet somehow, we are to believe that the authors and framers of the bible made a perfect bible and we are to just accept that.

I tend to prefer the Catholic version of the bible since it dates to 382 and for whatever reason, God seems to be communicating less and less with us over time or we are hearing less and less as the millennia go by. Maybe he has given up hope on us. Who'd blame him? Many Christians, at least in America, have become a most un-Christ-like lot. They are so quick to condemn those who commit all the sins that they don't enjoy committing, and many of them have cast their lot with a problematic political party that exploits them to win elections. I fear that the Christian church in America is headed to extinction if it doesn't reform itself very soon. Their eagerness to say they are pro-life while defending polluters, people who want to fill our streets with guns, extreme income inequality, harassment of immigrants and even, in some cases, racists, is sickening. There is NOTHING Godly about mistreating immigrants. NOTHING!

And sorry guys, the bible doesn't say Jesus was a capitalist. If anything, he, and his likely brown group of followers practiced, heaven forbid, something more akin to socialism! They say their white, blue-eyed Jesus condemns Gay people with no spiritual basis. Jesus did not reference homosexuality. He is quoted as referring to marriage in the context of a man and a woman, but that's to be expected when the manuscripts were written. In the scriptures, he did not explicitly address homosexuality. He also condemned one divorcing their spouse in order to marry another unless the spouse committed a sexual sin. I personally don't believe Jesus would have people stay in abusive relationships and forbid them to one day remarry. That's conjecture on my part, but the person who smiled at me on the beach that day, wouldn't expect a person to permanently stay single just because their spouse started beating them. I may be wrong.

I'm troubled that angels, which were common in the gospels, no longer make themselves visible to us. Did God redeploy his angels elsewhere? Or, are we too depraved to even see or hear them? I have often sat still to see if an angel wants to tell me something. Nada.

When I look at some of the colossal cathedrals in tiny villages, like Chartres, I believe that angels must have been a tangible presence to motivate those people to devote themselves to building these enormous structures with extremely limited technology. There weren't even railroads to assist with the transport of materials. The faith of these villagers was incredible. Their sacrifices were extraordinary. The Chartres Cathedral towers over the surrounding landscape for miles and miles. It is like a constant reminder that man and God were once closer. Europe is filled with huge Cathedrals.

Okay, so who the hell am I to write a book of the bible? Am I insane? Am I serious? Great questions. Well, I am a dude who has seen Christ and I am serious. The middle question, well I'm not sure on that one. I encountered Jesus on a beach in French Polynesia many years ago. He did not speak to me. He just looked into my eyes and smiled at me for a few seconds. Through that smile, it was like he "downloaded" something sacred into me.

He told me that his followers had gotten seriously off track and asked me to remind them what he said about love and to stop worshipping a book that man assembled. It was as though he was telling me that the book had become the thing, or even "the God" instead of his love and wisdom. Somehow, in my eyes, I heard, "And a few folks like Paul and Thomas Aquinas didn't always help matters. Does the Church realize that Aquinas came 1,200 years after I walked the planet? Super devoted and smart, but he read things into the scripture we didn't intend. Talk about placing a yoke on believers' necks. This has gone on long enough. Try to get the Church to focus more on my teachings please! If I didn't talk about it, it isn't a thing! I picked my word carefully, I am God after all. I didn't intend Aquinas or anyone else to add to my teachings!"

After staring into my eyes, this handsome Lebanese-looking guy, soaked and holding a surfboard, pushed his hair back and turned and walked away. My eyes followed him as he went his way down the beach until he just seemed to fade away.

I sat on that beach all day. I made notes in a journal I was keeping. I wanted to never forget what had just happened to me. I was in shock. I didn't completely understand, but somehow, I knew it was some sort of pivot point for me. I resolved on that day to study the bible and makes some sense of this.

So here is a draft of "the Book of Tiki," the fifth and final chapter (for now) of the bible. I know it's a silly name, but it does track with some things I take to be central to the tiki culture. Maybe I'll come up with a better name. Maybe, the book of life, or the book of Jesus? It is to be inserted right after the Gospel of John. It's really a summary of Jesus' core teachings. These seem to get lost in the bible and the mess we call society. The rest of the bible is of value...of course it is...but I think of it as more historical or reference than part of the bible. I mean have you ever read the story of Lot? He offered his virgin daughters to an angry mob of rapists! Huh? The Old Testament is often hard to digest and at times even seems disconnected from the New Testament.

The Book of Tiki (until I have a better name)
1 Jesus' Instructions To His Followers

1 As God as loved me, so I have loved you. Remain in my love.

2 If you keep in my commandments, you will remain in my love.

3 I have told you these things so that my joy may be in you and your joy may be complete.

4 This is my commandment, love one another.

5 You are my friends if you do what I command you.

6. Don't be anxious, trust my will for you.

2 Love One Another and Do Not Judge

1 Love one another

2 Let he who is without sin, be the judge of those on this planet. If you have sin, repair yourself. Bottom line is, don't judge. This is God's responsibility.

3 Jesus' Commandments Which All Reinforce His Central Commandment To Love One Another

Do not—
1 Judge others
2 Commit Adultery
3 Kill
4 Steal
5 Deceive
6 Neglect your parents
7 Be selfish
8 Mistreat others
4 Marching Orders
1 Be filled with joy

2 Deal with others as you would have them deal with you
3 Love all in the fullest sense
4 Judge not
5 Lastly, overcome the world and its worries, again, in short,
be filled with joy and love for each other.

Author's note: This book of Tiki is my honest perception of what Jesus shared with me on that sunny day on the beach. Catholicism and Christianity need to refocus, especially in America. I see the Book of Tiki not as a reformation, but a refocus. I don't reject the rest of the bible or most of the beautiful tradition of the Catholic Church. I love the Church and the tradition.

Some of these things just need to be better reconciled to the teachings of Jesus. It is a tough message (many would say heretical) but, the survival of the Church and Christianity may depend on it. A bit of the tradition and just Christianity in general has just gotten off track somehow. Please forgive me Jesus if I am sharing anything that is wrong. The future of the Church may depend on being more Christ and love-centric than ever before!

Who is this guy? Does Beach see himself as a prophet? This guy's got brass. I had no idea even how to process this. I know how most Christians would probably process it. He's a kook. He's a heretic. Yet, some, if not a lot of it, struck a chord. I wondered how long he'd been working on this. He didn't tell me what it was when he handed it to me. He handed to me between drinks at his bar with little explanation. Why did he give it to me? I only knew that I was going to have to read it a few times to fully absorb it and I would like to talk to him more about it.

I needed help dealing with this. Suddenly, Father Mike, a local priest I befriended on my last visit, sprang to my mind. I hadn't thought of him. When I left here last time, I thought I may never see him again. I resolved to meet with him soon. Meanwhile, I needed to get some soup and regroup. I needed to get some writing done if I could focus after this! And above all, I needed to help Pauline and me see a path forward if we were going to survive as a couple. I needed to know what her real concerns were. My "back processor," helped me to determine to have a good meal ready for Pauline when she arrived home.

22

While I was cooking, I was back processing my Pauline issue and to a lesser extent, Beach's strange document, which kept haunting me. I almost hopped in the car and drove down to Lunel where there was a Picard store to buy some frozen Indian or Thai food, but I decided I wanted to cook her something from scratch. I opted to make her some spaghetti and salad. I did splurge for a good pairing wine, *un Languedoc La Clape rouge*. Per my research, it was the best regional wine to pair with spaghetti, so at least there was that.

Just as I was wrapping up dinner preparations, Pauline came from work looking a bit tired. She kissed me. "*Bonsoir*. So sorry about this morning."

"I made us dinner."

"Excellent. I am starving." She looked just as good as when she left after a full day of work, just a bit run down.

"You're so beautiful, *ma cherie*."

"Thank you. Let me wash up. I'll be right back," she said with a smile. She seemed to be perking up. Making dinner was a good move apparently. It generally is, I guess.

After only a few moments, Pauline returned.

"*Finalement! J'ai été affamé toute la journée!*" She had changed into slacks and a sweater.

"Well, if you're that hungry, I'm so glad I cooked...hope you like it," I said as I was dishing us out our pasta dishes.

"I will. I want us to go for a walk afterwards. I changed, getting cooler out there."

After I filled her wine glass and we exchanged "*bon appétit*," she began to savor the meal. She liked it. I was proud.

"I can finally think. I can't even talk when I am that hungry. Thank you for making this meal. It's perfect. It marks the first time you have cooked for me."

I toasted her and said, "Here's to many, many more times."

We just smiled and communicated with our eyes. I felt like I really belonged here, with her.

"I know this wasn't a very complex meal, but you executed it quite nicely. Sometimes doing simple very well is a challenge. *Bien joué!* I'm impressed. And the wine, the wine is perfect!"

"Wait, I cooked for you in Marfa a few times. Did you forget?"

"*Non,* I just meant here, cooking for me here. Somehow, somehow it just means more to me, here. It really does. You are a good cook."

"Thank you."

"You are welcome, my love. Thank you for cooking." Her eyes sparkled once again. She did look genuinely happy.

After a quick clean up, we headed down the steps to take a walk. I had to run back and get a sweater as well. A cool front had come in.

The sun was just a thin line of orange to the west. The clouds were a mix of grays, brilliant blue and white. Stunning. The Sycamore leaves crunched under our feet as we walked along the river. I remained quiet. I wanted to give her thinking space. Belong long we were seated on a bench near the river. To our left, across the river, we could see the restaurant down river where we ate the night of my arrival, softly illuminated in the fading light.

Pauline looked me in the eye and stared at me a few minutes before she spoke.

"Steve, I want this to work so much more than any other relationship I have ever had. It is just complicated for me."

I just listened.

"I love you so much. But … I am in love with being French as well. It is who I am. Perhaps you are in love with being American. We must navigate this issue. It is so important to me. I want you and France."

I kept listening.

"See, I love the way you listen to me. Very few French men would sit and listen like you do. You want to understand how I feel, and I love you so much for that."

"I do."

She stared at a huge leaf at had just fallen on her leg.

"I don't want to become American. Not now."

"I understand."

"I want to live most of my life here. I want to die here. France is my home."

"I understand that, too."

"I know you may feel the same way about America."

"Pauline, before I say anything at all, I want to make sure I fully understand your concerns. I want to process them, and I love you for giving me your honesty, your trust and caring so much about how I feel as well."

"Steve, tell me what you are worried about?"

"Losing you."

"Yes, me too, *mais quoi d'autre?*"

"There is nothing else. Losing you. That's my only fear."

She suddenly hugged me so tight it almost hurt.

"We will work this out." It was almost dark, but by the faint light of a streetlamp, I could make out that she said that through moist eyes.

"Look, Steve, we're going to make this work, but there is work ahead of us. I know you have concerns and future dreams. I must know them. I want you to be happy. When you fall in love the way I have, your happiness is as important as mine, maybe more."

"I feel the same. Absolutely the same."

"I've…never felt this," she sighed, looking intently into

my eyes.

"Me neither. I thought I'd fallen in love before, but it was nothing like this."

We resolved that we would work through this over the next few days. She had a holiday on Thursday and would take the Friday off as well. We just sat there awhile and then she began looking at me almost as though she was studying me for the first time. Suddenly, we were making out like teenagers in the dark. Needless to say, we had an incredible night.

The next day, I resolved to find Father Mike. Pauline would have a four-day weekend after today. After I saw Pauline off in the morning, I decided to walk over to the church. I'd lost his number somehow. After a little more coffee I strolled up the Rue de la Monnaie to the church.

I had met Father Mike at the bakery during my first visit to this area. He heard my accent while chatting with the woman behind the counter and figured I might be American. From then on, we had short chats when our paths crossed, mainly at the bakery. At Father Mike's urging, I had attended Mass in the church a few times during my last visit. He was from Buffalo, NY, so we had the American thing going. He loved talking American politics and baseball. Plus, I was a struggling Episcopalian seeking some guidance and trying to make sense of the world. He was very tolerant of my Episcopalian faith, as it were, and offered me his best counsel, nonetheless.

The church is in a more elevated part of town. The site had been a place of worship back to the 11th Century though this church mostly dated to the middle 1800s. As I ascended the steps to the door, I smelled incense and the interior. It seems almost all Catholic Churches in France have a similar smell: kind of incense, kind of stone, kind of old, and hundreds of years of burning candles. The door was locked. I knew where he lived. The Parrish had a small house nearby for him. I had joined him for wine on his patio on my last visit. I rounded the corner and saw the house. I entered the gate and knocked on the door. No answer.

I went around and peered on the side of the house where the small, covered patio was. There he was, sleeping in his chair. I carefully approached him so as to not startle him.

I whispered, "Father Mike." He awoke with a start. He peered at me for a while like he couldn't believe his eyes. He pushed his horn-rimmed glasses back up his nose and looked again. Finally, he seemed to realize it was me.

"You asshole! Oh," he laughed and peered around as though seeing if anyone had overheard him, "Sorry. Steve! So good to see you. What are you doing here?"

"I came back for Pauline. We are engaged, I think."

"Well, that's great news, I think."

"It is father. We're just working some stuff out."

"Okay, so you need advice on that, so you came over here and woke me up?" Big smile. He was oddly enough, wearing a light yellow, Mexican guayabera shirt.

"Well, I don't know. Maybe not. Maybe we just need to work it out between the two of us."

"Glad to hear it. That's the way to do it."

"Yeah, well, I'm hoping so."

"Just came by to say hi then?"

"Well, yeah, but…"

"And…"

"I got this friend of mine; well, I guess he's a friend. Only seen him a few times. Seems like a great guy, he's from Texas. Anyway, he gave me a document that kind of has my head spinning. He thinks he's seen Jesus and has written a new book of the bible."

Father Mike started laughing.

"No, I mean it father, he really believes this."

Father Mike composed himself. "Okay, Steve. What do you think?"

"I don't know. You know I'm kind of spiritual, but I suck

as a religious person."

"I've noticed." Gentle smile.

"Father, well, I was wondering if I could show it to you."

"Well, there's really no need Steve. I think my beliefs are pretty well nailed down, as you might imagine."

"Okay. Well, just think about it. It really is haunting me somehow."

"Why is it haunting you? Your friend has a delusion and writes a story. It is probably that simple. I don't mean to critical of him. He probably really believes it happened."

"Yeah, I guess you might be right, but…"

"Spill it, Steve. What's his big idea?"

"Well, he met Jesus as a super-centered, surfer dude, who extols love over all."

"That's not quite as farfetched as I thought it'd be."

"Well, there's more."

"Uh huh. Go on."

"He thinks the bible as a whole really detracts from Jesus' core teaching of love, so he only embraces the gospels as sacred."

"Okay, well that's pretty original, but I've heard others express concerns a little bit like that."

"He wrote a book, he calls 'The Book of Tiki' to be the fifth and final book of the bible."

"Book of Tiki?"

I nodded.

"The Book of Tiki?"

I just watched his face. He started laughing again so hard I thought he might fall out of his chair.

"Steve, you came to tell me this and didn't even bring wine?"

"Look, I know it's crazy. It's just…as I read it, he made some good points."

"Steve, people have been trying to debunk the bible for a long time. It's a widow maker. Nothing has worked."

"Yeah, I know you're probably right."

Father Mike just smiled at me.

"Do you want to at least read it?"

"Nope."

"Okay, sorry I mentioned it."

"No worries, Steve."

Father Mike took a deep sigh and looked out into the bright sunshine. He changed his glasses to put on sunshades. "Tell me Steve, how do you think things will go with Pauline in the long run?" I felt kind of stupid for raising Beach's writing with him.

"I'm sure it's going to work out."

"Glad to hear it."

I spent the next half-hour or so getting him caught up with what's going on in America, our wacky politics and sports. He was very interested in hearing the latest.

Just as I was leaving, Father Mike called me back.

"Hey Steve, I ever tell you the one about the Guinness employee drowning?

"Don't recall that one." Father Mike was Irish and always enjoyed a good joke.

In his best Irish accent, "So Mary comes rushing in to tell Martha that her dear Seamus has died on the job. Martha says 'My heavens' and they both rushed down just a weeping and wailing to the Guinness brewery. A portly, bearded brewery worker walked up to them and says, 'So sorry Martha, Seamus fell into a vat and he drowned.' Martha, still sobbing, says 'Well, at least he went quickly. Thanked the blessed Virgin for that.' The bearded worker looked at her with a rather strange expression and said, 'Well actually, it took a wee little bit of time. He got out three times to pee!'"

We both laughed, and I turned to head back towards Pauline's place. It was so wonderful to see my dear Father Mike again.

I was soon walking down the street more confused about "The Book of Tiki" than ever, however, and decided to put it to the side for a good long while. I had more pressing business to attend to. I needed my full attention on Pauline and me. As I got further from the church, my full attention was on how to create a great environment tonight. It seemed maybe, a romantic dinner in a small restaurant might be in order. Just then, I got a text.

23

"Steve, I really need you to come back here. Weird stuff going on with the movie. And your railroad thing, if you care, is starting to really fall apart. And, oh yeah, our beer brand has been bought out by a big American brewing company. Come back as soon as you can. I'll try to keep things together as long as I can."

That was really rare for Amy to text with such a dire tone. She could handle almost anything. I knew she needed me back in Marfa, but I couldn't blow it with Pauline. Now that I was back with her and we were beginning to communicate, I knew she was the one. I made a simple lunch of more boxed soup and part of a baguette. As I ate lunch, thoughts swirled through my head. I'd let Amy know I'd call soon, but right now, I needed to think how to create a nice evening with Pauline. I also jotted down a few notes on a short story I'd been working on. Out of the blue, I'd come up with a great ending and wanted to make sure I didn't lose it. My back brain at work. I had hoped it would work equally well with resolving the "where to live" issue with Pauline.

All my thinking got put aside when Pauline called and told me to be ready at 6:00 to go somewhere nice with her. She'd just pick me up straight from work. That matter being resolved, I decided to call Amy. She'd be up and about by now in Texas.

"Good morning Amy!"

"Steve! So good to hear your voice." She sounded tense.

"Same here. How are you?"

"Good, but things are crazy of late."

"How so?"

"When can you get back here, Steve?"

"Not right away."

"Crap!"

"What's the worst thing?"

"I've gotten some nasty letters from the movie guys."

"Why?"

"They claim some right to lower our compensation."

"Huh?"

"When they did that, I played hardball. Yesterday, I had the Sheriff ready to arrest them for trespass for a breach of contract."

"Good."

"That calmed them down for now."

"Good."

"We'll see."

"Okay, then a major brewery has bought out the brewery in Chihuahua. They notified us that they are going to start distribution through their network as soon as our agreement runs out next year."

"Okay. That's a tough one."

"Yes. We may be out of the beer business."

"Not so fast. I have an idea, but it's going to take some real work. Let me chew on that. How's your Spanish, Amy?

"Rusty. Understand it better than I can speak. Spoke it a lot on the ranch. It'd come back if needed."

"Got it. What else?"

"The Union Pacific wants a demonstration that this railroad idea could work. They want to see a lot of studies and analyses, etc. The counties haven't done any of them."

"Ouch! That's not going to happen without me being there, I'm afraid."

"The good news is that the railroad has agreed to continue serving Marfa for now. Shank and Bud wrote a joint letter to DC and Austin. I guess County Judges still have some pull in

Texas."

"Okay. That's good. That buys us some time. I'm sure this will come back one day."

"Yeah, but we may not be bringing in beer much longer."

"Well, that's where my idea comes in. We might be bringing in something else. We'll see."

"Okay. Sounds interesting."

"May fizzle. Just want to think about it before I say anything. Maybe a crazy idea. Anything else?"

"You having a crazy idea? No way! Oh, Clark's in jail."

"Why?"

"He may be out already, but it seems he might have been using the cab for some extra fares that weren't reported to the cab company."

"What a moron!"

"I know. He'd probably gotten away with it if he hadn't started making frequent trips over the border. Somehow, Border Patrol reported it back to the cab company about the need to get a commercial border crossing permit or something like that."

"Your brother's an idiot."

"Tell me something I don't know."

"Gotta go. Look, I'll get back soon. I got something I got to focus on here."

"I didn't get to tell you about the art gallery controversy."

"That's gonna have to wait."

"Okay. Hurry back. The movie thing is going to get nasty. They were supposed to be done this month. They ain't gonna be close to wrapping it up. I'm going to hit them with more rental fees or up the royalty. I'd rather rental fee. I think this movie is going to be a dud! I've grown to hate Tito."

"Okay. I'll be back when I can."

"Good, we need to figure the beer thing out soon. We only have a few months."

"Copy."

"How are you and Pauline?"

"Good."

"Set a date?"

"Not yet."

"Why not?"

"It's a little complicated."

Amy was quiet.

"But, Amy, it's going to be fine. I won't let it not be."

"Good to hear."

"Take care, Amy."

"You too."

Time to get ready for our date.

Pauline was 15 minutes late, but gorgeous. She had kind of hurried out that morning. I hadn't fully appreciated the short black dress she wore and black opaque stockings. Her red scarf and lips were the perfect accent. She smelled so good.

"Sorry I was a tad late."

"No worries."

"Don't get used to me speaking in English to you so much."

"What do you mean?"

As she looked around to head out, she peered over and locked eyes with mine just a second, "We have some business to take care of. Best we do it in English, given your French, as it were."

"Thank you."

"*De rien,* I don't want you to forget how beautiful my language is."

"It is a beautiful language that becomes a very sexy language when I hear you speak it."

"I know, doesn't it? Glad you have an appreciation of that. That's important." She gave me a serious glance I didn't fully understand. A cultural divide still surfaced from time to time.

Within 15 minutes, we pulled into what appeared to be a farm, but it was a lot more as you approached the historic *château* that was just over a small bluff that hid it from the entrance. It was dusk, but the *château* was beautifully illuminated. Golden lights from the ground illuminated the beautiful stonework. A dozen or so cars were scattered about in front.

"*Bienvenue au château des Italiens.*"

"Interesting name."

"Interesting place as you will soon see."

The interior was what one would expect. Plenty of tapestries and large works of landscape art with an occasional portrait. No suits of armor. After several *la bise* with staff on the part of Pauline, we followed the maître d down a hallway to a small but well-appointed dining room. It was obvious, Pauline was well-known here.

The room was painted a rich red and had a couple of gorgeous tapestries depicting royal court life. The light in the room came from the illumination of a large landscape painting, a dim corner lamp and a candle on the table. The lighting was perfect to create a romantic environment.

"Pauline, this place is amazing."

"Yes. It is. Get ready for a long meal you will never forget."

"They seem to know you here quite well."

"I am somehow related to the owner. Way back. I bring my classes here often for an education in Languedoc cuisine, French etiquette, wine. They love me. I am good for business. My pupils are never disappointed. I dated one of the waiters way on back in Lycée. French teenagers don't date like American teenagers. We mostly go out in groups. At most, we stole a few kisses here and there, but we had a lot of fun. Growing up in France is very different than America. Gerard is a bee farmer, as well. That is where our honey comes from on my table, the lavender honey. What do you call bee farmers?"

"Beekeepers or apiarists."

"Yes! Strange term. One doesn't say 'cow keeper.'"

"Correct. One doesn't say that." I smiled at her.

As we savored the aperitif, I peered out the window to

my left and admired the last expression of the setting sun. Just an orange hint on the purplish tree-lined horizon. I couldn't get over how beautiful and even happy Pauline seemed. She was in her habitat. All was well. The gleam in her eye from the candle-light was captivating.

Before long, an *entrée* was placed before us. It was simple. Thin slices of bagette topped with green, maroon and black tapenades paired with a local rosé.

"I love this Pauline."

"Good."

"This is incredible, and I don't mean just the food or drink. I mean all of this. I am so happy to be here." I suddenly had a pang of guilt for my minor indiscretions in Paris. Nothing really happened, but it could have. Pauline was worth my being all in. She deserved the best. The whole Hemingway matter about "knowledge of life" was still a thing for me, but I needed to manage it better henceforth.

"Steve?"

"What?"

She smiled, "You were so deep in thoughts. What were you thinking about?"

"You. Us. How much I want to be with you."

"Good. But as I've said, we have work to do."

"I know."

"I don't want you to regret being with me. There will be a price."

"It's worth it. Tell me what it is. Don't hold back, I need to know what you need."

"I will. Don't worry. Enjoy *this* moment. Let me seduce you a bit *à la française*. Seduction is an art form for us."

"I've noticed. Believe me."

She reached over an took my hand and looked me in the eye. We just locked eyes. We talked with our eyes. We really did. I had never really looked into someone's soul before. If this was seduction, I never wanted it to end. We were from different cultures, different languages, different perspectives, but none of that mattered right then. As the *plat principal* arrived, she lifted her eyebrows, let out a big sigh and smiled.

After the waitress left, I whispered to her, "I felt like you were making love to me with your eyes."

"I was."

"Mission accomplished. I will follow you anywhere."

"I hope so."

The rest of the meal was a continual feast for the taste buds. The *plat principal* was *Clapassade*. Lamb, honey, olives and anise. Simple ingredients, complex tastes, even a trace of a licorice, which doesn't sound great, but it is.

The cheese plate was spectacular. Pauline relished educating me on her favorites. Most were goat cheeses. My favorite was the Pélardon--soft, ivory-colored, slight taste of hazelnuts. Pauline said it came from the mountains and high country in Languedoc. Food and wine are in reality national sports here, along with soccer that is.

I was enjoying a nice buzz, but Pauline had coffee to end.

As we walked out, Pauline pulled me towards the grounds of the chateau. The gardens and fountains were softly illuminated. So romantic. As we strolled, she said, "Follow, I want to show you something."

We entered a dark tunnel of vegetation. She pulled me into her and kissed me. I so wanted her to tell me what she wanted to hear so I could just give everything over to her. We had an adventurous walk about the estate and enjoyed each other by the light of the moon. I let her know that I was as seduced as I think I could be.

24

"Have I seduced you fully?" Pauline asked me with a flirtatious smirk the next day as she sat next to me in the sunshine.

The weather had finally warmed up. After a leisurely morning, we had packed a picnic lunch and driven to a site along the Vidourle River. We had spread a blanket and opened the wine. The weather was glorious. Seventy degrees and a super blue sky. Green grass and green hills in the distance. Pauline wore a pink and white shift dress and white tennis shoes. Her hair was pulled back by a white scarf. With her sunglasses, she looked like a 1960s movie star.

"You fully seduced me in Marathon, Pauline."

"Sure? I was pretty angry for a while."

"You got over it."

"Yeah, I guess I did." She winked at me; I think. Hard to see her eyes through the shades.

"Yeah, well, I have to say Pauline, I wondered if we were really going to be able to make this work a few times since then, but now that I'm here, I now know. Not because I didn't love you, I just wondered if our cultures were going cheat us somehow."

"Okay, so you are as you say 'all in?'"

"*Sans aucun doute.*"

"Nice touch saying it in French, loverboy. Some of us say 'loverboy' in French too. We stole that one."

She just smiled at me. Really studying me. As though she was working up her courage to say something.

"Do you really love me, Steve?"

"Yes. *Sans aucun doute. Je le promets.*"

"Good."

"Why?"

"Because I may be about to fuck things up."

"What?"

"I want you to move to France. I have zero right to ask this, but I want you to be French."

"Okay...tell me more."

"I want us to be self-sufficient in France. I don't want to have to share you with America. I want you to myself. I want you to move to France. I love you, and I love living here. I can't see us living in America. Not now. I don't understand America right now. It's barbaric."

"I will for you. I will do what is necessary to have you. I don't know if I'd said that before I arrived here. But after living with you only this short time, it fully confirms everything I felt when I saw you sitting in front of the Gage Hotel in Marathon. I can't see a future without you. I fell in love with you when I saw you in the fading light in front of the hotel. This beautiful, defiant, proud French woman who had come to the wilds of West Texas from the other side of the world for me. Your tearful eyes at the last of the sunset were the most beautiful sight I'd ever seen. I instantly plunged into a feeling for you I'd never felt. But then, after you returned to France, you became a little cool, which confused me. But when I saw you standing at the top of your stairs when I first arrived here the other day, it all came flooding back to me." I stopped talking and just sat there and admired her beauty and her "Frenchness."

"Look, it is complicated. I love you. I've loved you since you left me, to go back to Marfa, to West Texas," Pauline replied thoughtfully, and quite prepared, it seemed. "I was madly in love with you then. I just didn't think it'd matter if I told you. That is why I said we had unfinished business, '*inachevé*' when I texted you. I loved you since the moment I saw you and your topless Brazilian neighbor. I was so jealous! I've never felt that before. I guess you were like this white knight to me. I expected that shit, from Frenchman, but not you!"

"Nothing happened between us, between me and Brites! She had rented to place next to me. I barely knew her. She was a kid!"

"I know. But I was just so shocked how I felt seeing her topless next door! My mind raced. Sounds crazy...but I've known since then, you were the one."

"You were smarter than I. I didn't know it for sure until Marathon."

She just looked at me, like she still wasn't sure how much to share.

"Okay Pauline, I need it all out there. Tell me more on your thoughts about our future, France, America, us. Look, nothing is a deal killer, but you must be totally honest."

She just kept looking at me. The wind had tousled her hair. The wine was kicking in. God, I loved this woman.

"Okay. Remember you asked for it. And thank you for asking for it."

"I did."

"Okay, I thought I loved America. I studied English, just knew I'd marry an American and move back there one day. I loved all aspects of America. You know that. While not perfect, America has been this incredible force for good for decades. But I don't love the America I know at this time in history. The continuing racism, the irrational hatred of gays, the hatred of immigrants, the barbaric healthcare system, the embracing of polluters ... and the super stupid approach to climate change! You guys are going to get us all killed! America sucks right now! I won't live there. I just can't! I love you so much, but I absolutely cannot even stand the thought of living there right now. Have you all lost your fucking minds? You'd want to live in a society where an illness can wipe you out financially? What in the hell are you all thinking?!"

She just looked at me like she was mad at me for all this. Damn she was sexy when she was ranting! I knew I shouldn't be thinking that, but....

"Look Steve, I want us to have kids. I guess you can pay for their college, but what America does to middle class parents when it comes to paying for college! Again, are you all insane?"

I just listened.

"To hell with America! At least right now. You guys have lost your minds! I never thought I'd feel this way, but I do."

She just stared at me defiantly. She was pissed. I was slightly defensive at first but then I began to melt again. I was unable to get mad at her. Especially when I knew there was truth to what she was saying.

"Please Steve, say something."

"Agreed. We're nuts."

"And..."

"There's nothing else."

"What?"

"We're nuts right now. We've lost our way at the moment. I love you. That's all I know."

"Aren't you going to defend America?"

"Well, I might have in the past. And I might in the future when the younger generations finally take over. But for now, you're correct. I mean, I see things getting better someday in America and I have hope for the future, but we've been in a bad cycle for a while. Please remember though, many Americans, probably most, are still the good people you remember."

"You mean you'd seriously be willing to move here?"

"Yeah."

"Seriously? For me?"

"Yeah, if you told me that was a deal killer. I'm in."

"You'd leave America?"

"Yeah. I mean I'd want to visit my parents in America sometimes, but I guess I really don't need to live there."

"As you guys say, 'no shit?'"

"Yes."

"You'd leave America for me?"

"Yes, other than visiting. I don't have to live there."

She hugged my neck so hard that she was physically hurting me, but I didn't mind.

"Look, Pauline, I want to absorb this, digest it, but I don't see it as a deal killer. I have some people in the States I care about, even some causes. You know how I feel about saving West Texas, but I think I'd be fine here. I can make this work. If that's what it takes to have you in my life, I'm in. It's that simple."

"Are you really and truly sure?" She seemed surprised.

"Yeah."

"Absolutely?"

"Yes, don't you believe me?"

"I do. But…I want to make sure."

"What do you mean?"

"I want you to go back to America and make sure."

"What do you mean?"

"Look, once I get married, it will be for eternity. You will be stuck with me forever. I just want to make sure. If you go back and two months later, you are still 'all in,' I'm going to marry you. You won't have an option. You will be stuck with me. I'm not the best Catholic, but I agree that marriage is forever. I won't marry you until you and I know for sure though. I am so close to certain now, but I want to know for certain. And…I want you to know for certain."

25

A few days later, I was on a flight back to the States. I wanted to stay a while longer in Sommières, but she essentially kicked me out. Pauline was an odd combination of warm but super firm concerning the need for me to go back to the States. She said the sooner I left, the sooner two months would come. She practically catapulted me to the TGV station a couple of days later. I had long ago returned my rental car. I was essentially *persona non grata* until the two months were over. I tried to argue, but damn she was strong. She'd give me that look that made it obvious that resistance was futile. I loved her strength so much. I loved it a tad better when that strength wasn't forcing me to leave.

Still a bit in shock, I was back in Marfa a week later. I'd spent a couple of days with my parents in Houston but cut off that visit to get back west. I never expected to be dealing with Amy's concerns so quickly, but here I was in the bright white sunlight of Marfa. It felt good to be back, even if I missed Pauline immediately. I didn't really want to leave France.

"Hey, you thar...you go back. Closed...road." Dudley Morten, the former deputy sheriff who had consistently and without reason harassed me last year, barked at me as I tried to turn up the road to the ranch house where the movie crew was filming. He was standing in the middle of the road.

"Hey, you there, I own the land your standing on." He was quiet a second, just looking at me through his mirrored sunglasses like his two brain cells were feverishly working on getting close enough to rub together.

"I'm security. Film. Hey, you the guy, unfair to Miguel." I had fired Miguel at my distributor for giving away too much beer last year.

"Move Dud, you're trespassing on my land."

"Apologize, Miguel. Still sad." It was always hopeless to figure out what he meant.

"Sure, sure Dudley, can you please move?"

"You own here?"

"Yeah, I do."

"He gives me beer free…you own here?

"That's great, please move."

He just stood there as I got back in the car. As my car slowly approached him, he gradually stepped aside. He hadn't changed a bit. They had let him go at the sheriff's office after he accidently shot himself for the second time in six months.

As I neared the ranch house, I saw a couple of women near one of the outbuildings. Sid was talking to someone on the front porch.

"Thank God you're here Sammy, your assistant is impossible!" Sid in his magenta silk shirt and a gold medallion was standing with both hands up in the air.

"Hi Sid, it's Steve."

"That's what I said. I think. Anyway, I'm glad you're here."

"Look Sid, Amy's my partner. She's managing this effort. You have to work with her. I'm just here to check things out. Sounds like you guys have had a few disagreements."

"I'll say."

"Really?"

"She refused to let us film in your house!"

"Yep. You knew from the beginning I wasn't okay with that."

"Oh, that was you!"

"Yes."

"Oh."

"Well, now that you are here and see what an orderly operation we have, I'm sure you'll reconsider."

"Nope."

"Oh. Okay. Well, we'll be out in a couple of days to shoot on the outside of your house."

"That wasn't in the contract either. You have the ranch and the ranch house."

"Surely, that wouldn't be a problem?"

"Yes. It would."

"Look, we made you a partner. You are getting a lot of money from this."

"1%?"

"Yeah! One percent of 500 million is a lot of money."

"What did your last picture gross?"

"That's not fair. It was an indie project, really a vanity project for Tito."

"How much?"

"Not much. This one has the potential to be a real winner."

"I don't understand, I thought you recreated my home."

"Not the outside. Besides, its weak. Your interior is better. Love the orange paint!"

"It's terra cotta, not orange. You been in my place?"

"I like terra cotta even better!" I let it go.

"How much longer is the filming going to go on out here?"

"We are about to wrap up here on the ranch."

"Then why the big deal about needing it longer?"

"In case we have to re-shoot."

"Oh."

"We'll be filming in town beginning tomorrow, while the guys in California start processing the footage out here. I'm dubious about a couple of scenes. Your book was great as a book, but some of it was lame as a movie. Sorry. No offense, Sam... Steve." He just smiled.

Sid took his cowboy hat and sunglasses off and looked me in the eye, "Can we film outside your house? We make it big, you guys do too."

"Okay. Two days. No more."

"Sure, no problem Sam...Steve."

"It's...just...Steve. Just that one name. See you later." I started walking away. Sid followed me and called out. He made a big production of lowering his sunglasses to once again look me in the eye.

"Oh, Steve, do you know that idiot Clark?"

"Yeah, he's my cousin."

"I thought so. He's about to get cut loose. He's impossible."

"What's he doing?"

"The idiot keeps demanding more lines. He can barely remember the few he has."

"Sorry."

"He keeps changing them and saying good actors have to be able to improv. He improvs one more time, and Tito wants him cut. Tell him. He's really kind of disgusting anyway. We would have cut him already if he wasn't with you."

"I'll see what I can do."

"Thanks, champ!" Sunglasses back up and a big smile.

Amy thought it was critical that I show up at the ranch that morning. At least I got that over with. I had a ton of calls and research to do before my meeting with Amy at 3:00.

"Well, it's nice to know you still relax occasionally."

"Whatta ya mean?" Amy peered over her glasses at me as I sat down in front of her in our small office near the courthouse.

"Nothing. It's just nice to see you not all dressed up." She was barefoot in a plain black t-shirt and cutoffs.

"Yeah, well I dress nicely when I need to. Otherwise, this is comfortable, and we have a lot of work to do."

"Good. I have some ideas to pitch to you. You'll like some of them and maybe not the others."

"Fire away. I have all the latest financials."

"First off, is the brewery in Chihuahua really cutting us off?"

"Yes. They were bought out. They have no choice. The American company that bought them has a huge distribution network. They will stop distributing to us after March."

"Got it. I have a big pitch to make to you."

"Okay, you are scaring me, but okay."

"Look, this is big. I want us to relax. Can we get out of here, maybe sit over in the courtyard of the Paisano?"

"Sure, sounds good. Perfect day, but you are still scaring me."

A few minutes later, after we walked down the street, I felt like I could breathe. I wanted Amy to relax. Be open to new things. We both ordered a glass of wine. It was about 75 degrees, scattered, big puffy, white and gray clouds. Large deep blue patches of sky all about. Amy finally looked a little relaxed in her shades with a glass of chardonnay in front of her.

"Are you ready for my pitch?"

"Should we get Jim over for this?"

"Great idea!" Jim was our attorney and financial consultant. I had enormous faith in Jim. He took the cash assets my Uncle Clive left me and had already almost doubled them. I didn't really need any of these businesses in Marfa, but I felt obligated to Uncle Clive to make a difference here.

In a few minutes, Jim walked over from his office to join us. A slight breeze was making the afternoon incredible.

After catching up with Jim for a few minutes, I began the pitch, "Okay, I want us to simplify. Number one, I want us the shed the art gallery. It is our weakest performer. I have another use for it maybe. Besides, Marfa has no shortage of galleries. It was really just a Stacy thing anyway. I'm not even sure why I went along with that. Well, I know why, but it's irrelevant now."

"Good call Steve. I like it," Amy chimed in. "We lose

money about half the months, and the personnel headaches! Ugh!"

"Focus on 'eco-ranching,' beer, real estate leasing and philanthropy."

Amy and Jim darted concerned glances at one another.

"Okay Steve, you know the brewery is cutting us out, right?"

"Yes. We are going to start a small brewery here. We won't have a tap room. We will focus on boosting the economy of all the bars and restaurants around us by supplying them a world class beer. 'Puesta del Sol' brewing company will combine the best of Mexican and American brewing knowhow. We will seek to create an El Paso to Austin market over time, but just start right around here at first."

"You want to try a brewery again! You know that's a super competitive business, right?"

"Yes."

"We just lost a microbrewery over in Alpine a few years ago, Steve."

"I know. We will be properly capitalized. Plus, we are going to try to hire Esteban, the brew master at Chihuahua Brewing and bring in a friend of mine from Colorado, who really wants to quit as brew master up there. They're both magicians. They'll collaborate to make a bicultural suite of flavors."

"That's a great idea, but it will be super expensive, take a long time to happen and could easily fail."

"All true."

"Then why do it?" Jim queried.

"Because Marfa needs a brewery. It'll become part of the social fabric of this great town and region! Can you imagine smelling a brewery here?"

"Okay, I'm skeptical, but go on."

"We'll explore turning the ranch into a premier ecological destination. We'll explore turning the bunk houses and building a few more that are similar and look historic to provide overnight accommodations with a focus on birders and wildlife enthusiasts. Thanks to you Amy, we have those agreements with partners that bring a lot of people to the ranch already. Our restoration efforts have made our ranch an oasis for birds and wildlife. People will want to see this. We already have some of the best riparian areas for miles around. That's only going to get better. Let's capitalize on it!"

Jim nodded. "Solid. Proven. The tours are becoming more and more popular, which proves your concept."

"I want to explore producing high-quality bison on the place. But that's for another discussion. I could see the Gage and other restaurants around here one day offer locally-sourced bison. Oh, and James over on the Lazy T wants to do a little specialty breeding with his Highland Herefords. We want to keep that breed as part of the landscape out here too."

"Okay Steve, shedding the gallery and ramping up our efforts at the ranch makes good business sense. Brewery seems a little iffy, no, really big iffy. But I'm waiting for your super zany stuff." Amy was on her second chardonnay and not holding back, which is what I wanted.

"Okay, we continue to focus on leasing your dad's other properties in our portfolio like we have been. You've made that a cash cow most of the time Amy. We do beer and eco-experiences, with our hunting leases and movie leases when we can get it. We need some hunting to keep the deer from taking over. They love our ranch too much. So, to keep it simple, leasing, beer, and experiences."

"Yeah, I know there is more, Steve. I know you. And what about the railroad thing? Are you finally over that?"

"No, we'll use rail to bring in our products, such as hops and grain, for the brewery. If the brewery becomes an icon of the region, the Union Pacific will be less inclined to cut us off. Perhaps we can even do some joint marketing and things like that. Remember, they'll be bringing in freight cars out of Midwest and Northwest for us. They won't just be making a couple of pennies bringing the cars in from the interchange at Alpine. We'll see. It might make a difference. Perhaps one day, we might be able to do some outbound traffic on the railroad. I doubt it, but who knows?"

"Okay, you may be dreaming, but that sounds within the realm of the possible, maybe. Wait, where's this brewery going to go?"

"I'm still checking that out. I want to model it on a smaller version of the brewery over in Shiner. A few years ago, they recently redid their plant and tasting room. Maybe we could shoot for a brewery about 40% that big. I've spoken with the consultant, in Denver, who managed their overhaul. I don't want a boutique brewery, or a vanity project. I mean a real medium-sized brewery. Maybe 200,000 to 300,000 barrels a year. We have some research to do. I've requested some specs. That's going to keep you busy Amy. You're going to become quite smart about beer."

"Great. Thanks, Steve," in her best sarcastic tone.

"Is that it, Steve? Jim asked.

"Not exactly, I want to do more in philanthropy."

They just looked at me confused. I saw Amy point at her glass to the waiter. I guess I was driving her to drink.

"I want to focus on protecting the setting of Marfa and affordable housing."

"Huh?"

"Average folks have a hard time finding a place to live here, but I don't want sprawl to mess this place up. I don't want McMansions to pop up around the edge of Marfa, but important parts of the community can't afford housing, even the border patrol guys struggle, and they get paid decently."

"Okay. Good goals. What do you plan? By the way, the various Foundations around town here control most of the areas around Marfa."

"True. And I'm mostly grateful for that. But I've found two tracts unprotected. Neither is huge, but they are prime for development. I want to try to buy both so pretty much all the area around Marfa is protected."

"How's that going to help with housing?"

"I want to also buy vacant lots around town or crumbling houses and either build houses that look historic or repair old ones. Maybe even bring back a larger scale adobe building capability. I want to build houses that look like they've been here a long time, just well maintained. We'll make housing available almost at cost. It will be a non-profit. It won't solve everyone's problems but will help a lot of people out. It might help save a little of the Hispanic and ranching parts of Marfa's culture."

More stares from Jim and Amy.

"I wish I could reconstruct one of the old hotels here and make it modestly priced apartments. Can you imagine being a new teacher at the school here? Where the hell are you supposed to live?! Okay, that may be too much for now. Let's focus on houses for now."

"Okay. Not an easy lift, but okay. Don't know how it will work, but good goal." Jim was pretty community minded.

"I want to try to set all of this up as a non-profit foundation to help people."

"The housing thing, you mean?" Jim was puzzled.

"Well, maybe all of it. In other words, we pay the employees, but all profits go into conservation of the land around Marfa and creating affordable housing. We could let the city or county use our conserved lands for public purposes. Maybe the high school's FFA program or something. I just don't want Marfa surrounded by unfortunate development. It is beautiful the way it is now. Everything would change. Marfa would stop being the Marfa we know and love."

"Wow, Steve. This is a lot to absorb," Jim said. Amy looked a bit overwhelmed.

"Sure, I understand. We can call it the Clive Miles Foundation after your dad, Amy."

"That's cool. I like that Steve. But it's a lot to think about. We'd be in the beer brewing business, managing lands and tourism, leasing properties and then the housing philanthropy thing?"

"Yep. We can hire some folks to help you."

"Wow, Steve. This is a lot."

"I know. We could bring in a concessionaire to run the ranch."

Jim was a bit concerned, but not alarmed. I was encouraged by that. "But Steve, even the beer production would be part of the foundation?"

"Yep. I don't want any profit from this."

"Really?"

"You've done so well with my other investments, Jim, I don't really need it. Certainly not now, at least. I want to honor Uncle Clive."

"Steve, I don't even know if that's legal. Non-profit beer? I got to think on this."

"There are breweries run by monasteries that I'm sure are non-profit."

"I'll look into it, Steve."

"Good. I think the Clive Miles Foundation is going to be an incredible agent for good."

"That's great Steve, as long as you realize that we may not always be able to help a lot of folks every year. There will be ups and downs."

"I get that. Even if it is only two or three families some years, that still a big deal in a town this size. We will do what we can. But when the rental rates are good, that will be some decent income for the foundation. And we know that the ranch, under Amy's management, is growing into a nice profit center."

"Steve, it's the brewery that has me nervous," Amy chimed in.

"I know. Me too. But I think it can work."

"What if it doesn't?" Jim added.

"It will."

Amy and Jim just looked at me. They were a tiny bit in shock.

"We good, guys?" I was tired and needed to make a sandwich and go to bed.

"I guess, Steve. We'll start looking into this." Amy sounded like she was trying to be positive.

"Steve, I'll have to bring in an NGO expert to help set up the Foundation. That is not my strength."

"Good. We want it done right."

"Be thinking who you'd want on a board," Jim said.

"Do we need a board?"

"I think so."

"Okay, let's do this. And oh yeah, I'll be leaving to go back to France before long. I have unfinished business."

"Damn Steve. You are kind of hitting and running here." Amy was not too happy as she slipped her sandals back on.

"Okay, here's some relief. Take your time. The only thing that is remotely time sensitive is the brewery. Let's do this right, not fast."

"I'll need to bring in consultants. I know nothing about brewing beer. That will eat some profits from this year."

"That's fine. I blew up a brewery once, as you recall. That's about the extent of my knowledge. I'll give you the name of the guy in Denver. He sounded great when I talked to him on the phone."

"Can we meet again after Jim and I have a chance to process this?"

"Sure, but let's keep this moving. I need to head back to France in a month or so. I have a marriage to focus on."

That evening I felt a bit of relief. The Clive Miles Foundation was beautiful. I wanted to honor my uncle, Amy's dad. The thing I loved about this was that I could help run the Foundation from afar. I'd ease out of having day-to-day pressures back in the States. It would let me better meet Pauline's needs of primarily living in France. I had a good feeling about this. We were going to help people and Marfa. We were demonstrating stewardship at the ranch. We were making good jobs. I just wanted Amy and Jim to feel the same way. This was exciting. They'd get on board. This had to work. Since it was about 2:00 am in France, I'd call Pauline in the morning to let her know of my progress.

The next morning, after I had a cup of coffee in front of me, I called Pauline. I was excited to let her know I could return earlier if she wanted. It didn't go exactly as I planned.

26

"Hello Pauline! How are things? I have good news!"

"Hello, dear. *Les choses se passent vraiment bien. Mais tu me manque!*"

"I miss you so much, too!"

"What's the good news? I have news, as well."

"Things are going well here. I have figured out a way to get things somewhat on track here. I could actually come back earlier if you are okay with that."

She was silent. After she was quiet a little while, I became a bit nervous.

"Pauline? You still on the line?"

"Yes. Yes, I'm sorry. Well, things are complicated."

"Yes?" I didn't like this.

"Look, I want to make sure you are absolutely certain you can live in France, you know? More or less, leave America."

"We talked about that. I told you I could."

"I want you to be sure. You are giving up a lot for me. I want you to be certain this is what you want. I want you to be happy too. We agreed to two months."

"Okay, I guess."

"But my news might make you feel a little better. My colleague is still out, and my employer wants me to travel to the US in a couple of weeks to attend a trade show."

"Okay. Where?"

"A place in Louisiana, a town call 'Red Stick.'"

"Where?"

"Isn't Louisiana close to Texas?"

"Well, sort of. It takes about 12 hours or more to drive from Marfa to Louisiana, probably more. That's just to the state line."

"Wow! What's a state line?"

"It's like a border. Do you know where this town you're going to is? What's it near?"

"It says it is 130 km north of *Nouvelle Orléans*."

"Okay. Weird I've never heard of it."

She read to me, "*C'est la capitale de la Louisiane.*"

"Baton Rouge!" I laughed.

"Yes?"

"The name of the city is actually Baton Rouge. It goes by the French name. You don't have to translate it." We shared a laugh on that.

"Can you come see me? At Baton Rouge, or maybe *Nouvelle Orléans*?"

"I've always wanted to go to New Orleans. Just tell me when. I'll make reservations for us. I'd love to experience that city with you."

"I'll send the details soon. I look forward to seeing you, *mon cher*!"

"*Moi aussi!*"

Wow! New Orleans. I wasn't expecting that. Well, Amy'd be happy. I'll be here longer than I expected. I could help her a bit more. That's good. I wanted to pick Beach's mind about New Orleans. Soon I'd be making reservations. Beach said he felt the closest to France in America in New Orleans. This should be interesting. I didn't want to play that up too much with Pauline in case she felt strongly otherwise.

My days in Marfa passed fairly peacefully, after the movie idiots stopped filming around my house. I purposely tried not to hear what was happening on the set. The actress' lines did not match anything in my book. I wondered if I could have the phrase "loosely-based on" inserted when the movie subtitle lists my book as the inspiration. For a couple of scenes, the actress barged into my house, each time dressed differently, but immediately said sorry and excused herself. At least she was polite as she unknowingly butchered my book.

I tried to do some writing and do some of the front-end work with creating the Foundation. Amy tasked me with the brewery project. I had numerous discussions with the consultant making clear what I was looking for: capacity of the brewery, provision for rail service, need to make the building blend with the architecture of Marfa. I was pretty close to deciding we would incorporate the art gallery building into it. It was a large building that had been a feed store for decades. To protect the appearance of the old structure, we'd add on to the back of it. There was plenty of room to put a historically sympathetic building to the back between the art gallery and the old Godbold feed mill.

I also had numerous discussions with the Union Pacific about placing a new railroad siding in Marfa. The initial answer was no. The second answer was only if we'd agree to removing the siding to my current beer distributor building on the other side of the tracks. I wasn't ready to do that, for I might find a need for it one day after the beer distributor moved out. For whatever reason, the railroad called me back a couple of days before I was to leave for New Orleans to say they agreed. Of course, it was going to be expensive. I would have to use the contractor the railroad arranged. That alone blew my budget up.

Jim tried to get the foundation expert to come to town before I left for New Orleans, but she couldn't make it. As for my plans, Jim said that she told him it was novel, but likely doable. The non-profit brewery did throw her for a loop. She said she still had to make sure on that one. There were a lot of arcane laws about alcohol at the federal and state level.

I did have to deal with an additional movie fiasco before

I left for New Orleans. Clark texted me and told me to, "Shut the whole mess down."

I headed down to the area I knew they were then filming a few blocks from my house. I saw Clark off to one side sitting down glancing away from the action looking quite agitated. Once Tito saw me, he waved me over. For whatever reason, Paco was there as well, over across the street. Naturally, she discretely, for once, flipped me off and glared.

"Your brother is impossible! He did perfect on two scenes. I mean the way he shot the finger; it was beautiful! His glare at the art gallery was *perfecto*! Now we're trying to shoot his final scene, and he is holding out until we give him a girl to appear with! He says he won't shoot the last scene unless we let him kiss somebody!!! What are we supposed to do?" Tito looked to the heavens and once again made some kind of strange clicking sound, like he was praying.

"Sorry, Tito. Let me talk to him. By the way, he's not my brother. I just want to…make that clear."

While still looking at the heavens, he quickly peered over at me, "Shit! He said you two were brothers!"

"I'll be right back Tito."

I walked over to Clark. He sat, holding his head in his hands. He had his "movie star" sunglasses on.

"Can you believe these assholes, Steve?!"

"Look Clark, Tito is two seconds away from cutting you outta the film. He liked your work, but he said it ain't worth it." I kind of exaggerated hoping to motivate my idiot cousin.

"Stevo, don't you get it? I got them by the short hairs." Clark darted a quick glare at Tito. Clark then whispered, "I got them right where I want'em. He'll probably walk over here any minute and say he found my girl to kiss." He gave me a slightly deranged look over his sunglasses.

"Clark, do you wanna to be in the film?"

"Hell yeah, man!"

"I think you're blowing it. I see Tito talking to some other dumbass, I mean another person. He may be giving your role away right now."

"Never!"

"Clark, how much acting experience you got?"

"Not much."

"Not much as in zero, right?"

"Pretty much. I don't get it. What's your point, Steve?"

"This is your chance to have your first role! Most people never get this chance. Just do what Tito says, and you can be pickier once you get a film under your belt."

"Steve, you just don't understand power, do you?"

"Just trying to help."

"That's why you're farting around playing at being a writer, Steve. You wouldn't recognize big time with a roadmap!"

"That sounds familiar. You get that from a movie, Clark?"

"Huh?"

"By the way, why is Paco here?"

"Who?"

"Over there, short blond hair, glasses?"

"Oh, she's playing Molina, remember those crazy chicks you had out at the ranch house?"

"Of course she is."

"She's got the best Jamaican accent!"

"That's great, Clark. Go keep your part in the movie before Tito takes it away!"

"Steve, you stand back and watch how it's done. You just don't get it." With that, Clark bounded up and approached Tito. With his chest puffed out, Clark addressed him. Within about thirty seconds, I witnessed Clark dropping to his knees and holding his hands together in front of Tito, apparently begging him. Shortly thereafter, Clark sprang up and ran towards me.

"Got to get my hat! I really manhandled him. Sorry you had to witness that Steve!" He grabbed his hat and ran back to Tito.

"Yeah, me too Clark," I said to myself as I strolled away.

◆ ◆ ◆

I was able to get some great information from Beach on New Orleans. He told me about his favorite hotel, the Ace Hotel, on Carondelet Street. It was just a short walk into the French Quarter and the Warehouse District from the hotel. He gave me the next-door Maison de la Luz as a backup. The Maison de la Luz was according to Beach a bit more plush, but a bit less fun. Fun sounded good. I was able to get us into the Ace and booked it for the five nights as per Pauline's instructions. I actually added a night up front to let me do some reconnaissance before Pauline arrived. Beach instructed me to listen closely for echoes of France, Spain and the Caribbean in New Orleans. He said for him, it was "palpable." He said it was the only place in the US he felt those kinds of vibes.

While I was on the phone with Beach, he also asked me if I had read what he gave me. I told him yes and it was impressive. He asked me, "What the hell's that supposed to mean?" I told him I didn't know, but I look forward to sitting on a beach with him one day to figure it out. After wishing me a great time in the Big Easy, he closed with, "Steve, you're a writer. You can help. I celebrate tiki for its potential to help America, maybe the Western world: cut the materialism and hate shit and better connect with things that matter, have fun, respect nature, enjoy those around you and love. And for crying out loud stop being angry and have more sex!" I was struck by that and wrote it all down word for word. It was a great "Beachism."

◆ ◆ ◆

Amy was supposed to pick me up at 7:45pm the next day to take me over to Alpine to put me on the Sunset Limited to New Orleans. Having the time, I decided to take the train. Figured I might see some pretty scenery, learn something and maybe write a bit. It had been a while since I took a train in the

US.

I had a leisurely evening the night before. I sat in my house, drinking the last bottle of wine I had, and wondered if I'd ever live here again. I reflected on the silly guy who showed up here long ago and how much I had grown since I first met Stacy in Marfa, my first real love here so long ago. Here I was, after having published a novel, having lived and traveled abroad a good bit and having met the woman of my dreams who happened to be French. I was a changed person. I hoped I had grown enough for Pauline to want me in her life forever. I knew the act of living was the act of growing up and that I wouldn't be "fully grown" until my death, but I prayed I had "grown enough." I had gone to college, served as an officer in the Army and worked a few years in Congress, and yet I showed up here in many respects almost child-like and I was completely unaware of that at the time. I guess "child-like" people generally are.

Thanks to Uncle Clive, I had become more of a grownup...more of a man, as the military told me I would someday become. I was beginning to like myself. I was losing the self-doubt. For whatever reason, Sarah and Sofia popped into my head. It clicked that maybe the reason they both found me attractive was that women were able to sense when a man genuinely likes himself. In the past, I had had a few attractive women find reasons to embrace me, as it were, but it was definitely hit or miss. To have two attractive women express interest in me in Paris in such a short period of time, made me wonder if people in general are attracted to others who like themselves, that somehow people can tell.

I reflected on that awhile. It had to be a healthy "self-like" that was based on reality and avoided arrogance. Maybe that was why I was interested in Beach from the outset. He really did seem to like being Beach, but while he was playful, he didn't have an ounce of arrogance. It was as though he had no patience for pretense or game-playing. In a kind way, he was who he was, no pretense. Whatever it was, I was becoming more confident that Pauline was attracted to the emerging me, as well. Now that I had gotten to this place, I wasn't turning back. I know I found that trait in her attractive. She was definitely the person she wanted to be. In some respects, she and Beach were similar other than the fact she had a "French reserve," and Beach had an American openness. They were unabashedly themselves.

Regardless, I was grateful to Uncle Clive for helping me get to the point that I liked who I was. That's one reason why I was excited about creating the foundation named after him. I didn't want my name on it. He was the one who had amassed the wealth. He had caught some breaks for sure. He had inherited mineral rights himself from an uncle also. His uncle had owned a large ranch near Odessa, Texas. His uncle had the good sense to keep the mineral rights when he sold it. It paid off handsomely for Uncle Clive, but he was a good steward of that wealth and helped it to grow.

I had thought about selling everything and cutting my ties to Marfa, especially after Stacy and I broke up, but I just couldn't do it. I wanted to honor Uncle Clive but after my recent time with Pauline in France, I knew I would probably be only a part-time resident of Marfa at best. The Foundation would allow me to not have to be so involved but still make good things happen in Uncle Clive's name. And it would create jobs in Marfa, which was great.

No. I didn't want to sell off Uncle Clive's domain. I wanted to celebrate him and use it to better his hometown. He had a love-hate relationship with Marfa. He said it liked it better back when it was just "a good, clean ranching town." He didn't know what to make of the artists who started showing up in the mid-1970s. He didn't fully appreciate the good things that came with the artists.

Bouncing around in my uncle's pick-up as he'd drive me around the ranch, he'd tell me things, things that let me know me was a good man. He loved his deceased wife, my aunt Bess, so much. He loved his ranch and he loved "his" Marfa. He supported Saint Paul's Episcopal Church. He sponsored a little league team every year and handsomely supported several important civic causes. He was just quiet about the way he did it. I don't think many people in town knew, and he sought to keep it that way. He said he "didn't want to be hit up all the time for money," but I also think he just had a gentle modesty about him.

I understood that only the future knew of my relationship to come with this modest house I had come to love. I was lucky to have Amy keep an eye on the place when I was gone. She was grateful that I had brought her into my business when Uncle Clive had cut both her and Clark out of his will. That was unfortunate and didn't really reflect positively on Uncle Clive, but I wasn't going to let that overshadow his entire legacy.

Besides, I'd made it right. Amy had worked hard but was now financially comfortable. Clark was a bigger challenge. I'd tried to help him, but he had a propensity to tangle with the law. I wondered if Uncle Clive knew I'd make it right. I wanted to think he'd support what I did concerning his kids. I figured Amy would probably be the future leader of the Foundation one day, once I got her to love conservation, historic preservation and railroads! She liked beer already. At least she used to when we would sit on my front porch and drink together.

About 9:05 pm, the headlight of the train was just visible on the western horizon. It slowly grew until it eased into the station. It was a beautiful sight as it approached. It was totally dark by the time I boarded. The train was only in Alpine about ten minutes before heading east. I easily found my small cabin. It had a seat and with a little magic, the room could be made into a comfortable sleeping compartment. By 11:00, we eased into Sanderson, Texas. Shortly thereafter, even though I loved watching the moon illuminate the wide-open spaces we were racing through, I was out. The sway of the train, though rough, was kind of like a rocking cradle.

Around 7:00 am I awoke to some clanging noises. The sun was up, and the train wasn't moving. We were sitting at the San Antonio station. I left my little room and stepped out onto the platform. The train was being serviced. The beautiful Spanish style station was down the track in the dim sunlight. The huge

Alamodome with its strange towers loomed nearby. San Antonio was waking up as the sun was hiding just a tad below the horizon. The air felt heavier, wetter than the air of Marfa. I was reflecting on all the good times I had had in this city. The Riverwalk was completely contrived, but still a fun experience.

Suddenly I heard a whistle and train personnel were requesting passengers to board. In a bit, the train began to ease forward and gradually the train picked up speed until we were leaving San Antonio behind. It was uneventful the rest of the way, though we stopped and sat for no apparent reason four or five times. We stopped in Houston for an hour or so. It felt weird to be in Houston and not be seeing my parents. They didn't even know I was there.

Texas started becoming very green along the tracks as we pulled out of Houston. Some of the rights-of-way along the tracks were almost jungle like. I mainly sat in my little room and watched the countryside go by and did some heavy thinking. I was so excited to see Pauline. I'd occasionally get up and walk about the train or go to the dining car. It was a great thinking space. Texas sure looked different from a train versus the interstate. Way more interesting looking into forests and backyards versus looking at miles and miles of billboards and strip malls. For Texans to so often brag about how beautiful the state is, the State seem to be in a big hurry to cover it with parking lots and asphalt.

I dozed off after we entered Louisiana. I awoke to the train crossing the biggest swamp I'd ever seen and bridge after bridge, we finally started to near New Orleans. It was around 11:30 PM as we pulled into the station. My New Orleans adventure was about to begin!

27

By 1:00 am, I was finally in bed. The suite at the Ace Hotel I got, #902, was excellent. It was a two-story room, with the bedroom and main bath in a loft, and had sweeping views of the city. It was huge, with probably 30-foot ceilings. Dark brown hard wood floors. There was a well-stocked kitchen to the left with a retro dark olive fridge. A nice bar with three chairs delineated the kitchen. Straight ahead and to the right were tall French doors that offered exceptional views of numerous high-rise buildings. White and golden illuminated buildings dominated the horizon. The French doors to the right led out to a huge patio overlooking the city. A stairwell to the left led up to the loft where a king-sized bed awaited me and a very well-appointed bathroom. There was even a turntable with a wide variety of vinyl. It was stunning. Beach was correct in his recommendations, and I was thrilled that I'd be able to share this with Pauline.

The room was very promising as the perfect venue for Pauline and me to cement the American side our relationship. Other than the views from my ninth-floor balcony and short cab ride from the train to the hotel, I hadn't seen any of New Orleans really, but I already had a good feeling about "The Big Easy." The porter on the train told me that New Orleans got that nickname because it was so easy to for musicians to find gigs. I was looking forward to exploring before Pauline arrived from "Red Stick" the next afternoon.

After my early morning nap and a bite of breakfast, accompanied by surprisingly good coffee, I was on the street by 9:00. I had until 5:00 to do my reconnaissance. Following Beach's guidance, I started out by doing a walk by of a few of his favorite restaurants in the warehouse district. Most places were on Girod or Julia Streets or a block or so away. Nice mix of American, Southern, French, Italian and a few steak houses. I'd do some internet research later on each.

As I walked around, I noted a lot of historic buildings mixed in with more recent ones. Kind of a relaxed but rewarding approach to historic preservation. The historic buildings looked to be a mix of late 1800s to early 1900s. Lots of brick, many ornate window and door treatments. Lots of nice iron work. Made me think briefly of Marfa when I noticed so many art galleries along Julia Street.

The weather was perfect, middle 70s. The server at breakfast concerned me when she said, enjoy it while it lasts and that there was a hurricane in the Gulf of Mexico to watch. After I checked out some of Beach's restaurants and bars in the Warehouse District, I headed down Tchoupitoulas Street and then into the French Quarter. Beach told me about his favorite red beans and rice place. He said I had to have red beans and rice if I was there on a Monday. It was Monday. So, I headed to his favorite for red beans and rice and muffulettas, the Napoleon House.

On the corner of Saint Louis and Chartres Streets, the Napoleon House turned out to be a great place. The interior looked a thousand years old. The paint was peeling all over and ancient pictures randomly graced the walls from top to bottom. Opera music wafted about. Pauline would find this place most charming. I was going to have to help her understand why the city feels French in a sense, but French is generally, but not always, mispronounced. I was quickly corrected when I pronounced Chartres Street. In a flat, not so southern accent, the waiter told me, "It's pronounced 'char-ters.'" When I asked him where he was from, he said Chalmette, which I later learned was an area just east of New Orleans. His accent was a strange combination of Boston and southern.

I started to follow Beach's recommendation of the beans and rice, but at the last minute opted for a half a muffuletta and a Pimm's Cup. It was delicious. The Pimm's cup was good as well. It was fresh lemonade with a very generous splash of gin. The cucumber on the rim strangely added a lot of interest to the drink. Refreshed, I was ready to resume the recon mission. Perhaps Pauline and I would return for a muffuletta. Joseph, the waiter with the accent, had recommended I only order a half, as he said, "It's huge!" He was right.

The French Quarter was supposed to be nice as long as one stayed away from the half of Bourbon Street closer to Canal Street. I made a mental note to avoid that section. I feared that Pauline would have painful flashbacks of my cousin Clark were I to take her there. As Beach indicated, it was fine as you got closer to Esplanade where it became kind of a pleasant hotel and residential area with a few calm bars scattered about. For the most part, I was really liking the city. There was an energy to the place. Canal Street was a tad depressing, but not too bad. At least palm trees ran the length of it which was a neat touch. It gave the city a tropical feel and consistent with the adage that New Orleans is the northernmost Caribbean city.

Pauline would be here in a couple of hours. From Canal Street, I made my way back over Carondelet Street to the hotel. A shower and a nap were now in order. The text I had just gotten from her showed a 5:30 ETA to the hotel.

After a shower and nap, I was ready to meet Pauline. I walked over to where her shuttle bus was supposed to let her out in front of the Sheraton on Canal where she had stayed her first night in Louisiana. The trade show organizers had helped sponsor the attendees having a night in New Orleans before catching a flight the next day. Her trade show colleagues had planned a gathering for themselves in the French Quarter, but she'd be with me for what I hoped would be the first of five magical nights.

At the last minute she called and said to meet her at the Drury Plaza Hotel. Her shuttle driver said it was closer and four of the people who were also attending the trade show were staying there. Indeed, it was closer, just a block down on the corner of Poydras and Carondelet. I hustled down Camp Street and then walked up Poydras. I had watched a shuttle discharge at the Sheraton, and she didn't get off. I guessed she remained on it and didn't see me. Regardless, she was waiting in front of the hotel. She looked kind of small with her single large suitcase, but she electrified me as soon as I saw her. She had on a light gray sweater, black leggings, black flats and red lipstick. She was stunning and it reminded me why I was busting ass to get her. I ran to her and kissed her so hard. It wasn't optional.

"I have never seen a more beautiful sight!" Pauline just looked at me like she was surprised. Her eyes were locked on mine. She just stared at me and kept her arms around my neck.

"Say something Pauline!"

"I love you, Steve," and she planted a big kiss on me and smiled. Her look into my eyes was just the perfect love-filled look with just a trace of lust. I will never forget that look she gave me in the fading light in front of that hotel. Funny how your mind lets certain images burn more deeply in the memory banks.

"Let's get to our hotel *chère*! We have some catching up to do."

A sexy smirk came upon her face and she whispered, "*Pour certains*." She drove me insane when she flirted in French.

After a lot of "catching up," we were hungry. It was a bit late for a full meal, so we headed to "Alto," the rooftop pool bar. We sat on a couple of chaise loungers near the pool and split a few appetizers and a bottle of wine. The dusky view was so romantic. Pauline was taken. There were countless tall buildings across the cityscape before us. A few with many lights on, some with only a few lights. In France, this kind of view was rare.

Perhaps if you made the unfortunate decision to stay out towards La Défense, the business district west of Paris, you might see this. I didn't want her to be disappointed in the wine, so I ordered a known quantity, Chateau Ste. Michelle Chardonnay. Getting good was better than risking shooting for great in that moment. It had never let me down. Wine was so amazing in France, I didn't want to blow it.

"Actually, I like this. California?"

"Washington State." I was rather relieved. I had only given her some local wines in Marfa from the Alta Marfa Vineyard near Marfa. She liked the vintage I served her a few times while we were in Marfa.

"Washington? There're vineyards there? No."

"Not DC. Washington is also a state. Actually, a rather wonderful state in the Northwest."

"I think I'd like to visit this Washington State. If they make wines like this, I think I might like it."

"We can make that happen, my dear. It is a beautiful state with mountains; tall, green, lush forests and very dry areas too. They grow many apples as well. It's also a coastal state with beautiful islands and some ocean shoreline."

"Good. I'd like that."

"Anywhere else in the States you'd like to visit?"

She leaned backed and looked at the sky and said, "California."

"That too is quite possible."

She smiled. I got glimpses that her love affair with America wasn't completely over.

"Where'd you like to go in California?"

"You'll laugh."

"No, where?"

"No."

"Where?" I reached over at tickled her stomach. She was sitting back quite enjoying her *"vacance américain."* She giggled. The wine was kicking in. I loved when French people let their guard down. Smart and funny. A great combination.

"Disney."

"Really?"

"I've heard the California one is better than the park in Paris."

"It was the first."

"Yes. He was French you know. Disney…*D'isigny*"

"I heard he was from a French family."

"Yes. His family was from there. They have the best ice cream where he is from."

"Really?"

"Yes. *Isigny Sainte Mere.*"

"Where is it?"

"*Normandie.*"

"We could have gone there! I begged you to come!"

"Sorry, next time." She was reclining and looking sleepy.

I guess it was time to let her go get some sleep. At least, I'd try to let her sleep.

28

In the morning I snuck downstairs and got a couple of large coffees and a plate of jams and breads. I had it waiting on the table on our large balcony that overlooked the city. The air was fresh with a mild breeze from the north. Pauline must have been exhausted; she was normally an early riser.

I heard her stirring finally about 9:30. In a little while, she came out onto the balcony.

"*Bonjour mon cher. Vue magnifique!*"

"*Bonjour* Pauline. What a great morning. Welcome to 'the Big Easy'!"

After I explained the phrase, she gave me the little smile that would always confuse me. I think it meant, "I don't understand, and it doesn't matter."

"So, what is on the agenda today?"

"Well, we need to take advantage of the weather. I was thinking City Park and the New Orleans Museum of Art. The day after tomorrow may start to get messy. A bad storm is coming, maybe a hurricane."

Pauline looked a little concerned. "What would happen here?"

"Lots of wind, heavy rains, maybe some flooding."

"Should we be worried?"

"I don't think so. I lived through a few Hurricanes growing up in Houston. We'll just have to stay in. It could be rather romantic and exciting."

"Um. Maybe." Pauline wasn't convinced and looked a bit

apprehensive.

I was relieved that Pauline appeared to be enjoying breakfast. No commentary on the bread. She did compliment the hotel coffee though.

We finished breakfast, tidied up, and headed downstairs to the street.

To get the full NOLA experience, we took the Canal Street Streetcar up to City Park. Though a storm was brewing in the Gulf, the weather continued to be perfect. We got off the streetcar at the end of the City Park line and started walking up a long avenue towards the museum.

"What's in the rucksack?" Pauline asked.

"Lunch. A person at the hotel gave me some pointers."

"Nice. What's first?"

"Some art, some sculptures and then a little lunch."

We finally arrived at the steps of the impressive entrance to the museum. As we ascended the steps to enter, Pauline, touched my hand, "Wait, I want to tell you something."

"What's that?"

"I love you. I am very happy to be here with you."

"*Moi aussi, je t'aime tellement.*"

"I like this, I speak to you in English, and you speak in French." She smiled, "Seriously, it is important, I wanted you to know that. I am happy."

A little bit later we were standing in front of one of the two Edgar Degas paintings in the museum, *Portrait of Estelle Musson Degas*. Painted in 1872. She was excited to learn that Degas lived in New Orleans briefly in the 1870s. She enjoyed seeing a couple of his earlier works before he became famous.

After an hour or so, the beautiful weather outside beckoned us. We chatted as we took in the large sculpture garden.

"This is a great museum and garden. I wouldn't have thought a city this size would have all of this."

"New Orleans, thanks to your country, has been here a long time. The French showed up here and encountered American Indian tribes in the early 1700s. New Orleans was established shortly thereafter. That means the city is over 300 years old. Even though Spain controlled it for a few decades before it was sold to the US in 1803, it was still largely French in reality. Novels and newspapers were published in French well into the 1800s. So the city was effectively French for almost two centuries. For me at least, it does seem to have a different vibe. Beach told me to be on the lookout for the different feel of New Orleans. Maybe it is still a little French. And the arts are very important here."

"I like what I've seen so far. What's a vibe?"

"Short for vibration. Slang. Like a 'feeling.'" I paused. "So, Pauline, have you thought more about our discussion, the heavy stuff we talked about in France?"

"I guess I should ask you that."

"Let's go find a shady spot and share lunch. I can think better then."

We drifted away from the sculpture garden to find an intimate little grove of trees. I flung open a small red blanket out of the backpack. Pauline was very pretty in her short tangerine dress. Her lipstick and nails matched her dress. She had turned a lot of heads as we walked around. I knew, of course, what was inside her head, so she was sexy to me in so many ways beyond just her looks.

As I was opening the bottle of wine, she looked up at me at said, "I want you, Steve, to be the one. Are we going to make this work?"

"Of course." I handed her a glass and filled it for her, I wanted her relaxed for this.

"Will you give up America?"

"You mean altogether?"

"No, silly. I mean will you move to France? I can't live here. There're things I love about America, but I can't live here, not now. About half your countrymen scare me. So mean, so uncaring about society, about the world really."

I handed her a sandwich. I looked out at a group of people walking by in the distance. There was a red-haired woman in the crowd who reminded me of the Red Angel. I was suddenly struck by the fact I hadn't seen her since the night at the Honest Lawyer in Paris, and probably not even then. I snapped back to planet earth, looked Pauline in the eye and blurted out, "I told you I'd mostly move to France. I will do what it takes. I'm setting up a foundation to manage my holdings around Marfa. I'm trying to structure things so I can spend most of my time in France."

"What's most?" She lowered her sunglasses and stared at me with a smile.

"Look, my family's in the US. I do have some business interests here that will need a little attention. I might need to come back and do a few things that are quintessentially American occasionally, like watch a baseball or football game or get some really good Mexican food."

She laughed, "So Americans claim Mexican food. They just don't want Mexicans?"

"You know I'm not like that."

"Okay, seriously, I understand your needs. I really do." Sunglasses back in place as she stared out across the green expanse before us."

"My guess is I'll need to spend four to six weeks a year here. You okay with that?"

"Yes."

"Sure?"

She turned and looked me in the eye again, "Yes, I don't want you to give up your family and friends here. I do love you. I'm not that mean. I just want our relationship to be free of tension and resentment…and based on honesty."

"Me too." I deliberately stayed quiet to try to tease a bit more from her.

Nothing.

"Pauline. I want you to know, I'll do whatever it takes to make you happy. But please tell me your real concerns so I can work around them."

"Huh?"

"I mean, to make you happy, us happy, but also do what I must do."

She looked at me. She was beautiful in the speckled light filtering through the trees. She wouldn't speak.

I kept waiting. I figured if I didn't say anything, she'd finally speak. I knew there was more. We just sat there looking across the park, the sculpture garden was in the distance.

Finally, she spoke.

"Okay. Maybe this isn't fair. My girlfriend, Simone, she lives near me, in Aujargues, fell in love with an Australian guy. He actually kind of reminds me of you. But, oh, he had that sexy accent."

"Wait, you don't like my accent?"

She just smiled, "Do you really want me to talk about your accent or finish my story?"

"Sorry."

"Anyway. He promised her he'd move to France. All was well for maybe a year. Then he told her they needed to move to Australia. France wasn't working for him."

"What happened?"

"The bastard left her!"

"Ouch."

"Yes, ouch!"

"I wouldn't do that!"

She just looked at me, like she was sizing me up.

"Is that what you are so worried about?"

She just kept looking at me.

"Do you think I'd leave you?"

She just kept looking at me.

"I won't leave you. You'd have to beat me away from you. The look in your eye when I drove up to the Gage Hotel in Marathon...."

"Yes, go on, Steve."

"That look, I've been hooked since. In that moment, I knew you were the one. You have to believe me."

"I was so mad at you."

"I was madly in love with you. I've had no doubts since then."

"Look, I know you believe that. I really do. I just want to make sure."

"Please be sure."

"I would be devastated if you did to me what that asshole did!"

"I won't do that!"

"I know you believe that, and I know you love me. I just know you love your country, like I love France."

"Of course, I do, but that doesn't mean I could ever leave you."

"I just want you to be sure. We could have something incredible for the rest of our lives. I want to grow old with you."

"So do I!"

"I just want you to be happy long term. I love you so much that I never want you to be unhappy."

"Really Pauline?"

"Yes, you asshole!"

"Then why…"

"Why what?"

"I don't know, you didn't seem to be that anxious for me to get to you when I arrived in Paris. And, I don't know, some of our chats on the phone when I was back in Marfa, I don't know. You just seemed distant."

"It's complicated."

"I mean you, you introduced me as a friend to your neighbor. That stung like a bitch."

She laughed, "Bees sting, bee-ches do too?"

I laughed.

"Yeah, they do."

"Steve, you make up some strange expressions."

I smiled. "Look, Pauline, I'm not leaving you, so you can just stop that bullshit about me abandoning you right now."

She just deeply sighed and lay back on the blanket and looked up at the clouds. I knew to shut up and let her speak. The sigh was like a placeholder for keeping the floor.

"Steve, please just make sure. I am already in love with you. I'm so close to being hopelessly in love with you. Make very sure."

I had filled the glasses a couple of times. The bottle was almost empty. The truth serum was working.

"I am." I stared into her eyes. I was never surer of anything. I was proud I had finally become a man and knew with total confidence of what I was saying. I'd never hurt this woman.

"Good, just be sure."

"I am."

She thrust herself at me and hugged me. She smelled so good and felt so good in my arms. All seemed so right in my world.

"Are we good now?

"Yes, but…"

"But what?!"

"I am returning to France in a few days. I want you to stick to our deal. I want you to be super sure. This is forever, lover!"

"Okay, I guess."

"I want you to be sure."

"What does that look like? When will I be out of purgatory?"

"I want to celebrate Christmas with you in France."

"Okay."

"Wait, I'm thinking this through…"

"Tell me."

"Let me think this through. I think I know but I want to think about it before I say anything."

"Okay."

I waited to speak to see if there was more. Nothing.

"I just have one question, Pauline."

"Just one?"

"Well, for now."

"Okay." She removed her sunglasses and looked me in the eye and reached for my hand. I felt a bit of electricity as she

touched me. I felt closer to her. She was deliciously complicated which made me want her all the more.

"Pauline, this doesn't matter to me, but why do you not want to live here, I mean at all. I mean we could live in both countries. Don't you kind of like America?"

She just laughed and put her sunglasses on.

"*Mon cher*, you are hopeless, you know that?"

I smiled and said, "I know no such thing."

"Well, you are, and I love you."

"So, tell me!"

"I will. I mean I have told you a lot, but I may say more in due time." She looked at me and raised her eyebrows to emphasize it, "I will, I promise, but you know most of my concerns already."

"Okay."

"I really, I need to pee, love."

"Oh, sorry."

"No worries. *Plus à venir mon amour*."

"Yeah sure, leave me hanging!"

"It's that, or I pull my panties down right here and relieve myself."

"Wow, you can get salty!"

"You haven't seen anything yet. We French are like a huge onion. The layers just keep going! Now let's pack up and find a bathroom."

29

The next day we took in a couple of museums and we heard some music at one of Beach's favorites, Starlight Lounge on Saint Louis in the French Quarter. The hurricane was projected to hit the central Louisiana coast, but now seemed to be tacking east. Talk of it hitting New Orleans started to surface. The weather forecasts now projected a Category 2 storm upon impact.

The next morning, Pauline came down from the loft in her robe and a towel around her head. "How should I dress? When and where is this storm supposed to hit?

I smiled to reassure her. I was watching The Weather Channel.

"What does one wear for a hurricane?" she asked.

"Well, you mainly try to stay out of a hurricane." She was beautiful without a stitch of makeup.

She shot me a very mild glare. I quickly responded, "You sure are beautiful this morning."

"If this is some kind of foreplay, we met our quota for a while last night."

"No foreplay. Just making an observation."

"When is it supposed to get bad?"

"Not until later. We'll start feeling it about midnight based on what they are saying now. It's speeding up."

"Great."

"C'mon, this is exciting. So romantic."

"Okay, I hope my flight Sunday isn't messed up."

"I doubt it."

"What are we doing today?"

"Ever seen an alligator?"

"Yes. In Florida."

"Good. I wanted to take you to a National Park site called Barataria Preserve, but it closed today for the storm. Beach said the trails are incredible."

"What's plan B?"

"Sure our quota's met?"

"Yes. For now."

"Okay. I figured you'd say that. I have a literary tour lined up, then we're going to a bar Beach recommended. That sound okay?"

"Is it one of his 'tiki' bars?"

"It's a surprise."

She looked at me without much expression and wheeled back up to the loft to get dressed. I had learned that an absence of expression often really meant nothing with her. The *souris américain*, the fake smile, was generally not part of her repertoire.

On the overcast and windy afternoon, we enjoyed a pleasant literary tour. The guide named Sean, was a local, retired mail carrier. Interesting guy. He'd had a stint in the Peace Corps in Africa. His drawl was another one of those NOLA accents. Kind of Southern, kind of something else. Baltimore? Hard to place. Knew his stuff.

After walking around and seeing the many places Tennessee Williams and Truman Capote hung out and frequented, we visited Sherwood Anderson's Pontalba Apartment. From Sean we learned that Anderson interacted with pretty much the who's who of American writers. From here in the early 1920s, he interacted and helped promote many writers, including Faulkner, Dos Passos, Sandberg and Hemingway. Sean pointed out that Hemingway mentioned a place we visited earlier in the tour, the Hotel Monteleone, in his short story "Night Before Battle."

We concluded the tour at a nearby building at 534 Madison. It was here from 1937 to 1944, and at other times at the Saint Charles Hotel, that Lyle Saxon held literary court similar to Anderson. John Steinbeck had married Gwyn Conger here in 1943. As the tour wrapped up, I asked Sean, "Did Dorothy Parker ever come to New Orleans? I loved her book reviews of many of these writers."

Sean smiled and answered, "Funny you should ask. She came to see Lyle Saxon one time. She could be funny as hell, you know? Lyle just knew she'd light up the room. I guess she wasn't feeling it. She hardly said a word and left. She always knew how to make a statement, with or without words!"

He looked like he was thinking and then added, "She always had her say, if she wanted it!"

"Any bookstore around you recommend, Sean?"

"Faulkner House Books. Remember I pointed it out. That's where Faulkner lived for a while. Head back up Chartres and hang a right at the Cathedral. It's called Pirates Alley."

"Thanks, we will," I said, as we headed back from the tour.

The wind was picking up a little as we walked into Faulkner House Books. The store was in a narrow, three story light-colored historic structure with pale blue shutters. Beautiful iron works on the second and third balconies. The wind blew the door shut as we walked in.

"Sorry," I mumbled to the blond women sitting at a table in the middle of the story. The bookstore was stunning. The shelves went all the way up to the tall ceilings. A handsome golden chandelier hung from the ceiling. The place had that wonderful smell of noble and gracefully aging books.

She smiled, "Hi, welcome. Let me know if I can be of help." I thought of asking for my book, but quickly thought the better of it.

Pauline asked, "I am looking for the book Faulkner wrote while living here."

"Of course. Are you French?"

Pauline smiled, I am."

"*Bienvenue!*" The woman replied.

"*Merci.*"

"Sadly, I don't speak French very well, but we do get a lot of customers from France."

"That's okay. I speak English."

"Here is the book he wrote while living here. I might recommend another book he started here and likely finished in Paris."

Pauline enjoyed discussing the finer points of both books with the delightful woman. It was an engaging discussion and affirmed all the things I love about independent bookstores, but I was getting hungry. It was time to eat.

A few minutes later we walked into Latitude 29, one of Beach's top recommendations. A very brief squall had hit us as we had neared the place. A server promptly seated us near a window overlooking a courtyard and swimming pool. Latitude 29 offered a more modest tiki environment than Beach's bar in Paris. The décor included a bit of tiki iconography and a lot of "trader" paraphernalia, such as Japanese glass floats, fishing nets, lots of flickering lanterns and thatched walls. A highlight was the greenish map behind the bar displaying a wealth of tiki icons on a map of the South Seas.

"I loved that bookstore, Steve. So neat that Faulkner lived and wrote there." On the recommendation of the owner, she had bought both a copy of *Soldiers' Pay*, the book he wrote while living there, as well as a copy of *Mosquitos*.

"I was supposed to do a book signing there last year but had to cancel when a storm was threatening New Orleans. I was disappointed. I must admit I was excited because I'd never been here. *Mosquitos* takes place around New Orleans."

"The woman said that he may have written some of it here and some while living in Paris. That is really neat." Her expression turned serious, "You had better check the weather,

Steve."

I looked at my phone.

"Direct hit, midnight."

"Aren't you scared?"

"Nope."

"Why not?"

"We're 9 stories high! We'll be fine."

"If you say so."

"We will. Hey, I didn't want to tell our guide this, but my favorite Dorothy Parker quote was when an editor from the New Yorker was desperately trying to reach her, she told her friend to say, 'Tell him I'm too fucking busy, and vice versa.'"

Pauline laughed and said, "She was quite a brave woman, no?"

"The bravest. She took on some of the literary giants in her reviews. I'm sure Hemingway had mixed emotions about her. He probably hated her."

"What do we order…in a tiki bar?"

"I got this until you get the hang of it. That okay?"

"*Bien sur!*"

I started her out with a Mai Tai and I ordered a Suffering Bastard. Figured we ought to stick to the classics. The wind had started to pick up a bit more and it seemed to be getting a tad darker. I quickly checked my phone again. Still midnight the ETA of the stronger winds.

"This is exciting, huh? We are in a very cool tiki bar with flickering lanterns and a hurricane is bearing down on us! Like being in the islands! The lighting was romantic—dim and a few of the lanterns were really flickering.

"Yeah, I guess so." She gave me a sheepish smile.

Pauline just wanted something small, so she ordered the Lumpia. I had the Chicken Katsu. We shared some sesame green beans. All were excellent. Pauline seemed pleased. The Suffering Bastard was one of the best I've had. Maybe better than Beach's.

"So, what do you think, Pauline?"

"It's fun. The music is interesting."

"Tiki bars try to celebrate a few special genres to help round out the ambiance." The music was kind of a blend of surfing and "X-Files" music. Weird but it worked.

"Shouldn't we be getting home, Steve? It's dark."

"Sure."

"It's getting really windy too." Pauline looked concerned. I had wanted to continue our serious discussion from our trip to the art museum, but it'd have to wait. We were having fun, and she was nervous about the storm. I was glad I'd gone out that morning to buy some wine and snacks in case we had to hole up in the room awhile. I didn't tell Pauline, but when she visited the ladies' room, I checked the weather yet again. The storm had been upgraded to a potential Category 3. Time to get back to the room. It looked like the place was closing early anyway.

The weather had deteriorated considerably while we were in Latitude 29. As we walked up North Peters, there was a steady breeze with a few gusts. There was a slight mist in the air. I chose to cross over Canal Street and keep walking up Tchoupitoulas Street until we hit Lafayette Street. It was a nice way that led through to Lafayette Square. I wanted to point out the sign in French on the Saint Charles side of the park. We stopped for a moment, but clearly, she wanted to get inside as soon as possible. She looked a bit concerned that I found the weather to be exhilarating.

Within minutes we were on Carondelet Street, took a left and were in the lobby. She looked genuinely relieved. In a few more minutes, we were settling onto our sofa. I had opened a box of a chardonnay I had picked up around the corner.

"Better?" We clinked our glasses. She was sitting on the sofa with her legs tucked under her. She was wearing a light black sweater and grey leggings. She was always elegant. She had her dark hair pulled back in a hair band.

"Yes, but is it safe to have the doors open?" I had opened the French doors to the patio to feel and hear the wind.

"Yes, and I'm about to turn the lights off. You good?"

"Yeah."

"Only thing bad about the light off, is I can't see how sexy you are. You look great tonight."

"You don't have to flatter me, our 'quota' will likely no longer be met later tonight. But, then again, it doesn't hurt."

"I don't want to take any chances."

She hugged me and rested her head on my chest and watched the dark city and the wind outside. It was really starting to pick up.

"Could it flood here?"

"Probably not, the report shows it passing through pretty quickly. You have to be more worried when hurricanes stall out or move very slowly. In those situations, they can dump massive rain."

"You are right. This is romantic. Maybe it's the wine, but I'm feeling it now. Let's step outside on the patio."

"You read my mind."

The hotel staff had secured our table, chairs and small palms. The vegetation that ringed the patio was blowing violently with the gusts. New Orleans was beautiful by night. There was a wide variety of low, medium and tall buildings. Some dark, some well illuminated. There was a building down Carondolet Street with a columned dome on top. It was illuminated in orange. Some really strong gusts would hit every five minutes or so. Pauline was hugging me and trembling just a bit. She looked up at me with a smile wanting to be kissed. It was intensely romantic. Right then a downpour hit, the rain was laterally slamming into us. It rained so hard, that it sometime hurt your skin.

"Let's go in, I'm soaked."

Pauline looked up at me, "Just one more minute. *Je me sens si vivante!*"

"Wow! You changed." I stared in her wide-open eyes. "I feel so alive too, I feel so alive when I am with you, hurricane or not."

"*Moi aussi mon cher!*" and she dug her face into my chest.

The rain was so hard, the wind so strong, you could no longer see out into the distance. It was just a swirl of blacks and grays with a few city lights appearing at times. Lightning occasionally made a strange greenish light in the distance.

"What are you doing!" She had bent down.

"I want to be naked with you out here!" She was removing her utterly soaked clothes. I too was soaked all the through, and I also removed my clothing. No one could see. We could barely see to the edge of the patio. We threw our heavy clothes into the room, and just stood there embracing each other. At times, the gusts were so strong, it was a supreme challenge to stand up, but we persisted, soaked, naked, totally alive and in love. I ached to spend the rest of my life with this woman. One minute she was scared, and then this! She always seemed to have one more surprise for me.

She looked up at me very seriously, almost scary like, and said, "My skin is numb. It has hurt for so long, I don't feel it anymore. I love you, Steve Miles. You are mine. You are moving to France, you are becoming French and you will be mine forever. Do you understand that?"

"Yes. *Absolument.*" Our eyes were locked.

"Good. Glad that is settled. Now let's go inside and satisfy our new quota."

We made love as the rain and wind slammed into the windows all around us. I knew I would never forget this night. We both felt so utterly, incredibly alive. After our passions were spent, we went back downstairs. It had grown strangely quiet outside. The plants along the balcony were barely moving. We went back out onto the patio; it was eerily quiet. You could now see the city quite clearly. There was only a mild breeze.

Pauline looked confused, "What happened? Is it all over?"

I smiled at her, "I think the eye is passing over us!"

"The eye?"

"Yes, the center of the storm, where it's quiet."

"Really? Does it come back?"

"Probably. Before long, it will probably be wild again."

"You sure? That's crazy"

"Think of a hurricane as a donut. We are in the hole now."

"That is wild!"

"A friend of mine in Houston suggested to me to think of this as halftime."

"Halftime?"

"A football term, American football. *C'est comme la mi-temps au football?*"

"Oh. How long do we have?" She was standing there barefoot in a black t-shirt of mine looking so into this moment, into this experience. I'd never seen this side of her. I liked it so much.

"I'd say it's coming. See that strange lightning over there?"

"The weird greenish glows?"

"Yes. I think it's getting closer. The wind is beginning to pick up. Feel it?"

She just looked at me and smiled. Her eyes were so filled with wonder and excitement.

"Let's check it out from inside. The backsides of hurricanes are known to offer up some tornados sometimes."

She looked at me a bit alarmed, "*Comme des tornades?*"

I nodded as we re-entered the room.

We watched the "second half" from the sofa. She was in such a good mood, I wanted to have part two of the discussion we started at City Park a couple of days ago.

Rain was once again pelting the windows, this time from a different direction. While she was watching the storm like it was a movie, I asked, "Tell me Pauline, why you so fear living in America?"

She gave me a funny look I didn't understand.

"You know I am committed to you Pauline. We are going

to live in France. I just want to know where you're coming from."

"You want the truth?"

"Yes."

"America scares me right now."

"How so?"

"It seems half the country has gone nuts."

I just listened.

"Look, about half of America supports horrible leaders that want to abuse immigrants, remember I'd be an immigrant. Now I know since I'm white, maybe I'd be fine. Fine until France doesn't support some war or something."

I just stayed quiet. I was in a record only mode.

"They want to take healthcare away from you all! And these idiots support that! They want to pollute the air and water our children would need, and the crowds cheer them on!"

She did have a scared look in her eye.

"They want to discriminate against people who aren't white or not conservative or Christian! Doesn't that upset you? Where is your outrage?"

I started to speak, and she touched my arm.

"And climate change! Your politicians are fucking nuts! They are going to get us all killed! This tiny planet, is ALL we have!"

She just looked astonished.

"In short, many of your countrymen scare me. They aren't sane. I used to love America and I wanted to perhaps live here, but not now. Not with all this crazy stuff going on. Everything's a conspiracy. There are no shared facts. You all have some of the best scientists in the world, but half of America won't listen to them. It's like half your population hasn't been educated all of a sudden. No! I won't live here, not like this."

I sat there to make sure she was through. She wasn't.

"And all your allies. It is no longer certain that we are all friends who have each other's back! And your politicians just allow the worst behaviors. Some of your politicians are disgusting. They disgust me, and I won't give them power over me or you. Never!"

After a few minutes of quiet, I finally spoke.

"I know."

"You see why I won't submit to these idiots? To these crooks?"

"Yes." I was kind of crestfallen. She was right, at least half my countrymen seemed prone to believe any conspiracy their gurus told them to believe.

"Any more questions? I'll never live here as long as this is going on."

"We discussed all of this. I know you must be very concerned to raise all of this again. You know, over half the country doesn't go for this stuff, right?"

"Doesn't matter. Your constitution enables the idiots, the haters, the polluters, the wealthy. The majority doesn't matter. You have tiny states that have the same representation in your Senate as the huge states. That's insane. How is that even remotely democratic?"

"True."

"And your Electoral College nonsense! That is bullshit!"

I just listened.

"Face it Steve, your democracy is dying here. The structure of your government is resulting in minority rules, with no concern for the majority whatsoever."

"How do you know all this stuff?"

"Unlike much of the American media, we care what happens outside France. We must. If America fails, we're probably next. Your country is so important to our national security."

"All I can say is that America is still a young country. We have had dark chapters that we overcame, at least somewhat. It seems we keep fighting the stupid Civil War. I believe we will overcome this dark chapter too. Some people are just believing horribly false narratives. This will change. I know it will. Plus, it's complicated. You said we are critical to international security. Maybe if the US spent more on its people in terms of health care and college and less on the military, we'd address your concerns, but what would happen to the world? There's no easy answer. You think Americans like high healthcare costs and expensive college? Also, aren't taxes super high in France? And you guys are having some issues on immigration too."

"Maybe if Europe and the US formed an even stronger alliance, we could spend a bit more on the military and you guys could divert some spending to your people. You need that to survive! That'd be easier if you guys stopped cutting taxes for the wealthiest!"

"All true."

"By the way, France spends more on national security compared to most European countries plus we maintain nuclear weapons. We are not a slouch worldwide. Somehow, though, as you say, you guys spend about three times what we spend per capita on defense. Of course, your economy is giant. And yes, France's taxes are high, but look at the quality of life."

"I don't know the answer, but I am optimistic about the future. The US has always rallied when we need to. We will get better. I have faith in the next generation. Sure, we have real challenges, but I really don't think it as bad here as you are led to believe by the media."

"I hope so. The world is counting on you all."

"It will get better. Don't give up on us yet. Meanwhile, I'm happy to live in France with you." I hugged her so hard.

"Are you sure? I am giving my heart to you. Please don't hurt me."

"Never. I'm not saying we won't have disagreements, but I will never hurt you."

"I need you to become comfortable living in France."

I didn't know what I could do to get her to believe me!

"I am Pauline."

"When you return, I will only speak French to you until I am satisfied you are adequately fluent. It's tough love, but you need it. We need it."

"Okay." I didn't like that, but I knew she was right.

"I mean it, I will no longer understand English out of your mouth for as long as it takes."

"Okay."

"You sure?"

"Yes. My French isn't that bad."

"Glad *you* think so."

"Look, I want to wrap up some stuff out in Marfa, swing by Houston and come home to you in France. Should take two or three weeks."

"No. It isn't going to work that way. I must be sure. You must be sure. You will stay here until December, just like we agreed."

"December!"

"Yes. I have given this much thought. I must be sure."

"What do you mean? Why December?"

"I want you to be, as your Thoreau kind of put it, 'At the mercy of your own thoughts.'"

"You read Thoreau?"

"In university." She studied the rug on the floor before us. After a pause, she looked up at me, and said, "I want you to deal with your Marfa issues and spend your Thanksgiving with your family."

I started to say something but again she touched my arm and just looked at me.

"If you are still sure, absolutely sure by then Steve, I want you in France by early December."

"That long?"

"Yes."

"You are going to kill me."

"Good, I want you to know for sure. And when you get to France, no trips to the US for at least a year! Preferably two! I want you to become so French, you feel weird here! You got that?"

"I already feel weird here, especially after you so accurately indicted my country."

"Sorry. It will only get worse as you live with me in

France. At least unless the US gets back to its senses!"

"I'm game. But December!"

"Yes. And I urge you to spend a lot of time thinking about what you are leaving behind."

"I prefer to think of what I am gaining, you."

"Yes. That is true." She smiled then did her best to look arrogant and self-assured.

Then she looked me solidly in the eye, "So, we have an agreement?"

"Yes. I hope I can last to December."

"You will. Don't be silly, it's only a few weeks!"

30

Before I knew it, I was back on Amtrak heading West. As I sat in my little compartment, I had a lot of time to think. We departed New Orleans about nine on a sunny, breezy, cool morning. We were slated to be in Alpine around 10:30 the next morning. Lots of thinking space.

Pauline had a great rest of her stay. We never lost power at the Ace Hotel, but some parts of suburban New Orleans were without power. The power had been restored at the airport pretty quickly. We were able to explore New Orleans a bit more. Other than a couple of trees knocked over, the area around us weathered the storm very well.

I took her on an urban hike through the warehouse district. We visited the Ogden Museum of Southern Art and enjoyed some wonderful paintings. She liked the view of the World War Two museum from the observation deck at the museum. We resolved to return to New Orleans one day to take that museum in. We then walked around and admired the architecture of the area. The historic buildings were of particular interest to her. I was surprised at her interest in it. She seldom feigned interest. It was normally obvious if she was interested in something, or not. She enjoyed seeing all the ghost signs that indicated the former lives of many of the now condos and art galleries.

We happened to see a priest outside of Saint Patrick's Catholic Church near the hotel, and he gave us a short tour. I let Pauline know that while France may have stunning churches across the country, gorgeous churches like Saint Patrick's and the Saint Louis Cathedral in the French Quarter were not as common in the US. She found Saint Patrick's in some ways more impressive than the cathedral in the heart of the French Quarter. I had to agree with her. She did like the French touches at the cathedral, particularly the statues of Louis IX and Joan of Arc prominently displayed at the rear of the cathedral. She liked that Saint Patrick's also had a Joan of Arc statue just to the right of the alter.

We did get to go to Beach's old employer, Tiki Tolteca. I thought Pauline would be annoyed with a trip to a second tiki bar, but she seemed good with it and seemed to have a good time. She enjoyed the Zombie they served her there. It must have been strong. It lifted her spirits for sure. Tiki Tolteca had a different vibe than Latitude 29, but it was good in a different way.

The interior of Tiki Tolteca was rich with tiki iconography. The interior was actually more classic "tiki" than Latitude 29. The bar had a thatched roof over it. I could easily picture Beach behind the bar, mixing his many concoctions and holding court on his emerging tiki philosophies under the green Japanese glass lanterns and other "trader" paraphernalia. Some huge Moais, like one sees on Easter Island, gave the place a real tiki feeling. The lighting was dramatic. A lot of thought went into making this place quintessentially tiki. The food was great, the drinks were strong and good. It was a great place also. I could see how Beach found inspiration from his time here. Sadly, his friend I was to meet, "Drift," was out of town, but I did pick up a nice tiki mug. Beach would be pleased.

We capped off our final evening together by taking in some jazz infused with blues at the Ace Hotel bar that night. Or was it blues infused with jazz? It was great regardless. Beach was right. The Ace Hotel was a fun place.

The remainder of our time together was just fun and playful. Lots of flirting. Lots of growing even closer. We needed that after some very serious discussions to remind us what attracted us to each other in the first place. I learned a lot about Pauline. She was even smarter than I thought. Her interests were more varied than I imagined. She had an adventurist side I'd never seen before. After our time on the patio during the hurricane, I asked if she was in fact a closeted nudist. She said, "Not really. There's a first for everything. I figured that was a good time to break that ground." I asked her if she'd ever done anything like that. She said other than a little topless sunbathing in Spain, absolutely not. But she did warn me with a wink that more pleasant surprises could be in store. Americans would seriously benefit from studying the ways of French seduction.

As the train continued to race across Texas, I reflected on the challenges that awaited me in Marfa. I had to figure out how to disappear for a year or more. I hoped that Amy and Jim had made progress on my scheme to create my far-fetched foundation. Meanwhile I decided to catch up on my sleep. I'd missed a few hours of sleep in New Orleans, but certainly had zero regrets.

◆ ◆ ◆

"Sorry the train was so late."

I walked up to Amy as she was leaning on the car looking very business-like in her dark gray jacket and skirt in the white sunlight of Alpine. She looked up from her phone, "Steve! I'm relieved you're back! A lot has happened in a week! You hungry? Mexican okay?"

"You kidding? *Vamos!* New sunglasses?"

"Nope."

"Look good."

Fifteen minutes later we were surrounded by piped-in mariachi music and walls displaying a variety of Mexican blankets and sombreros punctuated with old Corona and Tecate signs.

"Three chicken enchiladas and iced tea."

"You got it." The young girl waiting on us disappeared.

"New owner here, Aim?"

"Not really. Just a new name. Paul took over from the mom. Staff pretty much the same."

"So, what happened while I was in New Orleans?"

"Well, Clark got arrested once again. He almost got fired again from the movie. Jim and I cannot figure out one aspect of the foundation thing, and the brewery in Chihauhua is trying to kill our exclusive contract early."

"In other words, everything is about the same?"

She took her sunglasses off, looked me in the eye and said, "Pretty much. How about you? You and Pauline work things out?"

"Yes. I'm leaving for good in early December."

"What?"

"Well, not for good maybe, but for a long while."

"Why Steve?!"

"It's complicated. But it's all good."

"Well, we have much to do before you leave. I set up a meeting with Jim in the morning. 10:00. The office. Okay?"

As our food arrived, she added, "I guess we should just focus on the Clark stupidity since that doesn't involve Jim."

I looked at her.

"Well, you know he got fired from the cab company for sneaking fares into Mexico?"

"Yes."

"Well, apparently, on his final trip to Ojinaga, he got busted for sneaking some pot back over the border."

"How stupid!"

"He claims he didn't know. He says he should have known something was messed up when the same guy kept asking him to take him to OJ. The guy would always offer to buy him a Mexican beer as he dropped him off. Clark figures they put the stuff underneath his wheel well when he'd go in the bar."

"What an idiot."

"He says he didn't really go for the beer. He did it because the girl at the bar always flirted with him."

"Like that helps somehow?"

"We're talking Clark here."

"He in jail?"

"Out on bail. I think Judge Forster took pity on him for being so damn dumb."

"What about the movie and Clark? He piss off Tito again?'

"Not directly."

"Uh huh, and?"

"It was just that Tito wanted him to redo a scene and Clark was in jail at the time."

"Oh no!"

"Yeah, well I had to lean on Tito a bit."

"How so?"

"Well, Tito needed to redo a scene at your house."

"Yeah?"

"I told him if he cut Clark out like he threatened, I'd call the sheriff if he set foot on your yard. Seems Tito and Sheriff already had a disagreement."

"So, Clark's still in the film?"

"Yeah. Clark got out and was able to reshoot the scene."

"That's good, I guess."

"Course I had to threaten Clark because he started talking about having Tito over a barrel again and bullshit like that." She pinched the bridge of her nose and grimaced.

She took a deep breath, let it out and added, "I told Clark if he didn't do the scene just like Tito wanted, I'd urge Tito to just move on. Clark believed me since Tito had already threatened that a number of times."

"Aim, your brother is a complete dumb-shit."

"Your blood cousin is a complete dumb-shit. Least I ain't blood kin like you."

"Touché. So, Clark is unemployed again?"

"Not exactly. The cab company hired him back. Seems nobody else would take the job."

"Unbelievable."

"Yes, unbelievable."

"They through with that damned movie?"

"Yep. They're packing up."

"Think we'll make any money on it, Aim?"

"I doubt it. Looked like a shitty movie if you ask me."

"Great book, shitty movie."

"Yeah Steve, something like that."

"Still haven't read my book?"

She smiled, "I finally started it!"

"Awesome! What page you on?"

She hesitated as she put a stick of gum in her mouth and started looking at her compact to reapply her lipstick. She glanced over at me and finally said, "Four, maybe."

"Shit."

"I'm a slow reader."

"Sure, Amy. Sure."

I walked in our office at 10:00. I'd had a good night sleep in my bed and was ready to get things tidied up on the foundation. Jim and Amy were already at the office.

"Coffee Steve?"

"Sure. I'll just help myself."

"Good, that's kind how it works around here, cuz."

"I don't get any respect around here at all, Amy."

"Steve, respect must be earned. Don't you know that?"

"I've heard that somewhere, I think."

Within minutes, we were well into the discussion. Jim had brought in a foundation expert from Midland who was due to show up shortly.

Jim gave me his fatherly look. "Steve, I think we can pull off what you want, but we have a revision to run by you. The 'non-profit' brewery is a bridge too far. Housing help, the land conservation, leasing buildings, the eco-ranch, all that works. And Amy can keep up with that. We recommend you give up the brewery."

"I can't do that. I'm passionate about Marfa having a brewery. I almost did it once you know."

"The one you blew up?"

"Well, yeah."

"Steve it is just too heavy a lift. Tina, the attorney coming in from Midland, she oughtta be here any minute, she can help us on all the other. Beer production is heavily regulated."

"I gotta have that Jim."

Amy jumped in. She looked at Jim and then spoke, "Look Steve, we figured you'd say that."

She paused and looked at Jim again. Jim nodded once. She continued, "There is one way. The Carmelites."

"Huh?"

"The Carmelites have to sell a monastery up north. It is huge and they are down to just a couple of dozen members. They are looking for a new monastery. They were looking over in Alpine because they want wide open spaces. They want to be left alone. Well anyway, I asked them if they would be interested in Marfa if we helped them find a monastery. Then we asked them if they'd operate a brewery. They seemed thrilled. I guess they operated a few breweries a long time ago somewhere and they are thrilled to do it again."

"That could be cool."

"How long's it been? Any of them still got experience?"

"I doubt it."

"Why?"

"It was in the 1700s."

"Oh."

"Yeah, but they seem super excited."

"Where would they live?"

"Well, they are used to pretty austere living. We were thinking we could let them use the old Danner homestead on the ranch."

"Damn, that's going to take work!"

"Well, apparently they are accomplished carpenters. And there's good water there."

"They'd have to outfit both of the buildings. They are in bad shape. And they'd have to install a septic. It'd be complicated. One of the buildings isn't too bad. Remember, the Army built one of them up pretty solid to use as an outpost when the raids were coming in from Mexico."

"True. Where they going to get the money?"

"Well, they have the money from the sale of their former monastery building but they may need to borrow a little. But before they do that, they want to make sure their place is secure. They want to buy the place or at least have a long-term lease."

"Okay, let me think on this. This could work, but it's complicated."

"Oh, there's Tina!" Jim got up to greet her.

After introductions, we jumped into discussing the rest of the operations of the Clive Miles Foundation. Tina did know her stuff. By our late lunch, Tina had most of the foundation operations mapped out. She felt all was doable. She also recommended leaving the brewery out of it. She said beer production, taxes and the like were super complicated. She did seem to think maybe, just maybe letting that be outsourced to the monastery could be an "elegant solution" if we had to do it. She'd draw up a legal structure and start working with Jim to put it in place. She asked me to be thinking who I'd want on the Board of Directors. After some discussions, we discussed a family foundation but there just weren't enough Miles family members to ensure continuity. I sure as hell wasn't going to put Clark on a Board. We opted for a small Board of Directors. I'd work with Amy on nominating the first board. I wanted this to go on after me. This was about Uncle Clive's legacy.

By the end of the day, the roadmap was established. There'd be a lot of follow up discussions, but we had a plan. Now I just had to think through this monastery thing. I had a few weeks. I wanted to be headed for Houston a week before Thanksgiving so I could spend some real quality time with my parents before heading to France.

I also wanted to spend some of the time left to the "mercy of my own thoughts" in Big Bend National Park or Big Bend Ranch State Park. Maybe even get a little writing in but getting ready to go to France had to be my first priority. I needed to see if my parents could travel to France for the wedding. This was getting complicated. I had a lot to think about. Did I need a VISA? Ugh! I'd have to let Pauline help me think through a lot of this stuff.

31

I'd just seen my fifth shooting star in about 15 minutes. All this was going on out here every night whether a human witnessed it or not. Total quiet, other than a pack of coyotes partying way off in the distance and the occasional breeze. I drew a map for the rangers at the park office where I'd be, but no one on the planet really knew where I was. It was probably kind of stupid, but I needed this. It made me feel alive like that hurricane in New Orleans. I could really think out here. Stupid stuff just kind of drifted away.

As I stared into the star-loaded sky, I felt so insignificant. Maybe ancient man benefitted from this. Maybe it helped keep man in his place. I dreamed of a time there were no arrogant asshole politicians or self-important actors or athletes. I longed for a life when I didn't have to suffer those people. Perhaps I'd be spared that a bit in France. Perhaps it was my limited language skills or the culture, but for whatever reason, I was so unplugged from mainstream culture there. Because of my lack of fluency, I probably had the awareness of a 10-year-old boy there. Regardless, it never bothered me. I didn't miss being aware of all the world's problems in the slightest.

The moon had not appeared yet, so the sky was brilliantly illuminated by the stars. They made light all around me. I could see a few lights way off to the south. Might have been in Mexico for all I knew. I was alone and I could hear my thoughts.

It was out here in the country I so loved that I decided a few things. One, I'd give the monastery a perpetual 100-acre easement if they did three things—

- actually use it to maintain a monastery,
- brew fine beer, and
- ship by rail as long as the railroad would serve them.

I'd give them an interest-free loan adequate to construct a brewery that had to be paid back by sharing five percent of their gross sales. No profits, no payment that year. After the brewery was paid for, assuming that ever happened, the five percent would go into the coffers of the foundation. I'd also give them a year of my brewery consultant's time. I know it had disaster written all over it and Aim would freak, but I had a good feeling about it. It would largely take Amy out of the beer business except to collect the five percent. I'd help the monastery out by renting the brewery to them for a dollar a year for five years. I'd want the rental to be 2% of gross sales from then on. I remember the Trappist beers I'd had in France being quite good. Maybe they could have a few travelling monks come help out from Belgium and France. The monks had proposed calling it "Soul Good" beer.

Okay, after I took a bath on the brewery, I'd turn Amy loose to be rapacious on our other properties to squeeze every dollar possible to fund the foundation. She'd done well on the ranch and various leases. Another movie production crew was thinking it over. They said they'd not seen such a lush riparian area anywhere in West Texas, so green, such lovely trees. It was gorgeous. Provided Marfa's economy stayed decent, the other rental properties should do well.

I was set moneywise as long as the Foundation was self-sufficient. Jim reluctantly offered that my monastery scheme could yield some significant tax benefits due to all the "donations" by offering so much well below market rates. I mainly just want to honor my uncle, do well by Marfa and be free to focus on Pauline and a bit of writing. But it did feel good to do good.

Okay, other decisions. I knew Pauline was my future. It

had taken both of us too long to see it. I stupidly thought she was getting cold feet while I was in Paris. I probably engaged in the "experience of life" thing a bit too much with Sofia and Sarah. All was well, but I may have flown just a bit too close to the sun with those two, Sofia more than Sarah. A bit more of temptation or alcohol and things could have gone differently. Fortunately, nothing really happened. That damn Hemingway! But I had to admit to myself that his saying about writing from the experience of life rang true to me. When I wrote about things I had experienced, it was so much better.

Also, I devoted myself to writing, including writing to save this country I loved and help people to understand what an international gift the Big Bend country was. I struggled to decide what was better: to help by letting the world know how amazing it is or to try to keep people from learning about it, the conservationist's eternal struggle. I also decided to write fiction that might help Americans deal with the many concerns Pauline raised. Much of what she raised in our chats made sense to me. I was alarmed how people could be so resistant to better health care, cleaner air, better climate policy, and all the other things she mentioned. The "muckrakers" made a big difference in the past. Could I mimic that?

There was an "undetermined thing" too. I still had a nagging feeling I could be doing more to help people who didn't have an Uncle Clive or the great parents I had. During my times around the courthouse in town, I had seen some prisoners being led out of the Sheriff's Department in Marfa a couple of times. I'd look at them and wonder how they wound up in handcuffs.

As I took in the zillion stars above me, I thought that those prisoners were, at one time, someone's little boy or girl, sweet and innocent. They played ball in the streets, they lit up when they saw a puppy, they hugged grandma's neck. How the hell did this stuff keep happening? They didn't come out of the womb a criminal. We all stood by and watched it happen.

We were all, in a sense, accomplices. I didn't know where to start, but I knew I had more to do in this area. This, and the fact we were okay seeing homeless and hungry people out there, all of a sudden seemed so wrong. The world's "wealthiest nation" and we seemed so incredibly insensitive to the plight of humanity. We're always ready to judge people for having failed somehow. Maybe Pauline was right, maybe we were barbaric. Maybe Beach's Tiki-Christ, focused on love, was more on point than I thought. At times, I didn't see a lot of love from the Christians I knew growing up in Texas. Some of them seemed a tad too busy judging to be able to take time to truly follow Jesus' teachings to "love one another."

As the moon began to appear on the horizon, just edging over the mountains, I took it as my cue to go to sleep and let my mind process this inner conversation overnight. At least that's what the stars and I decided. The coyotes must have liked it. They cheered a bit more. Oh, one more thing, I needed to embrace Pauline's vision of wealth—time, relationships, simplicity, avoiding stress, good food, good wine, good friends, caring. Way less thinking about material stuff.

I loved how her house was so free of crap. I could truly relax in her place. I really liked how her life was devoid of so much "busy-ness." I thought of seeing her there, on the sofa, reading a magazine or novel. Or, the "time" space, to take an evening walk! I had much to learn from her yet. I knew I'd make a great pupil!

A few weeks later I was over the dark Atlantic. The plane was peaceful and quiet. Most of the lights were off. The air was cool but just a touch musty. I was beginning my new life. I was surprised to have no doubts. It felt like what I was supposed to do my whole life. From playing on my high school football team in Houston, to attending Texas A&M University, to serving in the military, to working in Congress, to struggling with Stacy, my old girlfriend in Marfa, to hopping all over France. All that somehow felt like preparation for the moment I'd meet

Pauline in that bar in that small village, Saint-Côme-et-Marué-jols. I didn't blow that moment because I was finally prepared. I was ready to take advantage of that tiny opening to happiness. Maybe I finally had the right "experience of life" to let me capitalize on that moment.

I really knew there was something right between us the first time I saw her. We were standoffish at times, but gradually we grew on each other. There always a strong sexual attraction, but we just couldn't click personality wise. We kept giving each other little glimpses of what could be, and then I unwisely left. I knew it was a mistake. Something really haunted me. I felt the need to go back to Marfa for some reason. It wasn't entirely clear to me until I saw her on the front porch of the Gage Hotel in Marathon, Texas. Her moist, so wise French eyes looking into the fading West Texas sunset was it. That was also probably the last time I had seen the Red Angel, whoever or whatever that was. Maybe she was my guardian angel guiding me. Maybe she was my imagination. I guess it didn't really matter. The Red Angel doesn't hang out in Languedoc, my new home to be. Maybe she knows I don't need her anymore. Maybe I don't. Maybe she's off working on another "case" now.

After hours of wrangling with Amy and Jim, the Clive Miles Foundation was well underway. The monks were all in on the brewery and had indeed convinced some brothers from a beer making monastery in Canada to come live with them. I had a touching farewell with my Marfa friends. They called it my second bachelor party.

Fewer attended, but I had a great time. It would have been better if Clark hadn't kept crying. He did of course finally manage to spill his red drink on one of my nice rugs, but I didn't really care. I'd directed Amy to lease my house. I stored some of my better stuff in a backroom of our office in town. I wasn't entirely sure what would come of my books, art and statues. I didn't overly care, but I wasn't ready to part with them yet. They meant something to me. The proceeds from the rental of the house would also go into the Foundation coffers.

I loved spending Thanksgiving with mom and dad, but I hated leaving them for a year. They were getting on up there, as we say in Texas. I hoped that they'd come to the wedding. They said they would. I made it a goal to try to come for a good long stay each Thanksgiving with or without my love accompanying me. I would miss Amy and even that turd Clark. Clark was sure he'd make it big as soon as "his" movie was out. I half wondered if he was right. Somehow, he'd gotten a clip of one of his scenes. To my astonishment, he was truly extraordinary on film. Better looking, funnier, less repulsive. I could see a niche for him.

I finally drifted off to sleep while the Atlantic was still black.

32

My flight arrived at Charles de Gaulle airport around 7:00 am. True to his word, Beach was waiting to pick me up. He'd insisted I stay with him on my arrival in Paris. I was booked on the 14:14 TGV departure the day after next, Friday. I'd be in Nîmes around 17:11 that evening. I figured I'd get my jet lag out of the way, catch up with Beach and then head south. Nîmes was about a forty-minute drive from Pauline's place.

Beach lived near his bar. He lived on the fourth floor, better known as the fifth floor in America, of a beautiful late 1800's building. He parked in the basement a couple of levels below ground. His flat was probably huge by French standards. It had a great master suite and two other bedrooms. Twelve-foot ceilings, gorgeous hardwood floors almost throughout. He was proud that one could see the very tip of the Eiffel Tower if you leaned out the window just a bit.

"Do you live here alone?"

"At the moment." He harbored a mysterious smirk.

"What's that mean?"

"Well, that may change soon, my man."

"Tell me more!"

"Later. You probably need to wash up and maybe catch a nap."

"Yeah, that'd be good actually."

"Bathroom *est par là*." He pointed down the hall.

"Hey, how'd you rate this place? It's awesome!"

"I know. Kind of like you. Been in my family forever. My

mom left it to me. Believe that shit?"

"Unreal."

"Surprisingly the taxes aren't too bad either. Actually, they'd be cheap if the damn place wasn't worth over 1.3 million euro or whatever the cap is now."

"How much is it worth?"

"Who really knows."

"But over 1.3 million euro?"

"Oh yeah." Beach smirked and gave me a French shrug. He might sound like a Texan when he spoke English, but there was a real Frenchman in there.

A few hours later, I came wandering down the hall checking out his artwork as I went. Beach was sitting in his living room having a tense discussion on his phone. He looked at me and smiled and made a French hand signal for just a minute. I looked out at the views from his tall windows.

Beach got off his call. "Get dressed, bum. We are going to go eat steak and drink red wine!"

"What time is it?"

"Almost 17:00."

"Damn! I slept seven hours!"

"I guess you were tired."

"Where we going?"

"One of my favorites. Its quirky but incredible, Le Relais de Venise. Best *entrecôte* on the planet! Get your ass in gear. We got bit of a walk ahead of us!"

"Where is it?"

"Porte Maillot."

"Isn't that a good little way?"

"Not bad. Hustle. I want to get in for the first seating." I found out later what that meant.

We walked over to Étoile and then around to the Avenue de la Grande Armée to Boulevard Pereire. We mainly just got caught up on my trip to Texas and my glorious time in New Orleans. He had many questions about the tiki scene there. He was disappointed that I missed his friend.

As we walked up Boulevard Pereire, he pointed. "See that beautiful red awning?"

"Yeah."

"Remember this moment, the first time you saw Le Relais de Venice!"

"Okay, if you say so Beach."

"I say so my friend." And he hugged me. "C'mon, let's get in line!" The hugging thing was Texan, distinctly not French.

"How does this work Beach?" We were in line behind about fifty people. It was getting a tad cold.

"We're golden Steve, we're in for the first seating!"

"First seating?"

"Yes. When they open the doors, they will seat us all. Otherwise, we'd have to wait for the second wave, and I'm far too hungry for that."

"This is different."

"Yes, Steve, in a number of ways, but it's all good. By the way, you think any more about the Book of Tiki?" He smiled and lifted his eyebrows.

"Yeah, of course."

"And?"

"Well, it's kind of weird." I quickly added, "No offense, Beach."

"Steve, my man. I expected more from you. I've only shown it to a couple of people. I thought you had the capacity to give it deep thought." He looked disappointed.

"No, don't take it that way. Weird doesn't mean bad."

"Huh?"

Just then the line started moving. It moved fast. Within minutes, we were seated right next to a very well-dressed French couple. We were so close to them I could easily enjoy her perfume. Fortunately, she had good taste. We could hear almost everything they were saying.

"Again, different, Beach."

"The best difference is the food. *Attends juste!*"

The waitress came and took our order. The options were

few. Steak frites was it. The only choice was which red wine and dessert.

"That was simple."

"Yes. Most of these people are repeat customers."

"How do you know?"

"Did you see any confused people in line?"

"Just me."

"Okay, tell me about weird."

As total darkness descended on Paris outside the window near us and a gentle rain began to fall, I looked into Beach's expectant eyes. For some strange reason, like that earlier recollection, once again, a wave of mental images started flashing in my mind. Walking off the football field drenched in sweat on a hot August day in Houston in high school. Being in a foxhole one night in Fort Benning in Georgia. Wasting time trying to convince the Senator I worked for to support some environmental legislation. Never in my wildest dreams did I picture myself sitting in a restaurant in Paris talking tiki theology sitting three inches from a beautiful French woman I'd never met and talking to one of the most interesting and weird people I might ever meet.

"Steve, you okay?"

"Oh, yeah, just thinking Beach. Thinking how, I never thought this would be my life."

"Talk to me, think out loud, eh?"

"Beach, to be honest, I'm still absorbing your writings. Its heavy, you know?"

"Yeah, and…"

"I talked to a priest friend about it." We were picking at a delicious salad they had put before us. Greens and walnuts and an amazing dressing, vinegar and Dijon?

"And…"

"The dressing is amazing. Why the salad first? This is different."

"You keep saying that Steve. Get over it. This place is different. Does its own thing. Back to the priest maybe?"

"Oh sorry, Well, he wasn't a fan."

"Of course not!"

"The Catholic Church, of which I am a part whether they want me or not, is some of the problem."

"How do you mean?"

"Look Steve, the bible is largely the work of the Church. They can't refute their work. I'm sure many of the early fathers of the Church were well-intentioned, but it was a militant church trying to stave off the non-believers, Muslims and other competing religions. Above all, they wanted to make sure there were many Catholics, so they brought extra stuff into the teachings of the Church on abortion, birth control, what not. Probably even homosexuality."

He had my attention.

"Steve, the Bible was assembled in a particular era, maybe two or three or more eras. There's no way it couldn't reflect the thinking of the day, the worries of the day. No way at all."

"But your efforts are so radical. I mean, to dump most of the New Testament?"

"Not dump, just more accurately describe it as historical context. It was a bunch of dudes trying to interpret what Jesus said. Jesus was gone after the gospels. I'm just saying that perhaps what they wrote wasn't infallibly the "Word" of God. Valuable yes. Divinely inspired? Who knows? Are we going to trust that a bunch of guys, humans, 'the bible framers,' 1,700 years had the final word on what is divine and what is not? That's it? Why would we do that? I saw Jesus. Maybe I know more about who or what Jesus is about than Paul."

Beach sighed and then smiled as he continued, "Look, Paul was brilliant and so devoted, but he never knew Jesus as a human. And some of the most problematic teachings come from later theologians, such as Thomas Aquinas. Aquinas enters the scene 1,200 years after Christ, yet the Church allows him to take Jesus' teachings and make them impossible for man! All sex has to be for procreation? Where did Aquinas get that? Jesus *never* said that. Sex is one of many gifts God gave couples to help us form close, loving and exclusive relationships. In a loving relationship, two bodies merging in an act of extreme pleasure. It was a gift of God to cement a lifelong bond between spouses. To say it is just for procreation erodes the fullness of this gift. The Church I love dearly would be well served, and Christianity for that matter, to reexamine this dogma."

My head was spinning. "Beach, I don't know what to say. I'm just a piss poor Episcopalian trying to make sense of any of this."

"That's cool. The Episcopalians make a lot of great points. They see themselves as the reformed Catholic Church. I'm cool with them, but I'm telling you Steve, the Catholic Church is the real thing. I love it. It has just gotten off track a bit."

"If so Beach, haven't they been off track like a thousand years?"

"Not on most things."

Thankfully, the steaks arrived. I was almost getting a headache trying to follow Beach. All of a sudden, Beach and I were exclusively focused on the smell coming from the sizzling work of art put before us.

"Sorry Steve. I was losing you. I know. Enough on that for now. Now wait, Steve. Take a deep breath. Get ready. Prepare yourself. Cleanse your mind. Focus on your sense of taste alone."

"Okay." I started to cut a small piece.

"Steve, put the piece in your mouth and let it sit there a few seconds. Think of nothing but the pleasure you're experiencing. Then, slowly mix that flavor with a few drops of the Côtes de Bordeaux."

I did as he instructed. The result was incredible. I strived to give my sense of taste primacy as practically any good Frenchman can. It was like sex for the mouth. I know that's crude, but the best I can put it.

"And?" Beach looked at me so intently. I just smiled.

"Okay, Steve, I think you and that steak need to get a

room."

"Do they have privacy rooms here?" I laughed.

"Okay. Repeat that process slowly a few times. Savor this moment. Remember, surrender to your sense of taste, give it dominance. Many Americans have never mastered that."

"Oh, I have now, Beach."

"Good, a few more morsels of steak followed by a few drops of the Bordeaux. Then take a break and have a few of the *frites* to kind of reset your taste buds. The fries are perfection as well."

With a dark, rainy Paris and the smell of my neighbor's perfume as the backdrop, I was literally transported to another place for a while. Eventually, the euphoric shock to my taste buds waned just a bit so I could once again focus on my surroundings. Okay, maybe I'm exaggerating a tad, but not much. There was a multi-layered essence to what we were experiencing, immensely sophisticated, civilized and primal at the same time.

Just as I had slowly devoured my *entrecôte* and a mild let down was coming on, they brought another plate of steak and fries! I was the happiest man on the planet at that moment, knowing I'd have a few more bouts of ecstasy. Food is such a great way to focus on the now if you surrender.

"Wow! You were really transported, Steve. I thought I'd lost you."

"I was lost, somewhere. Somewhere I liked a great deal." I smiled.

"You have like a 'post coital' glow!"

"I do feel a bit groggy," I laughed.

"Happened to me the first time here, too."

"Really?"

"Yeah, I'm impressed. Never seen an American enjoy a meal so much. You were almost in a trance. Sure you're not French?"

"Bullshit. Really?"

"Okay, maybe I'm overstating it a little. Hard to tell, I was having kind of a thing myself. I always do here. I don't like to bring women here unless they appreciate it the way I do."

"The sauce on the steak, what the hell is that?"

"I don't know, think it has Tarragon maybe? I don't question it, I just let it bring pleasure."

We sat there and sipped the final drops of our Bordeaux. Resuming a discussion on theology was *hors de question*. We just soaked in the moment. We knew we had likely cemented a lifelong friendship somehow. For whatever reason, I'd likely know Beach the rest of my life. We had that kind of connection. The perfect time, the perfect meal.

On Friday I was on a silver train racing through the French countryside headed to meet my love. The green landscape was almost like a blurry abstract painting flashing by the train window. I had taken in a few museums on Thursday, before I met Beach for drinks that evening.

We resumed the "book of Tiki" discussion. Beach was so complicated. I could feel he was trying to make sense of life. For whatever reason, he felt comfortable sharing his innermost thoughts with me. He said that was super rare. He was now suddenly, practically engaged to a Spanish woman living in Paris. Their relationship was moving so fast, that marriage was already on the table. He was a mess. He was struggling to make sense of all this theological stuff and make sense of how their relationship was growing so fast. He said there were days he cursed his trip to Réunion Island. What he saw there keeps burning away in him. He wanted to talk all night. We had stopped drinking by 10:00, yet we sat in that bar until it closed a bit after midnight.

On more than one occasion, I wondered if Beach was a tad insane, or rather, maybe, just intensely human. I had never met anyone quite like him. I felt a closeness to him that was almost irrational. We hadn't spent that much time together.

I wondered why I had never had such strange encounters in America. Was I numb to it in America? Were people like Beach rare in America?

I must have drifted into a deep sleep. When I awoke, the train was already just a bit north of Nîmes.

33

I arrived in Nîmes awfully close to right on time, so shockingly unlike my experience with American trains. France was lucky to have such an amazing way to get around their wonderful country. I wondered as I continued this adventure, was it also becoming my country?

As I stepped off the train, there was no Pauline. I found a place in front of the station to sit with my two large suitcases. After I caught up on emails and texts, I looked at my watch. 5:40. It was now pretty much dark. At least it was a bit warmer here. No texts from Pauline.

Finally, about 6:00, I felt someone who smelled quite good hugging my neck.

"Je suis tellement desolée. Il y a eu un accident! Un grand camion retouré! Et la batterie de mon téléphone portable était épuisée!" Pauline was very excited. She spoke so fast.

"Are you okay? A truck turned over?" Her cell phone battery had run out too.

"Comment?" She just looked at me with a blank stare. Dammit, she meant it! She wasn't going to speak English with me. Crap! I told myself "welcome" to the real France.

From then on, unless she slipped, most of our conversation was in French. Occasionally, she'd help me just a tad, but her discipline was far better than mine. She really did want me to become French fast! She wanted me to become comfortable living in a French world before the bright shiny newness wore off. I had no idea how bad my French was until I lived in that world. But I grew fast of course. At times, I felt like a four-year old expressing myself.

The evening I arrived was pretty mild. After driving back to Sommières, we dined outside at the same place we'd gone upon my arrival last time, Chez Tibère.

"Welcome to your new home, Steve."

"I am so happy to be here, to be with you."

We were once again at the same table we were at before, overlooking the river. Lights on the other bank and the beautiful village of Sommières danced in the flow of the river. It was a little cool, but there was an occasional warmer breeze.

"So much different. The leaves are gone. It is cooler." Pauline was dressed in a black sweater and short grey skirt, opaque black stockings. Her thick, maroon scarf beautifully framed her face.

She just smiled and grabbed my hand.

"I'm so happy you're here."

"Me too. I liked it better when it was warmer."

"Last week was much cooler."

"Does it snow here?"

"Rarely, but it does snow in the mountains if you ever want snow."

"I like a little snow."

"Me too!" She smiled again. She really did seem to be genuinely happy. The same kind of happiness I saw in her eyes in New Orleans during the hurricane.

I was already starting to tire of speaking in French all evening. I was slipping and mixing in English or even some Spanish. By the time our Tarte aux Fraises and coffee arrived, I was mostly silent.

"You are tired, Steve?"

"A bit."

"Well, after dessert, we'll have to rush you to bed for a good sleep."

"Perhaps I'll revive about that time." I gave her a speculative look.

She laughed and said, "You turd" in English.

"Hey, I though you said, 'no English.'"

"Smartass." She replied also in English. She smirked. "I reserve the right to use English when the English word is so much more effective. Not everything translates you know. Besides, some French people use that phrase in French untranslated anyway. They just change the pronunciation a bit. Your damn language keeps trying to creep into my lovely native language."

I did revive and we had the most pleasant reunion that night. The next day would be the first full day of my new life in my new home.

◆ ◆ ◆

I fell right back into my Sommières morning routine. I got a pot of Carte Noire brewing then went up the street to get our baguette and picked up a *Le Monde* at the newsstand also. The people at the bakery and newsstand smiled at me as though they recognized me. The woman at the bakery asked where I had been. That felt good. I felt a sense of belonging.

I was on the patio with my coffee, baguette and confiture reading the newspaper as Pauline emerged.

"Aren't you cold?"

"Not too much. Do I look French enough for you with my *Le Monde*?"

"Not too many French people wear a Texas A&M sweatshirt my love."

"Oh, okay. I got cold. I didn't wear it out."

She mumbled no worries as she stepped back inside through the window that functioned as a door.

In a bit, she stepped outside with a nicely wrapped gift.

"I have a surprise."

"What is it?!"

"Open it."

I ripped it open.

"A soccer ball!"

"You asked for one last time."

"Cool, I did!" I hoped to be able to cross the river some-time and get some exercise on the fields over there.

"Thank you darling!"

"We can go play if you like."

"Really?"

"I'm pretty good."

"No kidding?"

"I have played off and on my whole life. How do you think I got these legs?"

I was learning something about her every day. I got up and kissed her forehead and said "I'd like that very much. I'd love to see you run!"

"It is supposed to get to 18 degrees today. Let's do it!"

"What's that in Fahrenheit?"

"I don't know, don't care. It is best you chuck off that stupid English system nonsense. And please never call it soc-cer again. That's a stupid American made-up word. The entire world knows it as football or, here, *le foot*."

A couple of hours later, we were on a pitch across the river. She'd actually worked up a sweat. Her tight legs were a sight to behold. She had put me through several drills she learned playing soccer over the years. She was good. She packed a kick. She was very pretty, glistening, sitting on the brown and green grass. The sun was brilliant.

"You're sexy when you sweat."

"You think everything I do is sexy."

"I do."

"And I love that...and you."

"When are we going to get married?"

"In my eyes we already are, you bastard, and don't fuck it up." She said in English and smiled at me.

"I love when you slip in some strategic English!"

She just smiled.

"I mean it. Should we make plans? I mean I guess there's no rush."

"We will soon, I guess. I just already see us as married. When you came back to France knowing what I need, I took it as if...this is permanent."

"It's in my eyes. I've never felt this alive and in love. I'm so happy to be with you."

"I know. I feel exactly the same." She reached over and hugged me. She was still a little wet.

"I like you sweaty."

"I know. You said that."

"Sorry."

"I like that you like it though. I don't stink?"

"If you do, it's a good stink."

She punched me in the shoulder and smiled at me.

"Look, let talk more on this. I am ready to marry you if you want. But I want us to process one more thing."

"What?"

"What we do when you're tired of this."

She walked over to her bag and grabbed her sunglasses and got mine.

"I'll never tire of you."

"I believe that. But you will tire of living in this village. I love it, but even I need a break sometimes. How will we handle that? I know you. You'll get wanderlust. I just want us to be in agreement about how you'll handle that. It's going to happen. I'd worry about you if it didn't. You are a writer. Writers are artists. They need new stimuli in order to create. They live to create. It is just something we should discuss."

"Okay."

"Let's go eat right now though. I'm hungry."

The next couple of weeks went very well, even though Pauline had to go do a workshop for English executives in Lyon for a few days. I assumed the role of Pauline's husband. Pauline's neighbors came to know me. She now introduced me as her "*fiancé.*" I took enormous pride in that. That was real progress over some of her previous introductions. I was also the local "*américain.*" People liked Pauline so much, I got some instant credibility. They almost became protective of me. I was their "*américain.*" They looked out for me. On a number of occasions, especially if Pauline was away, they'd drop by and ask me if I was okay? Did I need anything? I grew to love these people.

I wrote a lot during the day. As soon as I saw Pauline off, I'd drink coffee and make myself read the paper and then write. When I read the paper, my goal was to write down and learn ten new words a day. When the weather was decent, I might go play some soccer or shop for groceries. Somehow, I just fell into a rhythm: see her off, write, soccer or shopping, more writing, cook supper. It was a good rhythm I knew I'd like better when the weather was warmer, and I could regularly spend more time outdoors.

One of her neighbors asked me to play *pétanque* one morning with a couple of his friends. I obliged and I sucked. He loved laughing at how bad I was. I might get one of my metal balls within a foot or so of the *cochonnet*, the little ball you aim at. Of course, he or his partner would bomb my ball off the court immediately. He showed no mercy. I stayed a good sport. I had a hard time understanding him. I asked Pauline why and she told me that Monsieur Morlet is ninety years old. He mixes in some Provençal in his speech, a regional dialect. She said she had trouble understanding him at times as well.

The routine was good, actually very good. We were growing closer and there was really almost no wall between us remaining. I had to ask her to repeat herself sometimes, but our relationship had somehow transformed into a French only relationship. She was right. It accelerated my language acquisition enormously. I had way more confidence than I did than even when I arrived a couple of weeks ago.

However, we still had not discussed marriage or the other discussion she wanted to have that she mentioned on the soccer field. If I raised it, she'd channel us into a different discussion. I was starting to grow concerned but things were going so well, I never pushed. Actually, things were going incredibly well. We both seemed to be extremely happy.

It was about then of course, I got "the text."

34

After seeing Pauline off, I started my day with a couple of good hours of writing and a small lunch. I then took my walk. I'd shifted my walks to the afternoons with the cooler weather. I had just left Father Mike's church after having made plans with him for an afternoon happy hour for later that day. Just as I headed down Rue de la Monnaie the text bomb hit.

"I need to see you. I felt something when we kissed. Something real. Something incredible. I think you did too. I'm coming down. Beach said it's not too late. Sof"

Just when everything was perfect, well we still had a few discussions to go, but almost completely perfect with Pauline, this happened. What the hell did Beach tell Sofia? I started processing how big a deal was this. I immediately called Beach.

"*Ma chère!*"

"Beach?"

"Oh, sorry. Thought you were Gabriela. Steve, my man! How'a doin'?"

"What did you tell Sofia?"

"Huh?"

"Did you two discuss me?"

"Yeah, sorta. She came by a few days ago. She just asked how you're doing."

"What did you say?"

"Fine. Said you were about to get married."

"That's it?"

"Well, now that you mention it, there was something a

little weird."

"Yeah, what?"

"Well, we just chatted a bit more about our favorite tiki drinks, stuff like that, and then out of the blue she asked where you were now."

"Uh huh. Then what?"

"I guess that that caused enough of a concern, that I said something real general, like 'somewhere in the South of France'."

"Uh huh. That's it?"

"Well, here's the part you might want to know, she said something like, 'Well, I hope he's happy there in Calvisson or Sommières, wherever in Languedoc.' It was kind of like she was fishing just a bit."

"What'd you say?"

"Nothing, she then changed the subject herself."

"Why didn't you tell me?"

"I dunno. She just seemed so nonchalant about it. She was a little lit up. I thought she was just making small talk. I do remember I had just a trace of concern when she asked me where you were. I was on guard enough to clam up."

"Okay. Thanks Beach."

"Say, what the hell happened between you two? Why are you so nervous? I thought you said nothing happened."

"Exactly nothing happened."

"Okay, then why are you so nervous?"

"She just sent me a text saying she has feelings for me."

"Crap!"

"Yes."

"Where'd she get the idea there was something between you two?"

"Well, we did have a great rapport. On that stupid night I got drunk with her at your place. I'm wondering what all I told her."

"Did you guys bed down together?"

"No!"

"You two just left the bar and went your separate ways?"

"Yeah, well no, actually."

"What?"

"Shit, I spent the night at her place."

"Son of a bitch! What the hell were you thinking, Steve?"

"I was kind of drunk, but nothing happened."

"You just slept with her?"

"No, I slept on the sofa. Remember, it was that night it poured so hard?"

"Steve my man, you may be fucked. That's not a good look."

"I know. It looks bad. But I'm telling you, nothing happened."

"You sure?"

"Yes."

"Y'all never saw each other again?"

"One other time."

"You saw her again?!"

I thought of that damned Hemingway with his "experience of life" shit.

"Yes, but again nothing happened."

"Nothing?"

"Not really."

"Nothing? You sure?"

"Yeah, I mean she like held my hands and told me a bunch of stuff, but nothing really. I was pretty confused what she was after really."

"And that was it? She left then?"

"Yeah, well she came back and kissed me goodbye. And then she just strolled away."

"Okay, I not judging you Steve, but if what you tell me about Pauline is right, what the hell were you thinking even meeting her the second time? She was hot. You were playing with fire there, buddy."

"Look all I know is nothing happened. It was stupid of me to get drunk with her, super stupid to tell her where my fiancée lives, if I did, and it was stupid to meet her again. All she said when we met again was that she needed some advice. We met at an art museum, the Musée d'Art Moderne. It was all innocent."

"Look, I think I know you well enough to know nothing happened. I know you're crazy about Pauline. Look, she's French. She knows men can be pigs. Even if something happened, she probably won't care that much. I mean she'll be pissed, but she'll get over it."

"I'm not a pig. Just stupid sometimes."

"Join the club. Since I've met Gabriela, I've had to change my ways, my ways of thinking. Think of all the babes that come in my place. I can't flirt back like I used to. I don't love that, but if I want someone awesome like her, I have to knock it off. I mean all I get out of flirting is a tiny ego boost. Is that worth losing someone incredible?"

"I know. We have to change when we meet the right person."

"It ain't easy, bro. I know it. Look, maybe you should just tell Pauline. You don't want this shit to blow up."

"Maybe you're right. I'd just hate for her to assume the worst. Nothing happened except I was stupid to meet up with her again."

"We all make mistakes. Just level with her. You don't want her to find out the wrong way."

"Thanks for the advice, Beach. I'm texting her right back to put an end to this crazy shit."

I had to think. I wandered over to the soccer field and sat in the sun. It felt almost nice in the sun when the wind wasn't strong. Sofia had still not texted me back. I was hopeful my text to her made it clear she was wasting her time.

I reflected on my stupidity. I ignored my instincts. It didn't feel quite right meeting her the second time. What was I trying to prove? Was my ego so fragile I needed those tiny boosts Beach talked about? I took a bit of solace knowing I hadn't done anything like that since Pauline and I really began to cement our relationship here on my last visit and in New Orleans. Did I think we weren't solid before? I guess I could try to justify it by saying she wasn't exactly rushing me to get down to her when I was in Paris. She declined to come up for the trip to Normandy. I could do all the stupid rationalizations I wanted, but they felt hollow.

At the time then, I was I guess trying to embrace Hemingway's quote about "experience of life." Look where it led him though. He was a gifted writer and even quite an adventurer, but he killed himself and wrecked the lives of many around him. He couldn't have been proud of how many people he hurt, people who loved him.

As I stared over at Sommières across the river, I felt excited knowing that was where paradise with Pauline existed, but I felt a pang of despair knowing I may have put that at risk if I didn't handle this right. As I sat there though, something else hit me. Something was missing. Something profound I couldn't name. Even when all was well with Pauline, there was something missing. And it had nothing to do with her. She was perfect.

I just studied the ground around me. By focusing on what was in front of me, the now, the grass, the weeds, the sky, I hoped to understand this remaining emptiness. Some ideas were coming to mind. I looked at my watch and noticed it was time to go hang out with Father Mike. I was already late. I texted him to let him know I was running late. This was ladies' night at the Bar L'Alambic over in Saint-Cômes-et-Maruéjols. I knew Pauline would run late. I encouraged her to keep maintaining her girlfriends. I knew that was healthy for us to have relationships beyond our marriage, just not Sofia type relationships.

He was already on his covered patio, nursing a tiny glass of red.

"I'm so sorry, father, for running late."

"Not to worry, my friend. It let me finish my readings for

today. Wine?

"Sure."

"What's on your mind, Steve?"

"Funny, when I dropped by after lunch the other day, I really hadn't a care in the world other than just talking about the future, marriage with Pauline, all that kind of stuff."

"And now?"

I filled him in. He maintained a small grin the whole time. It strangely reassured me somehow. After I finished, he just sighed and looked at the ground a minute.

"What do I do? I mean I feel stupid asking this. I know I just need to tell Pauline. I guess I just wanted a sounding board."

"I'm thinking, Steve."

I too stared at the ground. It really wasn't that fascinating.

Father Mike at last spoke, "Steve, look, I think it's going to be okay. This is a wake-up call. Things like this may happen for a reason. Ponder this situation. It's making you think, right?"

"Oh yeah!"

"This is your first real test of your relationship."

He took his horn-rimmed glasses off and briefly rubbed the bridge of his rosy nose.

"You just have to tell her, Steve. This is a test for her as well. How will she handle it?"

"I don't know. I don't want to stain our relationship. It just seems so perfect. And it was just such a non-event. I don't want Pauline's mind to race thinking I did something."

"Well, not perfect, if you fear telling her the truth."

"True. I know I must tell her. Any advice how?"

"Humble yourself before her. Be prepared for her to insult you. Don't fight back, just make sure the conversation stays factual. That's it. Be prepared to answer any question and stay calm. Again, don't be defensive. Be aware she has every right to be concerned. Just correct anything non-factual and absorb the other. Hold her hand while you tell her. Human contact can mitigate anger."

"Good advice."

"I'm just glad you didn't really do anything too wrong. To me, you were mostly innocent, but be careful where you get your ego boosts."

"Me too. I just hope this works."

"It will. I'm confident. It might be bumpy awhile, but in the end, I think it will be okay."

"What about the other thing I shared with you? How could I have finally met the perfect person yet still fill a hollow place?"

"Remember, Steve, when we met here just before you headed back home the first time? What did I tell you then?"

I sat there awhile and thought, then shared, "You said to use my freedom wisely."

"Have you?"

"Not particularly, to be honest."

"Tell me more."

"Father, I thought I could write and make a difference. I've been stumbling around with that. Maybe it's just a vanity hobby. I mean my one published book has sold okay, and was, believe it or not, made into a movie. I still can't believe that."

"I suspect you have a lot of talent Steve. I know you're thoughtful and super smart. But maybe you need to give more, in different ways."

"I feel like you're right."

"Just think about it."

"I do feel super good about setting up a foundation to help with affordable housing back in Marfa."

"Tell me more about how that you made you feel."

"Awesome. Of course, I'm mainly paying others to do good. I'm just giving money."

"Well, that's important. I have a suggestion. It's just a suggestion. You could drop writing for a bit and just focus on helping those around you, not just money, you know?"

"Yeah, maybe."

"Just give it a chance. Maybe just try it a few weeks and

reassess."

"How do I do that, here?"

"Funny you should mention that…"

35

I knew I had to have "the talk" with Pauline soon. Sofia could show up at any time if she failed to heed my text. She was like a ghost stalking me at all hours. She had finally texted me back with something pretty incoherent. I wasn't sure what she meant by "This needed to be settled in both our minds" in her return reply. A subsequent text was just as vague. I was so on edge. I kept waiting for the right time to talk to Pauline. It was finally Friday night, and I knew Pauline was more relaxed on Fridays.

I cooked her the best meal I could. I hoped she be more understanding after a great meal I prepared for her. We ate by candlelight. Soft jazz in the background. It was perfect other than the ghost out there lurking. I had gotten another text from Sofia while cooking saying she couldn't wait to see me so we could get this resolved. I got goosebumps as a read it as well as an unhealthy dose of nausea. I again beat myself up for my lack of judgement. Why did I spend the night at Sofia's flat, even if I did sleep on the sofa?!

After the meal, I poured us a dessert wine and I had her sit on the sofa. I told her I had something very important to tell her and I asked if we could speak in English. She looked slightly alarmed.

I held her hands and looked into her eyes and told her everything. I told her all of it. I held back nothing and then apologized from the bottom of my heart. I told her I was very embarrassed at my stupidity. Though nothing happened, I acknowledged that it easily could have, and I was stupid for putting myself in that situation and that it'd never happen again.

I was concerned about her blank expression. A tear began to stream down her face that she quickly wiped away.

I added that I never want anything between us and that I wanted her to be the one person on the planet who knows everything about me, that one person where there are no secrets. That one person who knows exactly who I am, for better or worse.

As the candles continued to fill the room with flickering light, I saw another tear emerge. This one she didn't wipe way. I've never been more disappointed in myself, ever, that I caused that tear, that sadness. She just continued to stare into my eyes saying nothing. Seconds passed like hours. Her mind was racing.

Finally, she spoke. "Well, I'm disappointed in you, but this whole time, I've been asking myself if I love you. Of course, I do love you, Steve Miles. There is nothing I can do about that whether you were dumb or not. Please never let anything like that happen again. I'm fine with you having friends who happen to be women, but just be careful. I'm in the same boat. You don't think that my students hit on me? Happens a lot, but I navigate it. I never let it go anywhere. I'm never alone with them. I never get drunk with them. Follow those two rules and you'll be fine, dumbass. Don't fuck this up! What we have is amazing, I hope you see that!

"I do. I do so very much. I just want to spend the rest of my life with you. I have never experienced this kind of bliss. I just feel so stupid but am glad nothing really happened."

"Would you have told me if she hadn't started texting you?"

"I don't know. Maybe not because it just seemed so stupid and I was a bit embarrassed. I chalked it up to gathering material as a writer. The moment at Trocadéro seemed so surreal."

She just stared at me, then said, "Steve, don't mess this up. This doesn't happen for everyone. Many people go their whole lives without something like what we share."

"I won't. I know you're right. In fact, I've stopped writing. I'm going to start volunteering with the church relief program awhile. There are some people here who really need help. I need to stop being so into myself. I was sitting on the soccer field yesterday thinking how I can be so happy with us but still feel like there is a void."

"Huh?"

"I told Father Mike about this feeling I have. I need to give back more. I've been so selfish. I think I've been writing to make myself feel better about being so self-absorbed. Kind of like a self-indulgence."

"Well, I think you are overstating things a bit, but I understand. I mean you have a gift. I've read your damn novel. It's good. Sure made me think."

I felt a swell of pride when she said that.

"But I understand you wanting to give more. I support a number of charities. We've never discussed this. I give money and my time to a number of organizations. I used to volunteer at a domestic abuse shelter often. It makes me feel relevant, like I'm part of the solution."

"I know. It makes me feel like I am giving back. I like this Steve better. I don't know where I'll go with this but I'm thinking how I can re-channel my energies into something other than a bunch of damn novels nobody reads."

"Look, Steve, you do have a talent. Don't overreact to this woman texting you. You're a good writer. Don't give that up. Think of it as diversifying your contributions."

"You're right." I sighed and looked her in the eye, "You still love me, even if I was stupid?"

"You kidding? I love you all the more. I love your honesty even if it was belated. Many men around here would have sought to hide this. Who knows how that could have backfired?"

"True."

"Steve, this could have gone very differently had you sought to hide this. Always be honest with me. I can probably forgive anything but dishonesty. It's just how I am. Never lie to me. I need to count on your word. I'm actually impressed how much I believe you. I know that sounds strange, but it's true."

"Thank you, Pauline. I'm not perfect, but you make me want to be as perfect as I can be for you, for us."

"Do you think this person could be dangerous?"

"No. As far as I know, she works for the Danish embassy."

"You went for a cold-blooded Dane, when you have this hot-blooded French and Spanish girl? I even have a little Lebanese in me. It is like the perfect combination you idiot. Are you nuts?"

"I'm only nuts for you."

"Good answer, asshole."

"I have an idea."

"What?"

"I'll text her we're already married. You know all about her. And once again tell her not to come."

"What if that doesn't work?"

"I think it will, but if she shows, I'll tell her if she makes any more trouble, I'll be forced to report her to the gendarme and Danish Embassy. She'd likely be recalled to Denmark immediately if the gendarme report her. Ambassadors don't take chances with stuff like this. I hope she'll listen. I think she's just misguided."

Pauline leaned over onto me, roughly grabbed my face, and looked me in the eye. "You are mine," she said. "Do not fuck this up. Don't do anymore stupid shit. I'll kick your ass. You mean too much to me."

"I like this Latin side of you."

She tightened her grip a bit more, and whispered, "Believe me, you don't want to ever see it on full display."

I swallowed. I was both frightened and turned on at the same time. I had never seen this side of her. I liked it, even if it was a bit scary.

She leaned back and looked at me somewhat speculatively and asked, "We are clear now, no?"

"Quite."

"*D'accord. Je considère cette affaire close.*" And we went back to French just like that. We didn't speak of this again. I loved her strength. I came to love this woman more every day.

I texted Sofia what I said I would.

In five minutes, she replied, "Are you sure? You're married already?"

I replied, "Yes, in every sense of the word. I wish you all the best, but I'm happily and fully married."

After a few minutes, she texted back, "Okay. All the best to you as well."

I knew it was likely over, but I did get goosebumps when Monsieur Morlet asked me the next day if that "blond woman found me." I asked him what she looked like. It almost certainly was Sofia. I asked him what he told her. He said he spoke to her strictly in Provençal and she didn't understand a word. She got in her car and just drove way. He winked at me and told me, "*Étienne, tu dois être plus prudent, tu as déjà la reine de France!*" He was right, I did need to be careful. I did indeed already have the "Queen of France." I felt relieved suspecting that the Sofia fiasco was perhaps truly over. Somehow, something that was initially very scary, ended up being a blessing. I learned a lot about me, about Pauline, and about us.

A couple of days in, my volunteer work was so far considerably more satisfying than my writing, at least for now. I volunteered doing odds and ends around the charitable missions of the church. I noted to Father Mike that I was surprised to learn that there was no shelter for people experiencing homelessness in Sommières. It wasn't a big problem, but it was an issue from time to time. When a person needs a place to stay, they really need it.

With Father Mike's blessing, I worked with the Red Cross to start developing what I termed a transitional "micro" shelter in town. The church had at one time kept a home for victims of domestic abuse. With the blessing of the church, I paid to convert a small portion of it to a transitional shelter where people could stay until the larger facilities in the region had a spot. There were two in Nîmes. I even hired a person with no home at the time with a carpentry background to help, Pablo. We worked together to build out four very basic rooms with all the essentials and a men's and women's bathroom.

The Red Cross provided a consultant who also helped a few days and a local plumber in the Parrish donated some of his time. We had only put in one week on this project when I decided to break off for Christmas. One of the best gifts I got that Christmas was learning that just that week of work with me had enabled Pablo to get a government subsidized apartment and was no longer unhoused thanks to the job I'd funded for him through the church organization. I was enormously happy about that. He seemed so grateful. He told me that I'd given him a second chance at having a decent life.

I felt a change coming over me where I could actually feel shared happiness. It was a real transformation. I mean I wasn't a jerk before, but I realized just how unaware I was of all the need and pain right around me. Pauline was extremely supportive and proud of what I was doing to help people in need in her town.

36

Pauline and I were planning to head down to Spain, Llançà, on the Costa Brava, to spend Christmas with her sister, but at the last minute, she said she wanted our first Christmas together to be special and just us. There'd be time for family bonding in the future.

We'd visited the *Marché de Noël* in Nîmes in early December. I got to experience a variety of French Christmas traditions. *Vin chaud* smelled good, but I was reluctant until I tasted it. It was good, basically warm red wine with spices. The *marchés* offered lots of local wares: jams, foie gras and pastries.

I just flowed with whatever Pauline wanted to do to celebrate. She said she visited relatives most Christmases, so she was having to create "our tradition" on the fly. She decided we'd go for lots of "Christmas" walks to admire decorations and enjoy a few meals out. For the big day, she wanted to go the vigil Mass in town and then go for a contemplative walk about town Christmas eve followed by snuggling together to await Christmas morning. She bought a number of special pastries throughout the days leading up to Christmas and bought a us a special Bûche de Noël cake to enjoy Christmas eve.

She seemed to be very happy as Christmas approached. She really got into the spirit of the season. On December 22, we went for one of our many evening Christmas walks. I was surprised to see Pauline so eager to keep to this new tradition. She loved our walks. She'd notice something different about town every evening. She loved the nativity scene at the church. It kind of bothered me how little I knew about her spirituality and her parents. I had raised these subjects a number of times. She seemed very reluctant to discuss either subject.

As Pauline stopped and noticed a new decoration near her place, I took her hand and asked her how she felt about all of this.

"About what?"

"All these decorations? Well, I mean what is behind these decorations. Do you believe Christ was born so long ago in Bethlehem?

"My mother taught me to believe. My father was agnostic."

"Pauline, please tell me about your parents."

She turned and looked at me, almost as though she wasn't quite sure. She said, "Yes, let's go warm up," and quickly looked down.

Once back in her apartment, she made us a cup of hot chocolate. She sat on the sofa and put her stockinged feet in my lap.

"Please tell me about your family, your parents, will you?"

"Now that we are married, I will."

As I rubbed her feet, she began. "Only my family knows this stuff. We are kind of private people in case you haven't noticed."

"I've noticed."

"My mom passed away a couple of years ago. She was a semi-successful writer. She was born near here and grew up here and Marseille. In her later years, she lived in a tiny *chambre de bonne* in the heart of Paris, near the *Arc de Triomphe*. I have a few of her books here on that bookshelf. She was a brilliant woman and a bit of an alcoholic. She tried to teach, but it never really worked for her. She had a series of bad relationships. She and my dad were probably never really in love. They stayed together for me and my sister. My dad is still alive. He lives in Barcelona where he was born to a Spanish mother and a French dad. Hence my surname, "Ferrand." One of my names is Ribera, my grandmother's surname. Honestly, my dad isn't overly interested in us, my sister and me. He is a professor of literature. He will occasionally surface in my life and then drift away again. Once I left the house, he left my mom too. They sold their flat in Paris, split the money and then he took off. It was so business-like, completely devoid of emotion or even nostalgia. Perhaps that explains my self-protective ways."

"How has this affected you overall?"

"My sister and I basically became 'our family.' We're close. We're also close to an aunt in Lyon. That's it. That's my family. And now there's you."

"I am very happy to be part of your family. I'm sorry how your family life was."

"Well, I was in ignorant bliss until I was maybe sixteen."

"How'd you come to live here?"

"We lived here when I was in lycée. My father was on a faculty in Montpellier. He commuted."

"So how long have you lived here?"

"I went off to university in Paris and then came back. Well, I lived in Réunion Island close to a year."

I kept rubbing her feet. "So, this really is your home?"

"Yeah, well, I wasn't born here. I was born in Paris. Don't let up, I need this massage!"

"Of course. Your being happy makes me happy."

"I know, and I love that!" She smiled and moaned a little. "This apartment is really my aunt's. Well, I am buying it from her."

"When are we going to be married? I mean for real?"

"We are married."

"I know. Just wondering."

"We still have some conversations to have, but I'm thinking, if you must have a ceremony, let's consider late Spring or Summer. As I've said, in my mind, we've been married since you returned to live with me in France. Too late to backout now, lover."

"Okay. I know we're married, somehow, I'd just like to publicly acknowledge it. I guess it's old fashioned?"

"It's sweet. We shall be formally married."

"I hope my parents can come."

"I'd love to meet them."

"You'd love them."

"I think I would, too."

"I love you Pauline."

"I love you, too. You French is getting so much better."

"Isn't it?" I was proud to hear her say that.

"I must go to sleep, my love. Your massage made me very sleepy."

"Well, let's go to sleep. We have a lifetime to learn about each other. Thank you for sharing with me. I feel closer to you every day."

"Great news, lover boy!" Pauline said as she exited the bedroom the next morning. She had already dressed for work.

"What?"

"I'm off until January 4!"

"Really!"

"Yes. I thought we were going to have to do a bunch of reports and get ready for the classes next year, but my boss said he is in the Christmas spirit and wants to recognize our great year!"

"That's great! I was bummed you were going to have to work."

"You're stuck with me. What do you want to do?"

"I don't know...hmmm...you look pretty good in that short dress. I have some ideas."

"I'm most flattered, but I want to get out and do something!"

"Okay. What do you have in mind?"

"Let's see if my sister and her husband can meet us down the coast. I want her to get to know her new family member! She can't wait to greet you as her brother!"

"I'm game."

"Get dressed Steve, time to meet your sister."

"Sure, but I've met her." I had met her on my first visit to the area.

"You weren't her brother then. This will be different."

"Sure. I'll be ready in 20 minutes."

"I'll text her. I mentioned it to her a minute ago. She is checking."

We left at 9:00 and arrived at the restaurant in Cerbère at noon. The restaurant had an incredible view of the Mediterranean. It was cool enough we definitely needed to eat inside, but in the summer, it would be a glorious place with the breezes off the Med. Broad, beige beaches and blue water. Just a smattering of palm trees to make it look a bit warmer than it actually was outside.

"I guess we beat them. Let's grab a table. How many for them?"

"I don't know. She'll leave the kids with a neighbor if she can."

We got a table big enough either way. It wasn't crowded at all. It was one of the few places open given the off season.

"There she is!" Pauline got up and raced to the door to greet her. They briefly embraced and talked close. Pauline warmly greeted Yolanda's husband as well. No hug. Hugs are used very rarely by French people. Hugs are considered pretty intimate.

I stood up and Yolanda walked up to me, looked me in the eye and very seriously said welcome to the family with great conviction. Her husband, Raul, shook my hand with both hands and said welcome.

"We have a small family, but it's close," Yolanda smiled.

"Thank you, Yolanda and Raul."

"We are so excited this worked out. We and the kids loved you when you visited. But we didn't want to jinx things by coming on too strong. We are thrilled you and Pauline are together."

"As you might imagine Yolanda, so am I."

"The kids wanted to see their 'Uncle Steve,' but they get antsy in restaurants. They love having an American uncle!"

"Well, let them know I love being their uncle."

"Yo, I told him the story of our parents." Pauline confided.

"Wow Steve! She never talks about our parents."

"Well, he was giving me a foot massage."

"Oh, the foot massage trick, eh Steve?"

"Yeah, I had no idea how powerful it is."

"It's like truth serum for me." Pauline winked at me.

"I'll keep that in mind."

"Please do, lover."

I adored how comfortable Pauline was with her sister and brother-in-law.

"Yo, I just wanted us to see each other since we won't be together for Christmas."

"I'm glad you reached out, Pauline. It will be weird not having you around, but we understand."

"We just want our first Christmas to be intimate, be home, you know?" Pauline added.

"Totally!" Yolanda smiled.

"But you know Yo, we look forward to spending serious beach time with you guys this summer!"

"Of course, Pauline! Who knows, you might have an addition to the family on the way by then."

Pauline and I darted glances at each other. We hadn't even discussed that at all. Crazy.

"Well, we'll see my dear sister. We are just trying to get used to living together so far."

"Okay, Pauline."

"So far, it's been great." Pauline looked at me and winked again.

"So, Steve, are you going to be able to work here? What're your plans? By the way, your French has gotten so much better!"

"Thank you. Pauline has cut me off from English. Somehow, she can't understand my English now."

"If he's going to live in France, he must speak French," Pauline declared.

"Well as for work, I'm figuring all that out. I have a lot to learn. So far, I've just been doing some volunteering."

"Really?" Yolanda looked surprised.

"Yeah, I'm working with the church to set up a small shelter for unhoused people in town."

Yolanda looked impressed and raised her eyebrows at Pauline.

We had a great lunch. We bonded as a family for sure. Pauline was very happy. By 6:00 p.m., we were back in Sommières.

Pauline looked at me with pouty lips, "I'm too sleepy for our nightly walk."

"Let's get some sleep. Tomorrow is Christmas Eve!"

We nibbled on a couple of snacks and were probably asleep within the hour. I was wiped out, too. It was great but exhausting to meet my family members, speaking and trying to think in French the whole time. Raul's French had a Spanish accent so that made it even harder. By the time lunch was over, there was no doubt we were now family. It felt good to be in Pauline's small but special circle. I had effectively met her entire "family" other than her aunt in Lyon, and her dad, to the extent he met that description.

37

"Wake up, Steve! It's Christmas Eve!"

I was surprised she woke up first. That was rare.

"You must have been exhausted. You're never next to me when I awaken."

"I guess so."

"The coffee is ready. I have a little surprise for you on the table."

Pauline had made a trip to the bakery and brought a baguette and a couple of complex little pastries. She came over to the table to watch me try them. It was great seeing her so excited and happy. She was normally so in control and even in her emotions. As I was getting dressed, she had prepared my coffee. My white and light blue *Olympique de Marseille* mug she'd given me as an early present was steaming on the table. I sat and tasted the first pastry.

"And?" Her eyes were big. She was so cute like this.

"Very good. Okay, I know these are macaroons, but what's this?"

"Polvorones. Try one."

"Yum! Kind of like shortbread."

"Polvorones are really Spanish. The baker's wife is Spanish."

"I like them."

"My dad always had to have them at Christmas. Try the other."

I picked up a leaf-shaped cookie with white icing. "Wow!

That's good. Kind of orange taste. I like it. Spanish too?"

"No. That's French. They are Calissons. There's a couple of types, orange and melon. They are probably my favorite. They are associated with Provence."

"These are great."

"Don't eat too many. Kind of rich."

"Hard to stop myself!"

"I know, but I have a Christmas Eve treat for you. I want you hungry for lunch. I have some friends for you to meet, too."

After loafing around and sipping coffee and being lazy the rest of the morning, we finally set out for my surprise.

"Where are we going?"

"You'll see."

"Is it close?"

"Ten minutes."

We shot up D22 and were soon in a small, beautiful village named Souvignargues. Picturesque stone walls ringed the road. There were patches of vineyards extending into the village. We passed a winery on the right. The buildings got older as we got close to the center, lots of red tiled roofs. There were also several stone and light beige buildings with pastel shutters and doors. Very Languedoc. Some ornate ironwork on the balconies. We took a left and went up the aptly named Rue de Vieux Village. Pauline pointed at an old church nestled on a narrow street to the left, then she darted down a street that looked too narrow for cars, tall stone walls on each side, and we ended up in a wide spot. To the left was a beautiful, lavender-painted iron gate that had a wavy grill on a tall stone wall.

"That's where we're going!" She pointed to the beautiful gate. We parked up the way after going through another super narrow alley and walked back.

"That gate is stunning. Can I have a picture of you in front of it?"

"Of course." She was wearing a black cardigan and black leggings. Her undershirt almost matched the lavender of the gate. She was stunning.

"Where are we?"

"Welcome to one of my favorite little farming villages. My adopted godparents live behind this wall."

"Adopted?"

"Well, most people have godparents assigned to them. I said the hell with that and went and selected my own godparents."

"How did you know them?"

"Well, when my aunt lived where we are living, Yolanda and I would come stay a part of the summer with her before we moved here. The Martins are retired teachers. They are close to my aunt. They immediately fell in love with Yolanda and me."

"That's cool. You selected your own godparents?"

"Yes."

"That took some guts."

"I hope you're learning, that isn't a problem for me," she said as she opened the small lavender gate next to the large one.

"I've noticed."

She looked back, "Prepare yourself for a Christmas culinary treat. We are going to cheat and have *Le Reveillon* before mass! That's how the Martins do it."

"Works for me."

"Me too."

The meal was a true holiday celebration, and the Martins were wonderful people. We all enjoyed ourselves immensely, and a few hours later, we began our trip back to Sommières. I was miserably stuffed after feasting upon the most incredible combinations of turkey, oysters, chestnuts, foie gras, goose. Half the time I wasn't sure what I was eating, but it was all so good. And the wine pairings were incredible.

"I am so stuffed."

"No one forced you to eat so much."

"Yes, the Martins did. They didn't have to make food that good."

"Well, Madam Martin has a little help. Her daughters and sons-in-law actually help a good deal, I think."

"Was that their Priest there?'"

"Yes."

"Well, he cheated too."

"We must give the poor guy a break, after all. He goes home alone after midnight mass. He's the priest at many churches around here."

"Good point. I like their daughters. They were funny."

"Yes, they are great. I love the whole family. You have a great 'God family.'"

"That is a neat way of looking at it, Steve. And kind of true."

"How come you aren't into the whole midnight mass thing?"

"I think our whole midnight Mass tradition is kind of crazy. I'm asleep by midnight. I prefer the early vigil Mass. Always have. And often there are more kids, maybe a kid's program. I like that. I got into that habit with Yolanda since she has little ones. About every third Christmas, they've piled into my place. Getting harder as their kids get older."

"The early Mass thing works fine for me."

Just as we parked back in Sommières, she looked over at me, "Is there any little touch of America you want to bring into our tradition?"

"Funny you should mention that. I have a little surprise for you as well, plus let's open our gifts in the morning. I don't like the idea of doing it at night."

"I agree. Let's do it your way. Some French families do it in the morning too. Plus, there's no way I am going to do it the French way and load up on food after midnight. That's crazy."

As we got ready to go the Mass, I played the Charlie Brown Christmas soundtrack off my phone on her small sound system to help me get in the mood. Out the window I could see a number of buildings around Pauline's place were decorated, modestly, but festive, maybe a simple string of red and green lights. I was ready so I was just relaxing on the sofa soaking in the music. This was my first Christmas in France. For a bit of a secular country, Christmas was very real. On our evening strolls, I felt excitement building across the town. Even Pauline was excited.

Pauline emerged wearing a red sweater and scarf and a short black skirt with thick black stockings. She placed her boots near the door. She had her hair pulled back, fixed a little differently.

"You are stunning, my dear."

She walked over and proceeded to sit in my lap.

"I am so, so, so happy you are here. Merry Christmas darling." She lightly kissed my lips.

"Merry Christmas to you, as well."

She looked me in the eye and said, "I may have to let you open one of your presents tonight."

"I thought we said morning."

"Hush. Believe me, you will like your present once we go to bed."

"I bet I will."

"You will. Now let's get going. I'd rather not have to stand during Mass."

The walk over to the church was magical. The town was quiet but still abuzz somehow. Anticipation was high. Interesting aromas, fireplaces, cooking, *vin chaud*, spilled out onto the streets. Kids were running around grinning from ear to ear.

The church was decorated beautifully. The interior was very ornate, and statues of saints were all about. I'd never been in the church at night before. The illumination made the statues more apparent. The Mass became mystical during the children's play where they re-enacted the birth of Christ. The lights were dim for a while. Mainly by the light of a few candles were we able to see the beginning of the play.

Father Mike was there and helping, but a priest who appeared to be of African origin celebrated the Mass. I recognized most of the songs we sang in French though. I glanced over at Pauline from time to time. She was definitely in the moment. It dawned on me that this was the only time we'd been in church together.

As we walked home, I asked her if she was a believer. She looked at me with a strange look and said, "Let's add that to our list to discuss." I took it that she had no desire to discuss it further right then. She grabbed my hand and asked me again what I wanted to add to their new tradition from America.

"Have you ever heard of a show called, *A Charlie Brown Christmas*? I played music from it while you were getting ready."

"Vaguely. The Snoopy show?"

"Well, Snoopy was in it."

"It rings some bells. Maybe I saw it when I lived in the States. So long ago. I was 11 years old!"

"Why were you there?"

"My dad was a visiting professor."

"Let's go watch it! I bet I can find it online!"

She stopped and turned around hugged me and said, "Let's! I'd love to see something that meant a lot to you as a kid."

"Still does, Pauline. It's magical somehow."

"I can't wait then!"

I loved seeing this side of her.

Christmas morning Pauline awakened me with a very happy look on her face. She tugged on me. "I have more surprises. C'mon."

"On my way, darling."

Again, my coffee was waiting for me and more pastry surprises.

"More pastries!" I smiled, trying to keep up with her enthusiasm.

"Well, per Provence ways, we were supposed to have had 13 desserts last night! I'm just giving them to you over a few days."

"Thirteen?"

"Yes."

"Pauline, why are we speaking English?"

"Well, it is a tiny present to you. I figured you might forget how to speak English."

"Thank you. Speaking of presents, we need to open gifts!"

"Enjoy your coffee and pastries first."

We had put a limit on gifts. No more than twenty-five euro and no more than two or three. She gave me a pump for my soccer ball after she noticed it a bit low on air, a French dictionary, a Maigret detective novel and she got us a painting for the apartment. I gave her a scarf with a Matisse design I loved that I had picked up in Paris, some cologne I found to be wonderful on her, and I wrote her a short story just for her in English. I busted the twenty-five euro cap on the cologne. We had a fabulous very relaxed day. I loved our first Christmas together.

38

A warm spell arrived a couple of days after Christmas. Pauline decided we needed to go play soccer again. This time she was a bit more assertive. She clearly wanted to show me she could hold her own on the pitch. When we faced off, she was able to consistently push past me, until one time I decided to bring her down. She tumbled a bit more than I planned. She laughed so hard. I crawled over to her and began to passionately make out with her in the sun on the field in front of the world. She was totally fine with it. She was French and public displays of affection weren't a big deal within reason. She sat up and looked at me with a strange look on her face, a kind of sexy smirk.

"I wish we were home. You just lit my fire somehow."

"The first time?"

"No dumbshit. I mean just something special."

"Well, we can go home right now. I'm kind of feeling it too."

"Wait, I just want to enjoy this sun. I can't believe how warm it is for December. This is glorious."

I looked at her. Grass in her hair. She always looked tanned. I guess it was her Spanish or Lebanese blood. She was so glorious in the Sommières sun. With her hair tousled and grass all over her, she was the most beautiful sight I'd ever seen. Even messy and in warmups she was unbelievably sexy. I knew there was nothing I wouldn't do for her. It was both scary and wonderful to be completely enraptured by her. It was getting so warm that she slipped her warmup bottoms off to reveal her athletic shorts beneath.

"Okay, that's it, Pauline. We need to go home now."

"I can't tell you how much I love it when you call here home." She lunged at me to hug me. She stared into my eyes, into my soul really, and said, "Yes, let's go home now. This time, we both need to."

◆ ◆ ◆

The next morning, after my pastry surprise, I asked Pauline what we were going to do for New Year's.

"I'm not sure. I'm torn. I want you to meet the final member of my family, my aunt Lélia, but I also want to hang out with Yolanda. New Year's in Spain is quite special. Aunt Lélia has been after me since you got here for us to come see her."

"You decide, dear. I am fine with either. Hanging out with Yolanda and Raul sounds fun though."

"Seriously, Steve, I decided our Christmas. What do you want to do?"

"Pauline, to be honest, if I am with you, I'll be happy. I'd be fine just staying here and seeing what happens here."

"You know? I haven't stayed here in a while. Let's do that!"

"Works for me."

"That settles it. The weather looks great today. Can we go do a picnic somewhere?"

"Steve, I love that idea! I know just the spot."

After getting a fresh baguette and making some ham and butter sandwiches and packing a couple pieces of cheese and a few apples, we were on our way. Since it was still a tad warmer than usual, we celebrated that by bringing a bottle of one of the great local rosés.

After heading back up D22, Pauline left the highway and went down a series of one lane roads finally turning onto a dirt road in the middle of a rolling vineyard. We pulled up to the ruin of an old stone structure. It was a beautiful spot. All around, all one could see were mostly leafless grape plants on all the surrounding hills. It was a mélange of browns, grays, orange leaves and a few green trees here and there, but still beautiful and very peaceful.

"I'd love to see this place in the spring, Pauline!"

"You will, many times. A friend of mine, really one of Aunt Lélia's best friends, owns this vineyard. When I want to be all alone or just truly at peace, this is one of my hideaways. You're right, it is so beautiful in the warmer months. I came here after you left the very first time to just try to make sense of what had happened. I was so sad. I decided here, on this spot, that I'd come see you. I honestly wondered if it was a fool's errand."

"I'm so happy you came. It makes me love this spot all the more. What's the story on the house, or ruin rather, over there?"

"It was here when the owners' parents bought it. Who knows?"

"It is rather photogenic."

"The whole place is."

"I'm hungry already."

In a short while, with the red and white blanket beneath us, we were sipping our wine before beginning to devour our lunch.

"How common is a warm spell like this in December?"

"It happens, but it's turning cooler later today." She looked at the sky, "Enjoy it while we have it!"

"We have things to discuss."

"I know. I'm happy to talk. I'm in my happy place." She looked over at me. She was beautiful sitting there on the blanket next to me with her arms pulled around her legs as she sat up. She wore a floral dress and had her hair pulled back in a short ponytail. She had put on lipstick before we left. No other make-up.

"You look beautiful Pauline. You're just a natural beauty."

"Thank you. Let's talk more substantive things, not that I don't love your compliments."

"Okay, where do we go from here?"

"You mean in our conversation or with our life?" She smiled over at me.

"Okay, you said something about us needing to talk about my wanderlust or something like that?"

"Yes. You will tire of my beautiful village and want to get out some. What will that look like for me?"

"Mind if I speak English? I want to be precise. There are still many things that I don't know exactly how to say in French?"

"Of course."

"I don't know. I say that partly because I'm evolving. Helping to establish that shelter is doing something for me. When Pablo and I finish it, the work won't be over. The project is awakening something in me, it's making me like myself more. I like how as I focus on the needs of others; I see myself differently. I've been self-absorbed most of my life. I feel like I am transforming. I mean, I've always been a nice guy, at least I think so. And I've never gone out of my way to hurt anyone, at least off the football field. But I have seldom gone that far out of my way to help either. You'd think that inheriting some serious wealth would have awakened me. It really didn't. I did help a few folks right around me, and I am trying to help people in Marfa in my uncle's name with the foundation, but I have much growing to do in that area. I know when I was meeting with people in Marfa on the foundation, it gave me a glimpse of what I could become if I started thinking about the needs of others."

I paused to look over at Pauline. She was studying me and listened. I wondered if I was being too honest. No, I wasn't going to hold back. For once, I wanted someone to know me absolutely and hopefully accept me for who I am and who I wanted to become.

"I'm sharing this because I just want you to know, I am changing, I think. I hope. I'm trying to stop being so focused on what I want. I'm trying to be to more aware of what people around me need. I feel kind of backwards just now thinking about these things. Even the whole writing gig! It feels so self-oriented. What am I trying to prove?"

Pauline smiled at me reassuringly, "Keep on. I'm listening. Let me know when you want me to weigh in. Meanwhile, you have the floor."

"Okay. Stop me when you get sick of hearing me." She just smiled.

"So, here's the deal. I don't know exactly where this road might lead me. I mean I am wealthy but not so wealthy I can throw money all over the place. We will be financially secure for the rest of our lives if we don't go crazy. I have no desire to have high-end cars, a boat or a mansion, crap like that. We should be able to give our kids a nice chunk of money when we're gone if I don't develop some of those stupid rich person habits. I know you won't."

"Our kids?" She smiled and her eyebrows lifted.

"Yeah, I guess that's something else to discuss. Okay, but for now, back to the wanderlust issue. I want us to travel, but I'm not sure I'm going to want to be on the road that much. I like this. I like what we have now."

"I know. I love it, but I just figure you will want something bigger one day, Steve."

"I don't know, maybe. But I'd want us to make these decisions together. Look, I know we love each other so much, but I just want us to go into this with our eyes open. I don't want one of us surprised. And I always want you to be happy. At one point I thought I might be a big author. I guess in the last few months, I've started to revisit that. That goal feels at times like I was trying to boost my ego or something."

I looked all around at the beauty surrounding us and savored a sip of the wine. "Pauline, I am a rich man even if I had very little money because I have this and mainly because I have you. Why shouldn't I let someone else make the money, gather the fame? Why be selfish? I have more than what I need. Why not celebrate that and see how I can help others in need?"

"You have a creative side that needs to be expressed, Steve. I mean the story you wrote me for Christmas was powerful. I've been reflecting on it the last couple of days."

"You've read it?"

"Of course. I stayed up Christmas night and read it. I loved it. I touched me. You have a gift."

"Did you really like it?"

"Of course."

"Thank you."

"Thank you, my darling. I saw us in it. I liked your vision for us."

"Even the kids?"

"Yes, even the kids." She reached over to hug me and kiss me.

"Pauline, I guess my answer to your question is, I don't know. But I do know one thing. I never want to be away from you, especially for a long time to come. I want to help people. I don't know where that's going to lead."

"I think you should write, too."

"Maybe."

"Look Steve, you have a gift. You can help people through your writing to not be so selfish, so self-absorbed. You are an American. If you can reach Americans and help them to turn away from some of their darker impulses, you can help the world given your nation's importance."

"I'll keep reflecting on it. I just know I want to do more. I want to give more."

"Maybe give yourself a bit of a break. I think you are being a bit hard on yourself. Maybe you can focus on getting the shelter up and running, keep your foundation in Texas moving in the right direction, do some writing to help Americans appreciate the opportunities that await them if they can cast off their divisive ways and…being around to give me foot massages." She laughed.

"Maybe so. Maybe that's a good plan."

"You can start on the foot rub now." She smiled and spun around and lay back to put her feet in my lap.

"I like this. It isn't overwhelming. It's helping. It continues the journey and I get to hear you moan a little."

She looked at me with a smirk, "Huh?"

"I mean as I rub your feet."

She laughed, "You're kind of crazy. But I must say, you're quite good at massages. Hey, neck and shoulder massages are good, too."

"Anything to bring you pleasure, Pauline."

"I like that, but before we get too sidetracked, we have more to discuss."

"Gosh, we should have brought sunscreen."

"Look behind you."

A dark blue cloud was swelling up on the horizon.

"Oh, let's enjoy the warmth while we can."

"Yes. Let's." She peered up at me, "I suppose you might want to talk about marriage?"

"Yes."

"How about April? There's really no point in waiting much longer, and I want to keep it very small, very French, very traditional. That okay?"

"Good. I like simple."

"What prompted you to want to finally discuss this?"

"Well, I don't want to be pregnant in my wedding dress. That's not the best look."

"Huh?"

"No, I'm not pregnant, but for the very, very first time in my life, I am open to thinking about it. How about you?"

"Absolutely. I want to have children with you. I have only one request. Can you get away from work? I want us to travel some before. I'd like you to show me a place like Réunion Island or Tahiti."

"I probably can. I can take a couple of weeks off in February. Does that sound good?"

"You know, you don't have to work."

"We've been over this. You know that is not negotiable right now. I never want to be totally dependent on anyone. I love you more than anyone ever in my life, but I want to have some independence. Do you get that?"

"Yes."

"Maybe one day. Not now."

"I support you either way. I don't want you to change."

The wind was starting to have a bit of a cool edge as those blue clouds got closer. Pauline had let her hair down. The wind was tousling her hair beautifully. In the glow of the afternoon sun, she was beautiful and independent and free in her own way.

"You know my family will want to come, Pauline?"

"I would like that."

"Maybe, even the *plouc*?

"Clark? Ugh! What did you call him? Knuckleface?"

"Knucklehead."

"Ah, yes. The knucklehead."

"He's a big movie star now."

"No?" It was one of those French elongated, exaggerated "nos." She had taken her eyes off the clouds to peer over at me with the incredulous look that only a French person can give.

"Seriously Pauline, he's been getting attention. Somehow, he looks different on video. He already has another role."

"Hollywood! Ugh!"

Pauline sat up from lying back and looked at me.

"Crazy. Insane. He is the very definition of a knucklehead."

"I know. But you'll love my parents."

"I know I will, Steve."

"I love you, Pauline."

"I love you too. I'll take some neck massage now." She swung around and sat before me very quickly.

"Of course."

"I love the feel of your hands on me." After a long sigh, she added, "Have we discussed everything?"

"Well, just one more thing."

"Yes?"

"Are you still relaxed? Still feel like talking?"

"Yes, if you will get my sweater out of the car."

I retrieved the sweater and put it around her shoulders. I continued the massage under the sweater.

"Okay, Steve, what else?"

"Do you believe in God?"

"Why do you ask?"

"Look, I'm signing on to spend the rest of my life with you. I mean that's done. We are now married, but I was just wondering. I know your favorite color, your favorite foods, I know a lot about you, even about your parents, but I know nothing of your spiritual side."

"Well, it's complicated. But I'll try."

"Please do."

"I was raised a strict Catholic. The whole guilt thing and everything. For whatever reason, my mom drifted away from the Church as I got older. And my dad was never involved in that."

She paused, and asked, "Can you do under my shoulder blade? You can unzip my dress, but don't get any ideas. This is an important conversation."

"All right, you're no fun," I sighed.

"That comes later. Think of this as intellectual foreplay."

"Now, that's an interesting way to look at it."

"Yes. Yes, it is. Good. Well, anyway, when my mom drifted away, I guess I did too. That's common for teenagers. My Aunt Lélia and my godparents are always after me to be a better Catholic. So, like you, I'm a work in progress. I'm not an unbeliever; I'm open to it. It is kind of an artifact of being French, some kind of connection to the Church. Some of it feels right, like visceral truth, eternal truths, but I am just pretty disillusioned with the Church. You know the pedophilia stuff and their attitudes toward women. Plus, I think the Church likes to control people unnecessarily, like birth control. Some of it feels made up, you know? What about you Steve?"

"I believe, but like you, I'm on a journey."

"Perhaps we can journey together?" She spun around to look back at me and smiled.

"Yes, I'd like that. Perhaps, one day, you, Beach and I can have a chat on this."

"He sounds like a kook to me."

"Maybe so. I don't know, but what he shared with me continues to stay with me."

"I'm sure he's nice, but that stuff about a surfer Jesus? C'mon."

"Maybe he can explain it better than I. Maybe you and I can go talk to Father Mike to determine a baby step forward we can take together."

"Maybe so. One day at a time."

"Will you want our kid or kids baptized?"

"Yes, of course."

"Wow! Such confidence."

"I know Steve. Work my neck a bit more." She paused a second, "I'm French. It's what we do. We call on the Church when our kids are young, when we get married and I guess when we die."

"Yeah, I guess you're right."

"I know it's weird."

"Okay, we will continue the journey together, Pauline. I believe something. I don't think all this is utter random."

"On that we agree, dear. That's a start. I'm getting cold. And I just a felt a raindrop. Perhaps we should head back. You are going to have to drive. I'm too relaxed to drive."

We both stood to begin packing up.

"Wait Pauline, stand still. You were serious that this place, this ruin, the vineyards surrounding us is a special place for you?"

"Yes. It's my special spot. It's always been here for me."

With the wind starting to whip up and her hair flying all about and a bit of rain beginning to fall, without even thinking about it, I got down on one knee before her. She started laughing.

"Pauline, please, indulge me. This is the only time I will ever do this, and I can't imagine a better spot or a better time."

I looked up into her eyes and just stared into her eyes.

"Pauline Ferrand, will you marry me?"

She stared into my eyes and slowly smiled, "Well, if you can't figure that out from what we've been sharing, you must be a knucklehead, too, no?"

After looking down at me a few more seconds, she slowly displayed a cheeky smile and exclaimed, using my name in French, "*Oui Monsieur Étienne* Miles, I will marry you as many times as you like!"

Fin

AFTERWORD

The Sommières Sun is a sequel to A Moveable Marfa, published January 2020. CE Hunt didn't intend to write a sequel, but enough readers asked, "Then what happened?" He then began to explore were they right? Was there more to add? He hopes The Sommières Sun makes a robust case the readers were right.

CE Hunt was born and grew up in Houston, Texas. He has served in public service all over the United States and Europe, including his beloved West Texas and France. In his travels, he has taken close note of how people seek and find fulfillment in their respective cultures.

The Sommières Sun, though some of it is based on or informed by CE Hunt's observations and experiences, is a work of fiction.

CE Hunt would like to thank his brother, Carl, for his valuable editing and wonderful content ideas. This book would not have happened without his strong support and wise counsel. CE Hunt would also like to thank his friend, Elisa, for her excellent editing and content suggestions.

OTHER PUBLISHED WORKS BY CE HUNT—

Houston Atlas of Biodiversity, selected chapters
(Texas A&M University Press, 2007)

*Buffalo Soldiers at Fort Davis, Texas
(1867-1885)*, (BLACKPAST.org, 2007)

*Big Thicket People: Larry Jene Fisher's Photographs of the
Last Southern Frontier*, (University of Texas Press, 2008)

*Paradoxes of Power: A Collection of Essays on Failed
Leadership/Chapter author on Climate Change and
Environmental Challenges*, Amazon Publications, 2020

A Moveable Marfa, (Amazon Publishing, 2020)

Cover credit – La Vie by CE Hunt, 2017. All rights reserved.